FOUND

Gabby Skeldon

FOUND

For information contact :

Front Cover Design by : Saint Jupiter (@saintjupit3ergr4phics)
Editor : Gabby Skeldon (gab@authorgabskeldon.com)
Proof Reader: James Buckley (info@buckleysbooks.com)
Formatting : Gabby Skeldon (gab@authorgabskeldon.com)

ISBN : 978-1-7394170-2-4

Second Edition : August 2023

MERLIN'S HEIR
BOOK ONE

FOUND

GABBY
SKELDON

For Dad.

1

I expect the present sitting on my bed, even if it's a shock to see it there. I get one every year around this date, and it's always the same. A royal-blue box tied with a silky black ribbon. Inside, there'll be a charm, a butterfly, a bird, a beautiful silver daisy with a diamond middle, or something similar. When I went to shower, there was nothing. But now the box is waiting for me, perched on my pillows as if it belongs.

I grip my towel more tightly to my body, as if that can stop me from shaking, or the tears sliding down my cheeks, or the dull ache of grief pounding at my heart. Oh yes, I knew it was coming, the anniversary present marking ten years since Dad disappeared, but it still stabs like a knife. Worse. Hundreds of tiny needles poking every inch of my skin.

My breath fogs out in front of me in a fine

mist. It's cold in my room, especially in October, but not cold enough for frost to be rippling over the windows, or for my toes to be aching where they meet the floor. It can mean only one thing. A Shadow.

I don't know exactly where they come from, although I've wracked my brain trying to figure it out. One moment my room is empty, and the next it fills with grey smoke, taking on shape, like water filling a glass. The smoke runs into two legs, forming beneath a thin wiry torso. Bony arms protrude like tree branches. Huge, glittering claws hang from the tips of twisted fingers. It raises its head, a vaporous orb of grey and blue, with the beginnings of a nose and mouth. I can't take my eyes off it, even though that's what the doctors have told Mum to do. Tens of them trying to convince us they're just hallucinations.

"*It's grief. It* will *pass.*"

But it hasn't. At first, the dreams, manifestations, whatever they are, were Mum's to bear alone, but now they're *ours*. Mine and hers. Heavy on our hearts like stones. Growing rather than passing.

The long arms of the Shadow reach forward, cupping the blue box in both hands, offering it to me. It tips its head to expose a sickeningly long neck. In the smoke, there are shades of other body parts, of collar bones and sharp ribs. But this thing, whatever it is, isn't human.

I know better than to scream. I also know better than to take the box, but that's exactly what my treacherous hands are reaching for. Taking another step would be madness. Even so, I find my foot lifting and inching closer. The Shadow holds out the box again, swaying its head in approval.

"Merle, are you up yet?" My bedroom door clatters open,

2

making me jump so hard I almost drop my towel. Aunt Hazel stands with her hands on her hips, staring at me. "You're supposed to be leaving in ten minutes. You are working today, aren't you?"

I nod, unable to speak, the lump in my throat bobbing up and down; a buoy in a raging sea.

"Come on then, I'll give you a lift. I'm going that way. But you'll have to walk back."

"Thank you."

"Bloody hell, it's cold in here," she says, rubbing at the gooseflesh on her bare arms. "We'll have to get that radiator fixed before Christmas."

"Yes."

Hazel narrows her eyes at me. "Is everything all right? You're quiet."

"I'm fine, just tired."

"Hmm." She raises an eyebrow, unconvinced. "I'm going in fifteen minutes. If you aren't ready, I'll leave you behind."

"Got it."

"And you're sure you're all right?"

"Yes."

She shrugs and leaves me to get ready. With a sigh of relief, I check for the box, which is still on my pillow. I may be imagining the Shadows, but I'm not imagining that. I've asked Hazel about them before, if she or her wife Ali leave them for me. It's something Ali might do to distract me from the time of year. They both say they aren't responsible though, and for once, I'm inclined to believe them. I pick the box up with trembling hands and shove it into the back of my underwear drawer for later.

"Ten minutes, Merle!" Hazel shouts from down the hall.

Grumbling under my breath, I stomp to my dresser, sighing at my dishevelled appearance. I could be pretty if I wasn't so tired and terrified all the time. I've certainly inherited the bone structure for it. A small nose, angular jaw and a mass of unruly brown hair from Dad, high sweeping cheekbones and full pink lips from Mum. My eyes are my very own. They're hazel with tiny flecks of gold and green. Too big for my face, but wide and bright, and by far my most interesting feature. As it stands, dark patches are gathered under them, my cheeks drawn and thin. I look sick. I suppose I *am* sick, but not with something anyone can cure.

When I'm ready, I run downstairs to find Hazel waiting in the hallway, ruffling the fur of her beloved chocolate labradoodle, Alfie. We're not friends. Since Hazel brought him home five years ago, he's done his very best to make sure I can't get away with anything. If he catches me with my feet on the sofa, tracking mud through the kitchen, sneaking out, or one of the many other offences I get accused of, he'll run to Hazel and tell on me.

"I wish you'd do something about your hair, Merle." My aunt clicks her tongue against the roof of her mouth.

"You can blame Dad for that."

A small smile spreads over her face at his mention. Hazel is Dad's sister, and she moved in with us not long after he disappeared. For a while, Mum could manage. She sent me to school and made my lunches, keeping her grief at bay with the hope of his return. As the days passed and it became obvious he wasn't coming back, her sadness became a storm, a tempest that ripped us apart. Hazel had no choice but to step in. I suppose I'm grateful for that. We're not really friends either. I know she's done her best, but she doesn't

4

understand what it's like, to have everything taken away, including the sanctuary of my own mind. She still has a wife, friends, something I have never and probably will never have.

Our house, the Wilde Manor, as Dad called it, was bought by my parents about a year before I was born. It's a grand old house, and the true reason I suspect Hazel is here. Dad was an artist, and just before they had me, he became a famous artist. A collector picked up one of his pieces at a show, and for at least a decade after, he, and then *we*, were rich. They bought the manor house at Little Oulmarsh's edge, to stay close to the place where Dad grew up, and his parents before him.

"*Our blood in the very soil,*" he used to say.

Little Oulmarsh is a sleepy town with few people and lots of livestock. The largest industry here is farming, which accounts for the rolling fields and run-down country lanes. There's a high street though, a couple of schools, and a college. Lots of green space, parks and fields, woodlands that sprawl into the nearby countryside. That's where my house is, backing onto an acre of land and a small wood. There's even a little stream that feeds into the River Ure somewhere along its way. It's one of those towns people seem obsessed with 'getting out' of, although I can't see why.

"Come on then," Hazel motions to the door, car keys jangling in her hand. "We don't want you to be late."

It won't take long to get to the Java Bean now Hazel's dropping me off. I usually walk, but the long route takes almost forty-five minutes. Sometimes, when I dare, I cut across the field between our house and the one that sits on the other side of the treeline. I don't think I'm supposed to, or know who the land belongs to, but no one's ever tried to stop me. And there's something about the other house. Something that draws me in.

I clear my head of those thoughts, my mind wandering back to the box and the Shadow. Their visits are becoming more frequent. At least once a week now where before we could go six months without seeing one. Mum's convinced they're the cause of Dad's absence. She used to tell me stories about them. Evil beings that stole him away. How they were coming for us. Long claws and bony arms waiting to snatch us into the night, never to be seen again. I shared in her terror, lying awake, paralysed with fear. She put crystals and charms around our windows and doors to keep evil spirits away, but it only made things worse, feeding into my own nightmares, even though I couldn't see them then.

It wasn't until my thirteenth birthday, that I saw a Shadow of my very own.

I'd been dreaming about Dad, a horrible, desperate dream, being chased by something terrible. When I'd woken up, heart pounding, trying to reassure myself that everything was fine, I saw it, sitting there on my bed. A huge grey Shadow.

It looked exactly as Mum had described: human shaped, with long, gangly arms, spade-like hands and extremely sharp claws. The shape had flickered, grey running to steel blue, as if skin was growing over it, the claws glinting silver, coming to life. I'd jammed my fists into my eyes, screeching. When I opened them again, it was gone, leaving a neatly-wrapped blue box behind. I knew then we'd both lost our marbles. Shadows aren't entities that exist in their own right. Everybody knows that. But still they pursue me, creeping inside the walls unchecked.

"You've not forgotten about tomorrow, have you?" Hazel asks me when we stop, pulling me out of my thoughts.

"I remember." I don't remember, but I want to get to the Java Bean as quickly as I can.

"All right, go on then. I'll see you for dinner."

"Okay. Thanks for the lift." Then I'm out of the car, free at last. As I round the corner onto the high street, Nicky, the owner of the Java Bean, waves at me from the front steps. Nicky's a tall man at around six feet, with thinning black hair that rises and falls in the wind. I guess he's about fifty, although I don't know for sure. He has a few lines around his eyes, and pink flares on his ruddy cheeks. Every time he smiles, a gold tooth winks from somewhere behind his thin lips. Today, he's wearing a pale-green bowling shirt that emphasises his rounding middle.

"You're early," he calls when I'm close enough.

"No rest for the wicked," I say. "Hazel drove me."

"How's your mum?" he doesn't need to ask, but he always does, his voice full of concern. He knows how unwell she is and has probably noticed the enormous bags under my eyes.

"She's okay, but, you know."

"And how are you?"

"I'm okay."

"Is it almost the anniversary?"

"Tomorrow." I *hate* it when people call it that. Anniversaries are something to celebrate. The day Dad disappeared, taking Mum's sanity with him, isn't something worthy of that title. But the essence is right; she does always get worse the closer the day comes.

"Are you sure you're all right? You look a bit pale."

"I promise, I'm fine." I feel for the rough cord around my

7

neck, as I always do when I'm stressed. The familiar shape of the ring at my throat is cool on my fingers. It was a present from Dad for my eighth birthday; one of the few things he gave me before he left. It's made of heavy, yellow gold, set with a large stone that glitters and changes colour in different lights. An opal.

"Okay. Let's get to work then."

The Java Bean's interior is a mismatch of furniture. Some tables are metal, some hardwood and some plastic. Dotted around the room are sofas made of leather, ratty with age, and threadbare cotton armchairs of different colours. There's always a pleasant smell of coffee, the dark rich scent of ground beans, and fresh pastries.

I work only a few shifts a month, usually on call for when one of the other baristas can't make it. I like to help Nicky out when I can, and besides, I owe him one. When I was younger and I needed a place to get away from home, this is where I came. Nicky welcomed me with open arms, as did the other regulars, Shelby and Otto. They've become my second family. As an extra bonus, I also get free coffee and as many blueberry muffins as I can carry. It's a pity job really, but I'm happy for the distraction nonetheless.

I take my time cleaning down the coffee machine and stocking up the cakes, while Nicky deals with the tills, and it's about thirty minutes before our first customer rolls in. I recognise Marnie, eyes half-closed and hidden behind thick-lensed glasses. She always orders strong black coffee, barely even able to mumble "thanks" before she's had her morning espresso.

Next is Otto. He's in his late sixties, with white tufts of hair around his ears. I love Otto. He always sits at the bar, often regaling me with stories about his youth.

"Morning," he says as I pour his tea. "Our Marnie's cracking on with her bestseller I see?"

"Always."

"Your friend's back, too."

I peer over his head at the boy in the booth by the window. He must have followed Otto inside, because I don't remember hearing the door open a third time. I'm sure I know him from somewhere, his face eerily familiar, but I can't think where. He spins in his seat, catching me staring, and a smile appears on his face, laughing at me. Black hair falls into his eyes, which are dark like tar, although I can't tell their exact colour from here. Heat creeps into my cheeks.

"He likes you," Otto winks at me.

"Oh yeah, right."

"Why else would he keep coming back? The coffee tastes like crap."

"One, thanks for that. Two, you drink tea." I roll my eyes at him before going to restock the straws.

When the bell over the door rings, I re-emerge. As I recognise those waiting for me, my chest goes tight, stomach rolling like an uneasy sea. Three girls march over to the counter, all of them with long highlighted hair and perfect makeup, so similar it's almost impossible to tell them apart. I know them from school: Isabella, Amy, and Amelia, and I hate them all.

After Dad disappeared, I had to grow up instantly. I focused all my energy into figuring out what happened to him, or all the energy my ten-year-old brain could muster. Then, as Mum deteriorated, my investigation had to stop, attention turning to her care. I didn't have time for friends, or shopping, or getting manicures. But children are cruel, and they don't understand.

"Merle's away with the faeries again!" Isabella cackles, cutting through the conversation of the other girls.

"Can I help you?" I say, my voice dripping with sarcasm.

"Skinny latte and don't burn it. These two will have the same." She flicks her long, honey-brown hair over her shoulder, tapping her nails on the counter. It only takes me a minute to make all three drinks, but when I hand them over, Isabella's rolling her eyes and muttering under her breath about how slow I am. She gives me a ten-pound note and takes a sip of her coffee. Her face screws up in distaste, as I pass back her change, dumping it on the counter to avoid her outstretched palm. "It's disgusting."

"I hope you choke on it," I mutter.

"What was that?"

My face remains still, giving nothing away.

"No wonder your mum went crazy, having to deal with you all day. I don't know how she stands it." Isabella scowls and flounces over to an empty table. I'm frozen to the spot with rage. I've been dealing with Isabella and her minions for years, but that's a low blow even for her.

"Ignore them, Merle," Otto says as I grab a saucer off the side to throw into the sink.

My skin is hot and itchy, as if it wants to crawl off my body. How dare she say that about Mum! Isabella knows nothing about her. They don't have a care in the world! No responsibility, no Shadows. An easy life. Tears prickle in my eyes and I blink them away, refusing to show they've hurt me. I'm trembling, wishing over and over again that their coffee *was* burned, and they'd get what's coming to them.

A familiar tingle, what feels like a wave of sparks crackling from a plug socket, works its way down my arms. It happens sometimes, when I'm frightened or furious; an uncontrollable reaction. I've been accused of smashing windows and bursting lights, but that's impossible. Otto smiles at me wanly as I turn back to the counter. With all my heart, I wish they'd leave and never come back; I hate them, hate them, hate them—

Isabella squeals as her cup bursts into shards. The foam sprays from her mug, coffee and pieces of jagged ceramic fall into her lap. Amy's cup bursts too, then Amelia's. They all scream and push away from the table, chair legs scraping in chorus. Their outfits are stained brown, hair full of white flakes from the shattered mugs, coffee forming dark puddles on the table and dripping onto the floor. Otto and the boy whip their heads around at the noise. Nicky comes sprinting from the back of the shop.

"What the hell's going on?"

"Bitches one through three spilled their coffee. I'll go clean it up." I look down at my hands. They're shaking, but the hot itching of rage is gone. I take a deep breath, trying to stop the trembling. Out of the corner of my eye, I notice the boy staring at me. He tips his head to one side, lips pursed in a line.

"You did this!" Isabella barks, pointing her long, perfectly-painted nail at my chest, as I make my way over with a broom.

"Oh yeah, of course I did. And there's more where that came from. Next time I'll turn you into a toad."

She stamps her foot like a toddler, her face red and flushed, speckled with foam. Then she spins on her heel and walks out. The others follow her, scowling at me, and the door slams behind them. I sweep up the debris, still chuckling to myself.

When I check the clock, I realise it's almost time for Shelby to arrive, signalling the end of my shift. Shelby is my closest friend, more like a grandmother, and after I've finished helping with the morning rush I usually spend some time with her. I'm about to go and change when the handsome boy saunters to the counter. Close up, I can tell his eyes are brown, like roasted hazelnuts. They sparkle at me as if we're sharing a secret, something close and deep. When he knows he's got my full attention, he waves a sizable chunk of smashed china in my direction, and then lays it on the counter.

"Nice work, with the cups." His tone is light, but somehow, I know he's not joking. Maybe it's the way he's eyeing me like I'm a caged animal.

"Excuse me?"

"I saw what you did."

"I don't know what you're talking about." He can't possibly mean what I think he means. I had nothing to do with those cups earlier. I wish.

"Yes, you do." He stares straight into my eyes, unblinking. It's a little unnerving.

"Can I get you something?"

"No." Now he grins, giving me the full wattage of his smile. His teeth are white and straight and perfect. Maybe he expects me to melt, and maybe I would've if my morning hadn't already been so horrible. "I just wanted you to know I'm a big fan of your work."

"My *what?*" I protest. Then, behind him, something

flickers.

It's a large shadowy hand, creeping over his shoulder as if it means to tighten around his neck. My throat locks and I feel a little faint, blood rushing and ringing in my ears. This can't be happening. They can't be here, too. *No, no, no.* I can deal with it at home, in the dark, where it may or may not be real, but not here. Not here, not now—

"Merle?" the boy whispers, brow furrowed. His voice is so soft I barely hear it. It's enough, however, to snap my eyes away from the growing form behind him. When I look again, the figure is gone.

"Sorry," I breathe out shakily. He looks me up and down as if to check I'm okay and when he seems satisfied, he turns and walks out of the shop. It's only after he's gone I realise he called me by my name. A name I never told him.

"Well, that was odd," I say, trying to break the tension of the moment. Shelby waves at me from outside as she rushes past the window and bustles through the door.

"Told you he liked you," Otto mumbles.

"Can it, old man." I give him the finger and his sniggers turn into full gales of laughter.

2

Nicky tells me to sit down when Shelby arrives, fussing about how I've come over pale and distracted. I tell him I'm fine, but in all honesty, I feel a little sick. Seeing the Shadows at home is one thing, but here, in the real world, it's terrifying. I shiver and take Shelby's coffee over with my own. Her bright pink lips widen in a smile, pale face crinkled with lines. She's shorter than me, and I have to hunch over to give her a hug. Her gnarled hands grip at my back for a moment. A habit of hers is to pinch too tightly, knuckles like tree knots digging into my spine. Arthritis, she says, a consequence of growing old.

"How are you doing, sweetheart?"

"I'm fine."

"You don't seem fine."

She always knows when something's wrong,

and when I'm lying. I've told her a little about the Shadows, about how Mum's losing it, how *I'm* losing it, but after my scare this morning, I don't feel like explaining myself. It's exhausting for one, and every time I think about it, my insides squirm with shame. No, it's best not to dwell.

"Come on, Merle! Bottling things up only makes them worse!"

I yawn and rub the soft skin at my temple. "It's Mum."

"Ah," Shelby says. She knows Mum and was friends with Dad. Shelby told me they met when she bought one of Dad's paintings. She's been a rock for me; a grandmother and two parents all in one.

"She's been waking up a lot, waking *me* up. I'm not getting much sleep."

She pats my hand and pouts. "I'm sorry, love. And what about your nightmares?"

"On and off. You know how they are. Last week I dreamed I was late for work, and no matter how quickly I tried to walk, I wasn't going anywhere."

"Stress dreams," Shell muses. "And I wouldn't worry about being late for work, Nicky wouldn't mind."

"I should hope not. He's barely even paying me!"

Shelby slaps me lightly on the arm and laughs. She's into dreams and other psychic things. Sometimes she brings crystals and tarot cards so she can practise her readings. I don't put much stock in it myself, although it *is* interesting. Shell turns her attention to rummaging through her bag and I roll my eyes; she's looking for her dream diary. It's a battered purple book that she always carries with her. For the last two years, she's been writing down dreams, if people will let her, so she can analyse them when she gets home. Most of the entries are mine.

"Can I write that down?" She already has her pen in her hand. "And any more visits from Dad?"

I shake my head, and she bends her own to scribble. I have very vivid dreams, usually about the faery rings. They're in the forest close to my house. Hundreds of tiny mushroom circles, spinning over the landscape like stars in the night. I used to go with Dad and play in the flowers. I often dream of that, but sometimes it turns into a nightmare. Everything turns black and dies, and the ground splits open like a mouth. Usually I wake up as I'm sliding into the earth, screaming for Dad to help me.

I'm careful not to tell Shelby too much, though. She thinks they might be messages, Dad trying to communicate with me from wherever he might be. I think she means from beyond the grave, although she's never directly said it, which isn't a pleasant thought.

"Isn't there anyone you can reach out to? Who can help you?" she asks, putting down her pen.

"Hazel's been looking into it."

"Ah," Shelby nods. "Hazel will know what to do, she's always been a fixer." Then she pushes the cup of coffee under my nose. "Drink up, then go home."

"Yes boss," I nod and lean into her shoulder.

I leave after lunch, letting Nicky ply me with cheese toasties before I go. I'm grateful for it, as it's quite a long walk, especially when I'm dawdling along as I am today. When I get to the fork in the road, a strange sensation washes over me. As if someone's watching. I spin in a circle, seeing no one.

"Looking for something?" A voice says from beside me.

"Jesus!" I shout, startled out of my skin. "How did you get

there? I swear I just—"

The boy from the coffee shop is standing about two feet away, biting his bottom lip as if he's containing a laugh. Now I almost *do* melt.

"Following me, are you?"

"A bit." A cheeky smirk spreads over his face. "Can I walk you home?"

Absolutely.

"No thanks. I'm almost there. See?" I point into the middle distance. "Wouldn't want you going out of your way."

"It's really no trouble." Somehow, his smirk gets even more smug. He moves behind me, every step graceful, almost liquid, and takes hold of my arm, pointing a little lower on the horizon. "I live right there. It's on my way back."

I swallow, my mouth suddenly dry. "You live in the other manor?"

"Is that what you call it?" He wanders back to the path, motioning for me to join him. We walk in silence for a while, at least until I get my bearings. I'm not very good at interacting with people my age, especially when I find them extremely attractive.

"I didn't know anybody lived there."

"No? Even though I've seen you looking?"

"You've got a good imagination, haven't you?" I bite back, a little embarrassed. He *might've* seen me looking; I've always been curious about what goes on inside. Sometimes I've dreamt about the house too. Occasionally, that curiosity may have spilled over into trespassing.

"Or you're in denial?"

"We'll agree to disagree." We've reached the gates that mark the entrance to his home, which thankfully signals my departure.

"Want to come in?" he asks, his lovely dark eyes shining at me playfully.

Yes. More than anything.

"No. For all I know, you could be a serial killer."

"Well, if you ever want to find out..." He rummages in his pocket and hands me a piece of paper. On it is a phone number and a name: *Ren.*

"Thanks." I try to convey nonchalance, but my heart's beating hard against my rib cage. Even my palms are sweating.

"Come over anytime." Ren smiles, a breathtakingly beautiful smile, one that almost makes it irrelevant whether he is a serial killer, then he drops me a wink and sidles through the gate.

After I've composed myself, I march across the field and down towards my house, rivers of fire rather than blood pounding through my veins. It's almost three o'clock when I jam my key into the lock at the back door, fighting with the sticky keyhole, which only gives up after a hard knock from my shoulder. Weeds poke up through the dirty flags, circling my knees, leaving spatters of dew on my jeans and boots. When I push my way inside, I can smell food and clean laundry.

After saying hello to Ali and enduring an obligatory kiss on the cheek, I rush upstairs to check on Mum. She's sleeping, curled in a ball under her sheets, mousy brown hair sprawled over her pillow. Her eyeballs flicker behind closed eyelids, the light showing the spidery web of veins dancing across them. I remember when we used to spend time together, going for walks or playing in the garden. Dad scribbling in his notebook or throwing oils at a canvas. I bring my hand up to my throat, squeezing to take away the ache. It's especially hard to see her like this now, when Dad's at the forefront of my mind, looming like one of my Shadows. Sometimes I still read to her if she's up for it, but that's hardly ever nowadays.

"She's been like that for hours," Ali says from the door, startling me. "Come on, dinner's ready."

We eat together as we always do. I answer questions about my day and offer some of my own in return, but none of us really have our hearts in it. A black cloud has stationed itself over our house, at least for the next few days, bringing with it lashing rain and uneasy winds.

"And you've definitely remembered about tomorrow?" Hazel asks, making a last-ditch attempt at conversation.

"The 'anniversary'? How could I forget?"

"No, not that," Ali intervenes. "We're taking your mother away, remember?"

I'm confused for a moment, but then I do remember, and my cheeks flush with embarrassment. They're going to the Lake District, to take her mind off Dad in the coming days. "Oh yes. Sorry Aunty Hazel."

"It's okay." Her face softens into a smile, and grief tugs at my heart. She looks so much like Dad, with the same jawline and straight nose. It's difficult to see her, to be reminded of Dad's face when he's been on my mind so frequently. Suddenly, I think I'm about to cry. "And you're sure you won't come with us?"

"No, thank you." She's asked me about a thousand times, and I can't think of anything more boring than dawdling after my mum and aunts as they coo over pretty views and drink pale ale.

"Suit yourself, then."

With that, dinner is over, and I clear off to my room. I've got important business to attend to, after all. As soon as the door closes behind me, I wrench out my underwear drawer, searching for the blue box. It's still nestled amongst my socks, waiting. With trembling fingers, I open it and find a silver charm sitting on a velvet cushion. This time it's the faces of the sun and the moon, twisted together. Where the sun beams, the moon frowns. Minute crystals are glued to its cheeks, resembling tears. It might be beautiful if it wasn't so hateful.

I discard the box and take the charm to my dresser. In my jewellery box are more tokens, hanging from a delicate chain. Silver so fine it could be a spider's web. The bracelet came with the first charm; a notebook of ivory and glass, no bigger than my fingernail. There's ten in all now. Ten charms for ten years. Each a shard of ice in my heart.

It's late by the time I pull on my faded pyjamas and crawl under the covers and as soon as my head hits the pillow, my eyes slide shut.

When they open again, I'm not in my bedroom. Instead, I'm in the woodlands behind the house, sitting in the centre of a faery ring. It's freezing, no clouds to keep the heat in, or to keep the moon from shining on the figure sitting just outside the ring. It's Dad, staring right at me. Grief slowly replaces the initial jolt of surprise, like sand trickling through an hourglass. I'd forgotten the scar on his left cheek. How his teeth aren't quite straight. I can't stop the burning in my throat or the tears in my eyes.

"Dad?" I whisper, my voice small in the still night air.

He doesn't speak, but continues to stare from beneath

his bushy brows. A dull throb rattles through my chest, the ache like a rotten tooth, gnawing and relentless.

"Where are you? Why did you leave?"

He shakes his head. The grass where he's sitting turns black around his folded knees, the colour running as if through veins, until it hits the circle's edge. It pools there and I'm sure it'll seep over the boundary. He opens his mouth as if to speak, but dark crimson liquid spills from his lips and an acidic odour fills the air.

My first instinct is to reel away from him. The blood, if it is blood, makes my stomach roll. But what kind of daughter would I be, to abandon him now? I rock forward, but his flailing hands force me away. My throat is closed with panic, swelling like a balloon. I'm frozen to the spot as his cheeks fold inwards, decaying, skin flaking away from the bone. The muscles in his jaw peek through, a beetle scrambling between his molars. Dead then, he must be. I know I'm going to faint only a second before it happens, when my shrieking brain can bear it no longer—

I sit up in bed and cram my hands over my mouth to stop my screams from tumbling out. Cold sweat covers every inch of my body, the duvet clinging to my waist and legs, trapping me. I fumble for my bedside lamp, clicking it on with an unbearably loud snap. There's no mushroom circle or infectious grass. Nothing there. Just me.

It was a dream, I tell myself. *It was a stupid dream. Go back to sleep.*

I lay down and listen to my heart drumming in my ears. The haunting image of Dad's crumbling face wavers behind my eyelids. I throw my covers off and get up. There'll be no sleep until I forget about the dream, and if I'm going to be awake, I might as well make tea. After rummaging around for a bit to find my dressing gown, I head out onto the landing, thinking about whether normal or herbal tea would be best, when a black shadow blocks my path. It spins on the red-woven rug, the distorted shape rushing towards me. It's all long lines and sweeping grey arms. This is it then, the end, when it's finally going to attack. I wonder if it'll hurt, if I'll feel anything at all?

"Merle?" A voice echoes from the dark. "Merlie, is that you?"

I sigh with relief. Not a vengeful Shadow then, only Mum. The 'shadow' formed by her body blocking the dim orange light from the rising sun. It streams through the window, emphasising the sharpness of her bones, the awful thinness of her frame. It's not uncommon that I find her wandering around in the early morning light. Usually, she comes to wake me. As she hears my footsteps, she turns, revealing her pale face and the strained muscles of her jaw. Her hair fans out behind her, nightgown swaying with the movement. If I didn't know she was my mum, I'd believe she was a ghost. The long-dead lady of the house, coming back to haunt me.

"Do you see?" she whispers, turning back to the window. Her eyes, usually blue, are dark and fixed on something I can't see.

"Mum, it's nothing."

She points a shaking white hand in the same direction, veins running blue under her fragile skin. "It's them. Don't, Merle! They'll take you like they took your father."

"Mum, there isn't anything there, it's just the trees, look." I move towards the window, meaning to move the curtains.

"Don't, Merle! Don't get too close! I don't want them to take you too!" she cries, bringing her awfully bony hands to her mouth.

I go to the curtains, anyway. There's nothing there, and it's almost infuriating to have to prove it. I reach out for the fabric, and when I yank it back, the space is empty. Just like I knew it would be.

When Mum sees there isn't anything there, she cries harder, probably with relief. The sound of sobs wracking at her torn throat is enough to wake the house. I need to get her to safety, and quickly.

"Let's go back to bed, Mum. Come on, I'll take you." I wrap one arm around her ice-cold shoulders, and lead her back towards my room, forgetting about the creaky floorboard. The noise makes us both jump. I tuck her into my bed, pulling the covers up tightly around her chin. It's not ideal to leave her in my room. Hazel will know she's had another episode, but I can't think of what else to do.

After I'm sure she's drifted off, I run downstairs to make tea. As the kettle finishes boiling, there's rustling upstairs – my aunts waking up.

Oh no. They're up so early because they're preparing for their trip! If I can get Mum ready quickly, they'll never know what happened. My problem solved before it's really begun. I forget all about the tea and race back upstairs.

Fifteen minutes later, I'm guiding Mum and her overnight bag down the stairs to find my formidable aunt waiting in the foyer, hands on hips and an expression of slight annoyance on her face.

"You're up early, and your Mum wasn't in her room this morning."

"No. I remembered about the trip and thought I should help." I give her my most convincing smile and edge Mum forward. My fingers go to the ring at my throat, restlessly twisting the cord from which it hangs.

"Come on then, June," Hazel says, eyeing me suspiciously. "Ali's waiting in the car."

Mum hugs me, clutching at my back. "See you in a few days, sweetheart. I love you."

"Love you too, Mum."

"And be careful, Merle," she whispers so Hazel can't hear. "Watch out for the Shadows."

I nod and kiss her cheek, cold all over.

"Right then!" Hazel says. "The cupboards are full, laundry's done. I left money for pizza."

"Thanks, Aunty Hazel."

She comes to hug me and tucks a stray strand of hair behind my ear. "Just a couple of little bits before we go. I've circled a few job adverts in the paper for you to look at – and don't pout. It's about time you started earning, Merle. You're almost nineteen!"

"Okay."

"We're going to have a big talk when I get back. We've got some decisions to make."

She means about Mum, the house, my future. I groan internally. "All right."

"Good." She steps outside, almost gone. Then she pokes her head back through the door. "Oh, and we're leaving the dog! Just dry biscuits twice a day, and he's not allowed on the furniture."

"Wait! No—!"

"Bye then, Merle! Love you!" she shouts and slams the

door behind her.

Smart move, leaving that news until the last minute. The dog in question trots into view and flops down onto his front paws.

"I bet you think this is bloody great, don't you?"

He barks at me, as if he's laughing. I growl back and stomp off upstairs.

3

As well as the job adverts, Hazel's left me a list of chores. As I get to work, I find my mind wandering towards Dad: what happened to him, where he might be, if he's ever coming back? I know deep down he isn't, and the gaping hole he left in my heart isn't as tender as it once was. Mum's getting worse, though, and soon I won't be able to persuade my aunts she's better off here. Soon Hazel will decide we can no longer take care of her ourselves. Then what will I do? Stay here while Mum rots in some home? Will that be my life too once they realise I'm like her?

No. I can't let that happen. There must be a way to get rid of the Shadows. Dad would know what to do... and maybe there's a way to ask him now. If Shelby's even half right about my dreams being messages, it's worth a shot.

I need to take a trip to the faery rings. A place

where the fabric of the world is thin. And when better to go than today? Ten years from when it all began.

Dad used to take me there all the time, to the woods at the back of the house. I'd follow him up the garden path, over the crumbly old wall, and through the silver birches until we found the trail. In my earliest memories, he's carrying me on his back, my little legs unable to deal with the uneven terrain. Even when I could navigate the long grass and fallen tree branches, he'd still swing me over the small stream, planting his feet firmly on either side of the bank, flinging me into the spongy reeds.

"*Don't forget to thank the sprites*," he'd say, and every time I made sure I did.

Just beyond the river, the canopy of trees thinned out, as did their twisting roots, giving way to long emerald grass and bluebells in the spring. Dad's mission was always to find the faery circles. Hundreds of fat, white mushrooms, growing in perfectly formed rings. They're always there, rain or shine. Even in the snow rocks would take their place, the seasons of change nothing to them.

In the centre of those circles, Dad would sit for hours. Sometimes he'd draw while I played in the sun. Sometimes I'd sit beside him and he'd tell me stories of a grand faery palace, of the faery king and queen and all their tiny, magical subjects. The faery rings were our place. Mum came once, but they didn't impress her.

"*You mustn't fill her head with all that rubbish, Marcus*," she'd say.

"*Of course, love*," Dad would answer, but always with a wink in my direction.

The last time we went together, there was something

different about Dad. In fact, there'd been something different about him for a while. He'd taken to locking himself in the study, pouring over strange books and hiding his sketches. Suspicious, mumbling to himself, paranoid. Not the Dad I'd grown accustomed to.

I must've upset him, which was why he hadn't taken me to the woods for so long. So on the rainy Saturday morning when he'd knocked on my bedroom door, holding my mac and wellington boots, I couldn't have been happier. We'd taken our usual route, although not with our usual excitement, and didn't stop until we reached the clearings.

"*Now*," Dad crouched in front of me. "*You've got to listen to me very carefully, Wild'un.*"

His voice is so clear in my head I gasp and almost choke on my toast. 'Wild'un', or wild-one, is a name he used to call me. Not only because I like the wild, but as a play on our last name, *Wilde*. Nobody's called me that in years. I haven't even thought about it in years.

"*Yes, Dad.*"

"*We're going to play a game, a wishing game. Would you like that?*" He hadn't waited for my response. Instead, he'd picked me up, swirled me round and planted me in the centre of the largest faery ring. His face swims clearly in my mind. The expression I'd thought then was a smile, really a grimace. He'd taken a shabby notebook out of his pocket, furiously flipped through it for a second and then stuffed it back. His face flushed, eyes determined.

"*Come here, sweetheart. Yes, that's it. Now, do you remember the queen I told you about?*" He moved me further into the centre and took hold of both of my wrists so I'd be holding my hands out in front of me. "*Well, the legend says that the Queen of Faery will grant wishes to those who know how to ask for them—"*

"*Do you know how?*"

He'd taken a small penknife out of his bag, a penknife I still have, and pulled open the blade.

"*The queen gives wishes to people willing to give her a little part of themselves, like a trade.*"

For a horrific second, I'd thought he'd meant to cut his finger off, but he'd only sliced its tip, blood dribbling down the digit.

"*Does it hurt?*"

"*No, darling.*"

I'd cut my finger too, and it only stung a little. I don't think I really would've cared how much it hurt. I'd just wanted to make him happy.

"*Now, close your eyes. That's it. I'm going to count to three and—*"

"*What should I wish for?*"

"*Whatever you want. Now—*"

"*And what will you wish for, Daddy?*"

He paused. I couldn't see his face because my eyes were closed, but if I was to guess at his expression, I'd say it would've been guarded and dark.

"*It won't come true if we tell. Now listen, Merle! On three, we're both going to wish, we're going to concentrate as hard as we can, and wish. All right? One, two... three.*"

And I'd wished, with all my tiny little heart, to see a faery.

I think Dad thought something might happen, but nothing did. When I opened my eyes, he'd been staring at his hands and muttering under his breath. Eventually, he noticed me watching and made a fuss about what a wonderful game it was. It hadn't worked, though, whatever he'd wanted to happen. Even at eight, I'd known that.

In the time I've been remembering Dad, I've made my way outside, almost to the stone wall on the outskirts of the woods. I've only been to the rings once since then, and that was the day he disappeared. As far as I know, he stopped going. The place had lost its magic for him, I think. But on that crisp October morning, when the police turned up to take Mum's statement, I knew exactly where he'd be. He wasn't missing; he was playing a game. I'd pulled on my wellies and winter coat, and run as fast as I could to the rings.

He wasn't there. I waited all day, and he never showed up. Frozen to the bone, I went back to the house, and I never saw him again.

I haven't been there since. There's too much of him there, the journey too painful.

"This is stupid," I say to myself. "He won't be there now, either. Everything that's happening to you, it's all in your head."

But then... There've been so many weird things, like the shattering cups.

"*I saw what you did,*" the boy had said.

I didn't do anything, did I? That was a freak accident. A case of being in the wrong place at the wrong time.

How many times can one person be in the wrong place, though, Merle?

I rub my hand through my hair, scrubbing hard as if that will clear away my confusion. Did I smash the cups? Is magic real? How can it be? I need to prove to myself once and for all that nothing happened, or I'll never be able to let it go.

33

Then I can forget all about the ridiculous boy at the coffee shop and carry on with my life.

Taking a deep breath, I clamber over the loose stones and into the forest. The path is exactly as I remember it, littered with brambles and leaves, and all is quiet under the canopy of orange and yellow. For now, the trees still cling to their coats. Soon they'll be nothing but bones. There are no bluebells, and the spongy reeds are brittle with cold, snapping under the weight of my adult feet.

"Thank you," I whisper to the sluggish river as I cross. I know there aren't really any sprites, but it's best to be polite. Just in case.

I sense the first faery circle before I see it.

It's small, about the size of a dinner plate. The ring of mushrooms is dense, tiny white faces sticking up to the sky, their frilled edges shading the grass beneath. I consider them fondly; I love their delicate shapes, the way they're so strong and vital despite their soft appearance.

"*Marasmius oreades,*" Dad says in my head. "*You can tell because of the gills.*"

A lump forms in my throat, making it ache. It's hard being here, so close to his ghost. There's always been so much of Mum's grief, there was never any room for mine. Today I feel like I'm floating away, a ship lost at sea.

A hundred steps further and I find the ring I want. It's full of oversized white mushrooms with dark brown underbellies. Just like in the dream. I step into the centre of the circle, which is huge compared to the others. As soon as I'm inside the ring, the air changes around me. It becomes thicker, closer, and somehow shimmery. I smell lilacs, though there aren't any close by.

"Dad?" I whisper. "Can you hear me?"

No response. I expected none, but I'd secretly hoped something would happen. Yet another sign of my speedy descent into madness. He isn't here. Just like before.

And will you sit here all day like you did then, too? my own spiteful voice spits.

No. I came here for answers, and I know how to get them. I could make another wish. I could make a wish to find out what happened to Dad.

What a stupid idea, the voice jibes again, but I ignore it. It might be stupid, and it probably won't work, but people wish on ridiculous things all the time. Stars, wells, birthday candles, all to make their wildest dreams come true. Why is wishing on a faery circle any different?

I rummage around in the pocket of my coat for my key-chain and the penknife attached to it. Dad's old penknife, only a tiny thing, no bigger than my thumb. Aunt Hazel would go mad if she knew I carried it around, but I don't even think it's sharp. I tease out the blade with my nails, the oily silver catching the light. Sighing, I pause for a moment. By doing this, am I letting my imagination run a little too wild? I've seen in Mum what giving into delusions looks like.

You're already going mad, Merle. What more harm can this do?

And I've come this far. I might as well see it through. I take the knife and jab the point into the soft pad of my index finger. There's pain, but only a little. I press harder to make a cut, the blade not even sharp enough to break the skin on the first try. A tiny bead of blood forms on the tip of my finger. It swells there like a bubble, and then, as the flow increases, trickles into my palm.

I close my eyes tight and take a deep breath. Focusing all of my will, I whisper into the cold, "My wish is to know what happened to you, Dad. I wish I knew why you left us."

I don't know if this tiny offering is enough, but it's all I have to give. I tip my wrist and let the blood fall into the grass at my feet. There's a shift in the air, I'm sure of it. The scent of lilacs intensifies for a moment; a buzz as if something's happening; my wish being granted at last.

When I open my eyes, nothing's changed.

Exactly like before.

I sigh in frustration. Now I know what Dad felt like. Never admitting openly that he expected something, but hoping in his secret heart it would be so. The disappointment filling me is crushing. No wonder Dad was so hurt. But I should have known, shouldn't I? Magic isn't real.

As I move to make my way out of the circle, I catch sight of my blood, the dark red beads being sucked into the grass.

Wait, no, that can't have been real. I blink hard and look back at the droplets.

Sure enough, the shoots are stained crimson, slowly deepening to black. Colour runs down the stem and into the ground, turning the adjacent green to murky brown. It spreads like poison, as it did around Dad in my dream, the ebony running in rivers to the mushrooms. I hop out of the circle and spin, watching in horror as the rivers spread to the other rings.

No, no, no, this can't be happening.

Cold dread snakes its way through my body. I press the heels of my hands into my eye sockets and rub hard, trying to erase the image. With a deafening scream, the earth begins to shake. I open my eyes to see it splitting open, growling and slobbering like a hungry mouth. This can't be real. Blood doesn't make the ground shake and the earth crack.

You're dreaming again.

I want it to be true, and my dreams are vivid, but my legs ache from hiking, and the cut on my finger throbs. I know you can't feel pain in dreams. Sulphur burns my nostrils, and the ground is still making horrible creaking noises, like rotten floorboards breaking. It looks like a dream, but it isn't one.

Move it, Merle, or you're going to get infected too.

I can't imagine anything worse. Getting close to even a blade of that toxic grass makes my skin crawl. I turn on my heel and run until my lungs burn and my legs scream. The rumbling chases me, hounding me as I fly over roots and debris, fleeing like a gazelle from a lion. I can't even spare a moment to look behind me.

I trip over a loose stone and tumble to my hands and knees with a shriek, my leggings torn. When I make it back to the wall, the toe of my boot catches a stone and I fall to my knees again. I haven't quite made it to the field, but I can no longer see the clearing. I gasp for breath, my ribs aching painfully, my throat raw from gulping freezing cold air. I wait for the grass to turn black and the trees to fold in on themselves, but nothing happens. There's no sign the blood followed me down here. No sign it ever existed. Maybe I've outrun it?

"*I wouldn't count on it, sweetheart.*" Now Dad's voice speaks up. "*You can't outrun destiny.*"

"Oh, shut up!" I snap out loud.

I get to my feet and start towards the house, shivering uncontrollably. My leggings drip with ice cold water from the stream, my hair hanging in dark limp strands across my forehead. Occasionally I throw a look over my shoulder to check if I'm being followed. The trees sway as calmly and as vital as ever, not a single thing out of place.

Alfie cocks his head at me disapprovingly as I traipse mud through the back door and into the kitchen. He yips two high-pitched notes in quick succession. If Aunt Hazel were here, she'd hear those yips and come running, the dog making her aware of someone breaking her rules.

"You can shut up too," I say, throwing my damp coat over his judgemental face.

After a shower and a sandwich, I feel mostly back to normal. I read for a little while, then I go back to watching TV. Like earlier, I find my mind wandering towards memories of Dad. I'm used to thinking about him often, but not with the same nagging persistence. It's as if my brain is trying to solve a puzzle, constantly dragging me back to the scene of the crime.

About six o'clock, just before full dark, I whistle Alfie for his evening walk. I intentionally stay as far away from the woods as possible, but that means I find myself wandering towards the strange house. It looms in the twilight, surrounded by fog and high metal gates.

"Come over anytime," Ren had said.

I'm flooded with an overwhelming desire to do just that. To turn up on the doorstep and demand an explanation.

You're doing it again, Merle. None of this is real. Stop letting your imagination run away with itself.

Alfie must sense my anxiety, because he's as good as gold the entire way around the field. For a wonder, his excellent behaviour continues when we get inside. He eats his dinner in the living room next to me, then curls up by my feet on the sofa. At half-past nine, I decide to call it a night. There's no point dithering down here on the sofa when I could be getting some much-needed sleep.

The shrill ringing of the phone startles me so badly I jerk upright in my seat, sending Alfie rolling onto the carpet. My frantic heartbeat slows as I realise it'll only be Mum or Aunt Hazel, letting me know about their first day.

"Hello?"

"Hi, Merlie."

"Hi Mum! How are you doing? How was your first day?"

"Good. Me and Hazel went to see the otters, then for afternoon tea by the lake—" I tune her out for a moment as she goes on, following the peaks and troughs of her voice so I know when to comment. After about five minutes, she says, "And it's safer here, not as many Shadows."

I pinch the bridge of my nose between my thumb and forefinger, my anxieties stirring again. There's nothing I can do from here. I shouldn't have let her go on her own, I should be there to take care of her instead of chasing fantasies. While those thoughts are running through my brain at cosmic speed, I respond with only, "Good."

"You sound tired, Merle."

"I had a busy day. But I'm okay. I just need some sleep."

"Aunty Hazel wants a word. Can I put her on?"

"Sure." *I wish you wouldn't.* "Night, Mum, I'll speak to you tomorrow. I love you."

"I love you too, Merle," she whispers, and then leaves me to the dry, crisp tone of my aunt.

"Is everything okay?" I ask.

"Not really, Merle." I know Hazel's edging away from Mum's prying ears. The tinkling of the other guests fades a little. She must be in the hotel lobby. "All she talks about is the shadows she sees, something coming to get her. She says one was in her room, here of all places! I thought this trip away would help things, but—"

"It's not that bad! She always gets worse around this time of year. You know she does," I snap. The excuses sound weak to my own ears; I dread to think how they sound to Hazel's.

"We're going to have a serious discussion when we get back, Merle. Maybe it's time to consider getting her some help. It's what she needs, what *you* need."

"No. You can't, it isn't her fault she's sick! We can't just abandon her-"

"I would never!" Hazel hisses and heat creeps up my neck. "I would *never* abandon you or June. But what do you suggest we do now? This is out of control, Merle!"

I say nothing, tears prickling in my eyes and burning in my throat.

"Look," she says when she realises I'm not going to speak. "I know this is tough, that it's not what you want. I wish I could change things."

"Okay." I whisper. In my heart, I know it isn't really Aunt Hazel I'm angry at, it's the horrible feeling of helplessness. Of being able to do nothing.

"Goodnight then, Merle."

"Goodnight."

I put down the receiver, hand trembling slightly. There must be something I can do, anything to stop what's about to happen.

Alfie whines from the bottom of the stairs, then barks, testing me. I shrug and he bounds up the stairs, wagging his tail. I follow him, smiling. Maybe he isn't so bad after all. He's waiting for me in my room.

"You can sleep in here, but not on the bed, okay?"

Two minutes later, just as I get comfy, the springs of my matress creak and Alfie snuggles against my back.

That's certainly not allowed. But because I'm feeling that way out, I let him stay there.

4

I wake in the night shivering with cold. At first I think I must've left a window open, but when I rub the sleep from my eyes, I realise I'm standing in the woods.

I must be dreaming again.

As I get my bearings the cold seeps into my bones, turning to dread. The branches of the canopy reach for me like skeletal fingers, their trunks charred and crumbling, leaves forming black piles at their feet. I pick my way through the path, which is littered with charcoaled sticks and dead grass. The few leaves that remain on branches hang in dry and twisted curls. I'm a long way from the house, as far up as the river, which is dry. Puddles of mustard-coloured liquid that stink of sewage bubble in its place.

The blood I emptied into the faery circle has spread and killed everything. Something in my blood caused the entire forest to rot. Everywhere

I look, everything is dead.

"No need to panic, Merle," I tell myself. "This is just a dream."

Like earlier, it doesn't feel like a dream. The goosebumps rising on my skin along with the wet ground sliding underfoot, insist it can't be. That I must be here. Maybe I'm losing it faster than I thought. First the present box, then the episode at the coffee shop; now this? Have I really managed to walk this far, in my pyjamas with no shoes, before waking up? My bottom lip trembles and tears fill my eyes.

I'm about to collapse onto a blackened log and sulk when a twig snaps behind me. The crack is so crisp and clear it sends the bats from a nearby tree chittering into the sky. I spin around to find smoke rising from the ground. It twists in lazy tendrils, taking on a shape that resembles a human, but isn't one.

It's a Shadow.

I know I should run, but my legs freeze to the spot, mouth hanging open. The Shadow's wiry black torso changes, the colour transforming into a shiny blue, like it's growing skin. Hands, thin and flat as shovels, extend from its long arms, claws protruding from them. The moonlight glints off their razor edges. It lifts its head, sniffing the air. My legs go numb, wobbling underneath me. I've seen wolves do that when they're hunting. It's trying to locate its prey.

Me. I'm its prey, and still I can't move.

After a second sniff, the Shadow cocks its head and focuses its newly formed eyes on me. They're glossy like a bug's, bulging from sockets which are still solidifying. Underneath is a puckered hole, possibly its mouth. The hole creases into a wide and gruesome smile, the surrounding skin

44

guarding too many teeth. Rows and rows of lethal points.

With a scream, I clap my hands over my eyes, my breath coming in painful gasps as I stumble blindly backwards. The Shadow crashes through what's left of the undergrowth, gaining on me. I step on something and a sharp lance of fire runs through my foot. I shriek as I fall onto my hands and knees.

The hard thud shakes me awake. I'm in my garden, the flags under me are damp, freezing my limbs. My foot is throbbing, and the cut on my finger has reopened. I don't remember walking outside, but it's a relief to find I'm not in the faery circles. Gasping for breath, my throat and chest burning with cold, I push myself to my feet. Then something flickers in the moonlight.

In front of me, barely visible, is the huge black Shadow from my dream. It looms over me, the grin twice as gruesome, reaching for me with those lethal, scythe-like claws.

A sharp yip from the doorway stops it in its tracks. It turns its head, sniffing again.

"Go back inside, Alfie!" I shout at the dog.

He stands his ground, growling through gritted teeth.

There's no air in my lungs. It's stolen by my hammering heart and ragged, screaming breaths. I can't give in to my panicked desire to flee. If anything happens to the dog, Aunt Hazel will kill me, and it turns out, I'm more afraid of her than whatever this is. I get to my feet and stand between It and Alfie. A sound rumbles from the creature's chest; it's laughing.

I reach for the stick I stood on and brandish it in front of me. Now I've made some kind of peace with the fact I'm going to die, it doesn't seem quite so—

"Merle!" The shout sounds like it's coming from far away, and it's not a voice I recognise instantly.

I turn my head, everything moving in slow motion. The boy from the coffee shop, Ren, sprints from the corner of the house and stands between me and the Shadow. He pulls a knife from the belt at his waist, the metal reflecting the moon's sickly glow. Then he snarls something in a language I don't understand, words low and harsh in his throat, and the Shadow reels from him. Ren lunges for it, the blade flashing before it plunges into the creature's body. The monster lets out a hollow moan, a terrible screech of pain. One moment it's there, bearing down on us, and the next it's flaking away on the breeze, ash littering the sky.

The boy lowers his weapon, breathing a sigh of relief.

"Ren?" My voice comes out as a harsh, frog-like croak. "What are you doing here?"

"Are you all right?" He's much calmer than I am, as if he deals with this all the time.

"Yes." I look from his face to the knife in his hand. The blade is a dull grey and about six inches long. It looks to be sharp on both edges.

"It's iron," he says, twisting the dagger in his fingers and dropping it back into his belt. "They can't stand it."

"Who's 'they'?"

"Let's go inside." There's a strange look in his eyes I don't understand. As if he's exhilarated from what's just happened rather than terrified. Somehow, it puts me at ease. At least someone's in charge of the situation. "You must be freezing."

As the adrenaline coursing through my veins wears off, I realise I'm shaking uncontrollably, my teeth chattering. I nod curtly and motion for him to follow me inside. My first course of action is to get changed into something dry and warm, so I leave Ren in the kitchen with Alfie. On my way back down the stairs, there are tiny smudges of blood on the carpet. I check the bottom of my foot and find a shallow cut there, but right now that's the least of my concerns. Back in the kitchen, Ren boils the kettle and puts a steaming cup of tea in front of me.

"Thank you," I say and clasp it in my chilly hands.

He shrugs and takes a seat opposite. While he's dealing with the sugar, I've got enough time to get a good look at his face. His jaw is sharp, hair falling around his ears, slicked back to his temple from the rain. I know his eyes are dark, though I can't quite remember whether they're the colour of the deep ocean, or varnished mahogany. They sit above a straight nose, his lips in a thin line underneath. Ren is beautiful. The trouble is that he certainly knows it.

"Enjoying yourself, are you?" he says and my cheeks flame at the embarrassment of being caught.

"Don't pretend you aren't."

His grin widens, and he slides me a plate of biscuits. "That's beside the point."

"What was it, that thing?"

"Straight to business, huh?" He looks down at his hands, struggling with his words for a moment. When he looks back up, his face is much more serious. "Now, this is going to be hard to believe, but I need you to be open-minded."

I nod, urging him to go on.

"That thing in your yard just now was a faery."

My mouth slowly opens. A faery? Ridiculous.

"The organisation I belong to sent me to keep an eye on you," he continues. "I'm Ren Du Lac, descended from

Lancelot Du Lac, the Lord of the Lake, Knight of the Round Table."

"What?"

His face pulls down in a frown and he narrows his eyes at me. "You heard me. I'm descended from Lancelot, *the* Sir Lancelot."

I take him in for a full thirty seconds. There are no lies on his face, no shadow of a joke in his eyes. Still, it can't be true. How can it be? He might be mad. "The one who ran away with Guinevere? The one from a thousand fictional years ago? But they're just stories!"

"To ordinary people they're stories." His face takes on a wicked grin that makes me shiver. "But not to you or I. To us, it was all real, it all happened. We have a duty to our ancestors, to keep good on promises they made."

"What do you mean 'we'?"

"Me, Joth. You." His eyes don't leave mine. Brown, not blue. The colour of espresso. "We suspect that you, Merle Wilde, are the descendant of Merlin Wyllt, the greatest wizard and royal advisor the kingdom of Camelot ever knew." I see him hold his breath, waiting for my reaction.

From the way his face falls and his eyes go wide in surprise, I realise my laughter isn't the response he was expecting.

"I mean it, Merle." His voice is so serious, the giggles die in my throat.

No, no, no. This can't be real. My thoughts spin out into the silence. The descendant of Merlin Wyllt? Camelot? It must be a joke, it has to be.

"No," I choke out, shaking my head. "No. I don't believe you."

"Marcus believed us."

"Impossible."

I would've known wouldn't I? If Dad was involved with these people? Would he have hidden it from me?

You know he wasn't himself at the end.

"Our Guardian Joth says so. He says Marcus believed, and he has no reason to lie."

I stare straight at him. I hope he can read on my face what a low shot this is. Not that he's to know how much Dad and his disappearance have been on my mind lately, or what it led me to do earlier. "Who's Joth?"

"The Guardian of the Templar. That's what the building is, the one you call the 'other manor'. I've seen you looking. That's what put Joth onto the both of you, you know? He remembers you and your dad standing at the end of the drive and just looking."

"What's a Templar?"

"It's where we live and what we call ourselves, the descendants of the Knights of the Round Table. We protect each other, and the relics and status garnered by our ancestors. It's our job to take care of Arthur's line as the knights took care of Arthur." His voice is soft and dark. "And to find you, Merlin's heir, to claim your magic and—"

"Magic isn't real."

He shrugs, puts his mug down, and laces his fingers together. "Magic is rare. That's true, so rare it might seem unreal. But I've seen you do it. And you can see the fae rings. People usually can't, like your mum—"

I bristle noticeably at her mention. Ren must've expected it because he holds up his hands in a calming gesture. "Your mum only sees empty clearings. She's asked you before, hasn't she? What's up there? You can see them though, and you can open them."

"You've been following me?" I ask, but don't need to wait for his answer. "And that, what happened there, it wasn't real. I was dreaming."

"Is that what you told yourself?" He reaches across the table and takes hold of my wrists, turning my palms face up. They're scratched and red from my earlier fall. "Then how did you get those?"

I snatch my arms away from him and cross them over my chest. "I haven't been feeling well. Mum's been keeping me up, and it makes me imagine things! They could be from anything. I was dreaming."

"Then why did you ask if I was following you?" His voice is still soft, coaxing my anxious brain to admit what it's been hiding from itself. "If it was a dream, Merle, surely your first question would've been how I knew?"

Cold shivers run through my body, my fists and jaw clenching painfully. Once again, he's right. He shouldn't have known about it, *couldn't* have known about it if it was all in my head. Dizziness sweeps over me, and I close my eyes. It can't be real, the wish and the decay, the 'faery', the Shadows; but neither can Ren know about it. Nothing makes sense.

"What made you go into the woods?"

"I had a dream. Dad wanted me to go there."

He says nothing. With my eyes still closed, it's hard to tell what he's thinking, although if I open them I might be sick. "I can see them, the Shadows, for years I've been able to. I thought if I pretended they weren't there, then Mum would stop seeing them."

"It's okay, Mer."

"I saw one in the coffee shop when you were there. It was..." I trail off, reaching to my neck and squeezing. The memory of that huge black hand around Ren's throat makes me shiver. Now my eyes open to check one isn't there behind him.

Ren's deathly pale, the colour drained from even his lips. "The Shadows aren't shadows. They're faeries, a dark form of faery. Dangerous." He swallows, Adam's apple bobbing up and down. "They've always been able to slip through the cracks between their realm and ours. But the one in your yard, I've never seen one that big, not that I've seen many. I think you might've severed the protective magic around the ring an—"

"So this is my fault?!"

"No!" He leans forward to grab my hands so fast he almost upsets the sugar bowl. "No."

After a long look in his eyes, I nod for him to go on.

"You didn't know," he continues more calmly. "And no one could ever expect you'd be able to... I mean, we've never seen magic that powerful! I came here to help. Whether or not you realise it, you're important. We can't afford for anything to happen to you."

My stomach flips at the intensity in his eyes. It's a lot to take in and I need time to think.

"Merle, I realise I'm asking a lot, and I've thrown you in at the deep end. But let me show you, give me a chance to prove what I've been saying is true.".

"The real question here, Wild'un, is whether you believe him. Do you?" Dad asks in my head.

I can't help but note the hopeful lines around Ren's mouth and the tenseness of his shoulders. "Okay."

51

Ren beams, and it lights up his entire face. "How's tomorrow?"

"I'm not expecting anyone back until the afternoon."

"Then I'll be here at nine-thirty."

I snort and follow him to the door. As he steps off the stoop, I reach forward and grip his shoulder. "Thank you for saving my life."

"Anytime."

I squeeze my fingers, hard. I'm sure he winces. "And if you're lying to me, Ren Du Lac, you'll wish you'd let it kill me."

The next morning I wake to Alfie licking the bottom of my foot, and grey sky like polished silver peeking through the curtains. Stretching the aches and pains from my limbs, I get ready for the day. What I learned from Ren is almost impossible to believe; that the Shadows are real beings, faeries sent to haunt us, and that I have magic. Deep down, I know I wasn't dreaming earlier when I saw that thing. Alfie wasn't dreaming either. He was growling at it, he could *see* it. And how could Ren have known about it? If it was all in my head? At the bottom of the stairs, I check myself in the mirror. My face is too pale, dark circles under my eyes making them look sunken and tired. I pad through to the kitchen and flick on the kettle, pour some biscuits into Alfie's bowl, and pull milk from the fridge. I notice Ren at the back door when I'm washing up last night's cups.

"Hi," he smiles when I open the door, the action pulling at the corner of his mouth, dimpling his left cheek.

"Tea, coffee?"

"No, thanks." He shoves his hands deep into the pockets of his jeans, ruching the material of his green parka up around his elbows. "How are you?"

I bite my bottom lip and nod. "Mostly, I'm okay, although I'm still not one hundred percent sure I'm not in a coma." Ren snorts as I fill a flask with coffee. "I need to walk the dog."

He waits patiently while I put on my coat and boots, then I fiddle with Alfie's collar for a minute, debating whether he needs a lead. I decide against it; he was well enough behaved yesterday. When I'm finally finished, and there's nothing else I can do to delay the inevitable, I meet Ren's eyes again.

"Ready?" he asks.

I'm not. Which I'm sure is one hundred percent clear on my face. I'm not ready to have my whole life changed.

Yes, you are. You have been for a long, long time.

"After you," I say and push open the kitchen door.

5

Alfie bounds out ahead of us, his long brown fur tangling in the grass. Not for the first time in my life, I wish he could talk, to ease the growing tension between Ren and I.

"Where did they go, your mum and your aunts?" Ren asks.

"To the Lake District, to visit the otters. Hazel was trying to get Mum away, to see if she feels any better. These last few months have been—" I break off, swallowing the lump in my throat. I'm always crying nowadays. Everything sets me off. I haven't yet really admitted this to myself, never mind out loud, but it's time. "Mum is past the point of no return. They've driven her insane, those things she sees. They took Dad away, they've cost Mum her mind, and now—"

"They've come for you," Ren finishes. He looks worried. The expression marking the lines of his face like a ghostly hand.

We've reached the wall again, and today I won't be taking him any further. I never want to go near those rings again if I can help it. I shuffle up onto one stone and sip at my coffee. Alfie yaps a sharp high note, but when I wave my hand at him to carry on playing, he disappears into the long grass. Ren leans back and stares over at the house. It looms through the fog. Rather than grand, it looks old and run down, exactly as it is.

"Tell me about the heirs," I say.

"There are a lot of us, scattered all over Britain. The Templar tried to keep a handle on it as best they could, but people are tricky. They get married and create offspring and don't record it. Now it's a little better, but can you imagine trying to keep track of a fallen dynasty in the middle ages with pieces scattered to the wind?"

"I imagine it's difficult."

"Yes, but we've got a historian for that now. That's Willow, you'll like her, everybody does." He takes the flask from my hand, drinks, and then hands it back.

"I could have a disease."

"I'm willing to risk it," he chuckles. "Anyway, we have Templars all over. That's what the house is over there." Ren points off into the distance. I let my eyes follow the straight line of his arm, and just above the treeline, there's a slate roof. "I met Joth when I was six. He came to find me and explained that he thought I was the long lost great-great-great..." Ren rolls his eyes. "You get the picture. Anyway, the great-grandchild of Lancelot and Guinevere. They'd traced my bloodline back from my birth mother."

"You didn't already know?"

"No, and not many of the heirs do. There are some families that have always known about the Templar, like Sir Kay's family, and Joth. They've always been a part of it, hoarding information and relics." He frowns, tiny lines appearing at the corners of his mouth. "But most of the lines were lost. That's what Willow calls them anyway, and she could explain this much better."

"You're doing fine," I whisper. I don't think King Arthur himself would have a hope in hell of convincing me, anyway. "How could Joth know about you, Ren? After all that time? It can't be real."

"Some of it isn't. Most of the stories you find in books aren't, but they're all based in fact. There's no actual knowledge in the public domain because the Templars have it all. According to Joth, Guinevere and Lancelot had a child, a little girl called Galiere. They sent her to a nunnery to keep her away from them, in case the remaining knights found them. Galiere stayed with the nuns for most of her life, but when she learned her mother had fallen ill, she went back to her home. She fell in love with the healer who was caring for Guinevere."

"What illness?"

He looks into my eyes and then flicks his own away, a flush on his cheeks. "Lancelot died, and Guinevere's grief... she was heartbroken."

I've seen what grief can do to a person. How they fade into a pale imitation of themselves, then into an unrecognisable ghost.

"Did they get married?" I ask before I let my thoughts run away with me.

"Galiere and the healer? Supposedly. Anyway, they had

children, and all of them married into various families. Joth couldn't tell me very much about the middle period of my family tree. He could only trace one child, Galethi."

"Galiere, Galethi, and Guinevere? It all sounds pretty made up to me, Ren."

"I know how it sounds, just listen," he snaps, "and they used to do stuff like that, with the names! It's recorded by the knights that Galethi's son married into the court of Cerdic, the King of Wessex. After his marriage, it's easier to keep track. To cut a long story short, I'm a child of that line, and the knights brought me to the Templar so I could join them. During my training, we found a record of my entire family tree." A smile breaks over his face. "Somewhere in their hoard of books, there'll be a record of you, too. A proper one, at least." I snort and flick a strand of hair out of my eyes. Ren scowls at me, but then carries on. "If you decide to join us, then you'll learn all about that part of it, all the stories, what's a myth and what isn't."

"What do you mean 'join us'?"

He looks at me as if I'm entirely stupid. "You're the heir of Merlin. You have a duty to protect the Pendragons, like I do."

"The Pendragons?"

"As in Arthur Pendragon? King Arthur. Well, their line's actually been traced back to Anna, but..." He must see the confusion on my face as he stops and shakes his head. "Sorry, I got carried away. Lux and Lore are the Pendragon twins, but Joth didn't want me to tell you about them yet. In case you refuse. But I won't tell if you won't."

"How do you keep track? And how did your historian even know where to start?"

He pauses for a moment, looking up at the dwindling leaves. "I'm not the best person to explain all that."

"Try it."

"The way I understand it is that the heirs of the knights are unlike any of the family trees Willow ever traced," Ren begins cautiously. The wind whistles by us, picking up strands of his dark hair and casting spindly shadows on his cheeks. "She says that there aren't many survivors, as if only one person from each generation becomes a 'chosen one', so to speak. So take Galethi, for example. He and his wife Crierwy had six children, *six*, but only one of them ever had children of their own. It's the same way for most of the lines. No matter how many kids are born, only one person in that generation will create any offspring." He trails off. "Willow said it was a lot of guessing..."

"So you can't prove what you're saying is true?" I splutter. "This might all be a lie?"

"I told Joth he should have come!" Ren whispers almost to himself, then stares at me again. This time, I don't blush under the intensity of his gaze. "And it isn't a lie. I told you Joth met your father, didn't I? He'd traced enough bloodline for it to be worth the risk of contacting him. He explained who he was, about the Templar, and your father agreed to meet."

I cast my eyes forward, unable to look at him any longer. He keeps saying that Dad agreed to this madness, that he knew about it all and kept it from me.

Well, why would he have told you? I ask myself. *You were a child. And you know he wasn't right at the end. You know that.*

"Then, just before the meeting, your dad changed his

mind. He said he didn't want to get his family tangled in all this. Joth agreed to stay away. We didn't know that any Pendragon heirs still existed then. No point uprooting him," Ren continues, oblivious to my lapse in concentration.

"You're still here, though, watching me. There must be more."

"There is," Ren nods gravely. "On the night of his disappearance, he contacted Joth and told him he wanted to reconsider. Something had happened, and he needed to meet. Joth never got the chance to see him."

"Because he disappeared?" I close my eyes and put my fingers to the bridge of my nose, dizzy for a moment. I remember the night. Dad pulling on his coat, kissing me on the cheek and saying, *"in the desk Wild'un, something for you."* I jolt, as if I've been shocked. *In the desk.* I've never checked there, the memory buried far away under the strain of everything else.

"Merle?"

"Sorry," I shake my head. "Mum thinks a changeling took him."

"Probably not a changeling," Ren muses. "Maybe a faery."

I bite down hard, clenching my teeth together. No, it can't be, not after all this time, all the doctors, all the tests. It's driven her to madness, and I'm not far behind her, and it could all be real? We could have put a stop to this years ago, and I might've been able to save even a sliver of her mind. It can't be real.

But it would explain everything.

Ren sighs and the sad look on his face dampens my frustration a little. "Joth wouldn't have sent me if he didn't think something was wrong. Our job, mine, the Templar's, it's keeping the fae in their realm. We can't allow them to come through. Their sole purpose is to destroy what remains of the Pendragon line, which isn't much."

"No! No, it's all in our heads, the doctors said—!"

"You saw one!" he yells. "Last night, one almost killed you! The fact she can see them, your mum, a human with no royal or magical blood! It means they're getting stronger! If they get through, the world as you understood it yesterday morning won't exist anymore!"

I roll my eyes at him. The world as I understood it yesterday already doesn't exist. Not for me.

"So what you're telling me," I spit, "is that I'm descended from the greatest fictional sorcerer of all time? I'm being chased by Shadows that are actually faeries? And not only are they trying to kill me and Mum, and whoever the Pendragons are, but they're intent on breaking through from their realm to destroy the world? And somehow it's my job to make it go away?"

"Wow," Ren leans back on his elbows, "I didn't think I was making sense but..."

I slide off the stones and spin on my heel so I'm facing him, my drink flying and almost covering him. "You're insane! Magic isn't real!"

"I saw you break those cups." His voice is low and calm, daring me to challenge him.

"That was an accident!" I didn't do that. It's impossible, isn't it? But then there's what happened yesterday at the rings. Can I deny that too?

Ren rushes forward and grabs hold of my arms, twisting me so I'm looking into his eyes, which are wide and desperate. No lies in them though, none that I can see. "I promise you,

I'm telling the truth!"

"This is the craziest thing I've ever heard. I'm going home. Alfie, Alfie! Come on!"

"You might not believe me now!" Ren's voice is low, "but one day you will, and I hope it isn't too late when you decide to trust me."

"Are you threatening me?"

"Don't be an idiot! I'm not threatening you! First, if I was, I don't doubt you could obliterate me where I stand if you put your mind to it. Second, if I wanted to hurt you, I would have let that thing kill you last night!"

"Leave me alone, Ren!" I pull my arm from his grip and stalk forward. Alfie bounds to my side, a growl rumbling low in his throat.

"I can't! Even if you don't believe me, you're still in danger!" Ren's still now, put off by the dog, I think. He keeps flicking his eyes towards Alfie's sharp, white canines.

"There is no danger!"

"You can feel it, Merle. I know it! You've been feeling it for months. Haven't you? What if another Shadow comes back and I'm not there? Please, come with me to the Templar and speak to Joth. He can explain!"

"Why should I trust you? I don't even know you, and you don't know me!"

"Maybe not." His dark eyes bore into mine, making him impossible to ignore. "But you don't know you either. Come and meet Lux and Lore."

"No! I'm going home, Ren." He's staring at me as if I owe him something, hurt by my refusal. That only makes me angrier. He's blindsided me, given me information about Dad I never knew, the task of protecting two children I've never heard of, and that's if I choose to believe him. Tingling runs down my spine again. It's both hot and cold, spreading through my arms, to the tips of my fingers. Usually the feeling scares me, but not today. Today, it feels powerful.

"*Magic would explain everything, wouldn't it, Wild'un?*" Dad muses.

Alfie barks, high-pitched whines ringing in the quiet.

"All right, Merle," Ren holds out his hands in front of him, and takes two steps back, "go home. But I'm not lying to you! When you're ready to know the rest, to see the life that's waiting for you, come and find me. Like it or not, you need us. Almost as badly as we need you."

I turn from him and storm away.

"And be on your guard!" he shouts after me. "Do that at least! Be on your guard!"

I run most of the way home, which luckily is only a few hundred metres, as I'm already out of breath from shouting. Alfie keeps close to my heels, occasionally circling back to check we're not being followed. There's still a prickly feeling in my fingers that's not altogether unpleasant. Like pins and needles.

My mind is racing. How can it truly be real? Everything Ren's said is based in fantasy, knights and magic, fictional kings! How does Ren expect me to believe *any* of it?

"*You* do *believe him though, don't you Merlie?*" Dad's voice in my head again. "*How do you explain what you saw last night? What happened at the fae rings? Something isn't right.*"

"*Shut up!*" I spit back at him. "*If you hadn't kept secrets from me, we wouldn't be in this mess!*"

To that, there's no response.

I slam through the kitchen door and lock it firmly behind me, leaning my forehead against the cool glass. That didn't go as planned. I expected answers, not more questions.

After a moment, when I've stopped shaking, I fill Alfie's water bowl and head upstairs. If I want to figure out what Dad was thinking, there's only one place to go.

I haven't been in Dad's study for years. It isn't forbidden exactly, but we don't go in there. Not even Hazel dares touch it. Maybe it's in case she disturbs the memory of him? In case he comes back and finds things changed? I don't know. But it's the last of him, of everything he was, stamped into the pages of those books, faded into the walls. I make my way to the large rosewood door, stained as red as blood, laying my palm against it, unsure of what to do.

If I go in, I might find proof that everything Ren says is true. That Dad really believed he was Merlin's heir and decided to join the Templar. That he believed in magic and faeries and King Arthur. Or I might find nothing. I'm not sure which I want it to be.

"*Go on, sweetheart, in you go.*" Dad's voice echoes behind me, and I do as he says.

My fingers tremble as the door swings wide, and the familiar musty smell of old books and ink hits my nose. I'm sure I see him sitting behind his desk. Not dead after all, not gone, just here the whole time, hiding from us!

No. No, it's just his hat on the back of the chair, tilted at a jaunty angle.

I stifle a scream with both my hands as the door creaks behind me, but then fur tickles my calf; Alfie.

"You almost gave me a bloody heart attack," I snarl.

He tilts his head on one side and bangs his tail against the carpet, sending up a cloud of dust. I roll my eyes and go to the desk. It's varnished with the same red as the door, all the wood in here is, and covered with a thick layer of dust. I daren't sit on the chair in case it gives way under my weight, but I remember him sitting here. Sometimes with sunlight pouring through the windows, shining on his sallow cheeks. Sometimes with the lights dimmed so low his face became lost in shadow, eyes glinting like a beetle's. Like those things.

Stop it, I chide myself. *Stop that. He wasn't one of them. He was never.*

Still, I can't stop the shiver running down my spine.

As Dad was left-handed, his pens and pencils are still lined up on the left side of the desk. The fountain pen I could never touch, the pencils standing to attention, points sharpened with deadly precision. On the right is a stack of papers and notebooks. I ease the sheets from the top, and as expected they show nothing of interest. If he was hiding something precious, keeping something from me, he wouldn't have kept it here in the light. No, he would've locked it away somewhere. *In the desk, Wild'un. Something for you.*

I pull on the left-hand drawer, which slides forward, albeit a little stiffly. Nothing in there other than dust. The right one pulls about a centimetre before stopping with a metallic click. This is it then. I drop to a crouch, and Alfie licks my cheek. I push him away gently. No time for him now. Right at the back of the underside of the desk is a white envelope taped to the wood. I peel it off carefully and flip it in my shaking hands.

Merle is scrawled on the envelope in his hand, the 'M'

looping underneath the final 'e', the line curling with a flourish. I sit back on my heels, no longer caring about the dust. His handwriting is very similar to mine, and my gut wrenches at the sight of it. Words of his delivered after so long, bitter and sweet, almost unbearable. I peel back the folds of the envelope. The paper inside is so thin it's translucent, brittle like spun sugar.

Hello, sweetheart.

I'm glad you've found this, my parting gift, as I knew you would, you clever girl. I don't have time to tell you everything. There are ears everywhere, even in the walls. But I've not set you on without a little help. I--

There's a splotch of ink on the page, as if he'd been interrupted.

Never mind. Maybe I'll never need to give you this, my darling. Maybe I'll have explained it to you all in person and we'll laugh at what a silly thing I've done, as if I was a detective in an old noir.

But just in case, I leave you the key to the desk and everything else in the study you have use for. Be careful, Wild'un.

All my love,
Dad

Tears spurt from my eyes and run down my cheeks. He knew then that something was wrong, that something was coming for him. Alfie whines, sensing my distress.

"It's all right, don't worry," I say, patting him on the head, simultaneously pushing myself to my feet and tipping the envelope so that a small golden key falls into my hand.

After a few twists, the lock clicks and the drawer pulls open, revealing a dusty stack of books. I lift them out with trembling hands and place them on the desk. I want there to be more notes, but I don't think they'll be any. Not if he thought he was being watched.

I find a promising book, thick and bound with red leather, the pages ageing and yellow. I open it in the middle and am met with a large drawing of a king. His long hair frames a kind and open face. He's wearing a crown and holding a broadsword. The words '*King Arthur*' are written above him in Dad's steady hand. I flick through the pages and find hundreds of other drawings. Beautiful Guinevere, first at Arthur's side, then at Lancelot's. There's a portrait of a young boy with golden hair holding a wooden cup. He's shining with light as a choir of angels sings around him, above his head the name *Galahad*. There's also a picture of Merlin. He's not old as I've imagined him, instead he has dark, waist-length hair and shining eyes of different colours, one brown and the other gold. He stands in the forest, surrounded by leaves and grass which snakes around his calves. In fact, he's standing in the centre of a faery ring.

"They're just drawings," I whisper to myself.

As I rifle through the last few pages, I find one missing, leaving only a jagged yellow edge. The rest of the book is so neat and pristine, this sticks out like a sore thumb.

Maybe he made a mistake and ripped out the drawing, my mind offers. *Or he ripped it out because there was something he didn't want anyone to find.*

I stop myself. Speculating is just going to get me in more trouble, worked up over something that can't possibly be true. Dad was a fan of stories about King Arthur. Thousands of people are, so what? And he was paranoid, making wishes and hiding notes.

Underneath the first are two more hardback books, cloth covers fraying at the edges. They feel ancient in my shaking hands. In the first book there's nothing of note, only elaborately illustrated stories of The Knights Templar. The last one, however, is full of black, spidery handwriting.

As I flick through the pages, I find hundreds of smaller notes, harshly scribbled half-words, underlined phrases. The ramblings of a madman. Only one thing truly catches my eye in the topmost corner of the last page: *Call Joth.*

I'm certain my heart skips a beat.

I close the book and clutch it to my chest, head spinning. If everything Ren's told me is true, then I don't have any idea who I am, who Dad was, or any of my family who came before him. I close my eyes and take a deep breath. When I open them, everything will be the way it was before. I'll just be a regular girl. There'll be no Ren Du Lac, and no talk of magic, faeries, or Shadows. Mum will come home and she'll be happy. *We* will be happy.

When I open my eyes, everything looks the same.

I sigh and run my fingers along the pages of the book, gasping when I give myself a paper cut on an odd ridge. When I flip it open again, I find a piece of folded paper. It's a drawing of two small children. Their skin is pale and as smooth as a statue, blonde tresses of hair framing their faces. They're both wearing golden crowns. Above the picture, it says *'dream??'* in big letters.

A dream is exactly right. Everything that's happened in the last few days might as well be a dream. I rub my hands over my eyebrows. What I need is some time to relax, to think through everything that happened today, and decide what to do. I want to trust Ren, but everything he told me is so far-fetched. The only thing that sticks in my mind are the two words scratched into the side of Dad's book.

Call Joth.

Dad wanted something from him, and I asked for answers. Joth might be the one who has them.

"What do you think, Alf?" I ask the dog, who's looking at me in a troubled way. He huffs and drops his head onto his folded paws. I gather up the books, the note, and the key, and when I get to my room, I dump them on my bed before rummaging for my jeans in a pile of dirty clothes. I find them, fish out the crumpled piece of paper, and run downstairs. As I dial the first few numbers, I hesitate. Should I actually call Ren to ask for advice? I curse myself for leaving things in such a bad way earlier. Dad always used to say I was too hot-tempered.

Well, there isn't anyone else to call.

I finish dialling and wait. It rings a few times, so long that I don't think anyone will answer. Maybe that's for the best...

"Hello?" Ren's calm, deep voice says on the other end of the line.

I take a deep breath. "Hi—"

"Merle?"

"I need to see you."

He pauses for a moment; I imagine him biting his full bottom lip between his teeth, and a flush creeps up my cheeks. "Meet me at the wall. I'll bring you to the Templar."

"Okay, I'll be there in ten minutes." I don't know if I've made the right decision, but it's out of my hands now.

6

This time, I leave Alfie behind. He grumbles until I throw some sliced ham in his bowl with his biscuits. Then I don't think he could care less that I'm going out. I make it to the wall before Ren, and sit peering into the gloom of the trees, waiting for him. I think there's a path through the woods to the other house, as if they've always been connected.

"What are you looking at?" a loud voice says from behind me and I almost jump out of my skin. When I turn around, Ren's smirking, pursing his lips to hold in his laughter.

"Oh, ha ha." I slide down off the bank. Ren holds out his arms to catch me, gripping my elbows tightly. My forehead bumps against his chin sending a shower of sparks coursing through my entire body. Does he feel it, I wonder? The electricity between us? Or is that in my head too? As I lean back, he squeezes his fingers peering down into my eyes, searching them intently.

"There's something different about you," he says.

"Yet you look exactly the same."

He laughs and lets go of my arms, taking two steps back so we're on the flat.

"Come on, if we're going. Mum and Hazel will be back soon."

"What's she like? Your Mum?" Ren asks, picking up the pace. He shadows the wall for about thirty yards before finding a small path concealed by bracken and leaves.

That's quite the question, and I'm not sure how to answer. I only remember snippets of her from before. She was beautiful until she got so thin, her pale ringlets piled on top of her head, eyes shining with love and kindness. I remember her dancing by the fire with Dad's arms around her waist, the flame light shining on their faces, making them glow. Smiling up at him as if he was the most wonderful thing in the world.

"I'm sorry," Ren whispers. "I didn't mean to upset you."

I brush my fingers across my cheek and find them wet with tears. I turn away for a moment, the wind cold where it touches them. "She's not here anymore. She's been gone almost as long as Dad. Maybe not her body, but her mind."

Ren's a few steps in front of me, but he doesn't interrupt, so I take it as a cue to go on.

"I already told you about the changelings, didn't I? She's always been superstitious, she wouldn't let me dress up on Halloween, didn't want to anger the ghosts. She even used to make me put bread in my pockets when I walked to school."

"To keep the little folk away." Ren looks over his shoulder, smiling.

74

I start. Nobody's ever understood Mum's delusions before. His eyes stay on mine for a little too long. They're soft as he regards me and colour comes into his cheeks. After a moment, he shakes his head and turns back to the path.

"She wakes me up all the time, convinced something took Dad, and that it's coming back for us." As I say the words out loud, I realise the weight of them. All this time she's known. She's seen them in the darkness, the faeries, biding their time and waiting to pounce. They might have driven her mad, but never did she stop her warnings.

We've come out of the small band of woods and into more long grass. The Templar's much closer now, its stone walls the same colour as our manor, although its face is painted with ivy. Ren's still keeping a steady pace, and as I'm trying to catch up to him, a horrible thought dawns on me. I rush forward and reach for his arm, but he's already turning. He grips my wrist in midair, pulling me to him again.

"Promise me," I say. "Promise me this isn't some kind of horrible trick. *Promise.*"

He studies my face, looking for something. I hope he understands what I'm asking. If it were just me in this, at risk of being made to look like a fool, I wouldn't care. It would hurt, but I'd get over it.

Not her, though. The one thing I couldn't bear would be a joke at Mum's expense.

He relaxes his grip on my wrist. "I swear, Mer. I swear on Lux and Lore, on the Templar, and on anything else you'd have me swear on. It isn't a trick."

Now it's my turn to study him, and I find him honest. I tug my arm out of his fingers, rubbing the sore spot there.

"And don't sneak up on me like that."

"I'm sorry," I whisper, and I mean it. He turns his back on me and starts walking again. I fall into step beside him. "What about your parents? Where are they?"

Ren's quiet for a long time, so long I don't think he'll answer. The look on his face keeps shifting between misery and pain, and I wish I'd never asked.

"I don't remember my mother, I never knew her... and my dad died when I was small."

"I'm sorry. I didn't mean to..."

"It's okay," he smiles, although he doesn't look at me. "It was a long time ago, and I don't really remember. Joth's been all the parents I've ever needed."

"What's he like?"

"Kind and fair. He loves us like his own, even though he has no obligation to do so. You'll see for yourself in about five minutes."

We've now come up to the grounds proper, the huge old house surrounded by iron bars riddled with rust. The sprigs of long, unkempt grass drops off into a perfectly cut lawn. It feels spongy beneath my feet.

"Why don't you cut this bit?"

"Because it's the wild grass," Ren says, as if that should explain everything. "Most of the Templar's ground is consecrated, blessed. The wild grass only grows where holy water hasn't been spilled."

He motions to a gap in the metal fence where one bar twists out of shape. He bends down and slides through, waiting for me on the other side. As we round the corner, I notice the door is varnished oak, decorated again with twisting spirals. "What's with all the metal?"

"You're full of questions today, aren't you?" He raises an

eyebrow, although he's smiling. "Iron, it stops the faeries coming too close."

"Really?"

"Do you remember the knife I had? It works the same as that." He pushes open the door. The entrance hall is immense. In front of me is a grand stone staircase covered by a red rug. A crystal chandelier swaying slightly on its chain, casting fragmented colours across the walls. It's cold in here, with the high ceilings and uneven floors and it smells like a museum. Our footsteps echo as Ren guides me through an archway and into another corridor.

"Where are we going?"

"Joth's office." He flicks a look at me over his shoulder. We get to another large oak door, and Ren knocks twice.

"Come in," a deep voice sounds from the other side.

An older man is sitting behind the desk. It's the same as Dad's, although a deep brown rather than blood red. There are lines around the man's eyes, as if he's smiled a lot. A beard frames his chin, the same shade of grey as the hair pushed back from his temples.

"Hello, Merle." He offers his hand across the table, his fingers warm and dry. "I'm Joth."

"Hi." I shake his hand and he motions for me to sit. I don't know what to say. I have questions, a lot of them, but they all escape me now.

"I suppose I should welcome you to the Templar." He says. "Do you know much about what we do here?"

I shake my head. "I know you think I'm a witch or something like one. You think you're protecting King Arthur's line, something to do with tw—"

Ren kicks me sharply under the desk. Right. I'm not

supposed to know about them yet.

Joth raises his eyebrows and chuckles. "Well, you've got the right of it, and seeing as you've already heard about the twins," he gives Ren a scathing look. "We are the last remaining ancestors of the Knights of the Round Table. Our duty is to protect the children of the Pendragon line and make sure that, when they're old enough, they can resume their throne in Avalon."

"Avalon?"

"Yes." Joth's eyes take on a misty gleam and seem to turn inwards. "You may also have heard it called Camelot. I've only seen it once. The kingdom across the shining sea, blessed by Christ himself, the legend says."

"And what is it you want with me?"

Joth's eyes instantly focus. "Didn't Ren tell you that?"

"Yes. Ren told me you think I'm descended from Merlin, that the Shadows Mum and I see are faeries who are trying to kill us. But I still don't really understand what you want."

"Well, surely that's obvious?" A deep line appears on Joth's forehead as he frowns. "We want you to join us, to learn about your powers, how to control them, and use them. We want you to become the Templar's advisor, in law, magic, everything and anything. It's your birthright, Merle."

"Then how come I've never heard anything about it before?"

"Your father—" Joth starts, but stops when I hold up my hand.

"Ren mentioned him too, that you knew him. I believe you did. I found something that changed my mind about you both, but it might mean nothing." I pause, looking into Joth's eyes with what I hope is my most formidable stare. "He wasn't right at the end, locking himself away, talking to himself, seeing things."

"I know," Joth says, which surprises me. "I met Marcus at least three times. The first was when we found evidence of your bloodline. We're always researching how to find the lost heirs, and on this occasion, it led to your family. It was my duty to make contact, in case your father wanted to be part of it, so I scheduled to meet him. I explained the situation, that we suspected he was connected to us. Mind you," he dips his head at me, "we weren't sure he was Merlin's heir, only that he was *someone's* heir. That came a little later. Anyway, Marcus reacted like most others do; overwhelmed, confused. I asked him to come to the Templar so I could show him, but—"

"Dad said no?"

"He wanted to think about it, he needed some time, which, given the circumstances, was understandable. However, he was quite sound in his mind. A little eccentric maybe." Joth smiles, as if he's talking about an old, old friend. "But he was reasonable, if a little shaken. A few days later, he came back to me and told me he had a family. Even if he could be persuaded to believe, he didn't want to put you or your mother in danger."

"Well, that turned out great."

"Don't be so hard on him, he loved you very much," Joth whispers, and the sincerity in his eyes quiets me.

"What about the next time?"

"I know from your reaction that your father told you nothing. You were only young, so I'm not surprised. He likely said nothing to your mother, either. One night, he called me here. It'd been a few months, so it was quite a surprise. He sounded upset and angry, babbling about ears in the walls and being watched."

I jolt again. That's what he said in the letter, that he knew someone was watching him; ramblings of a madman. Except now I know it might all be true.

"He told me he might have been too hasty in rejecting the Templar's offer. I went to the meeting, but he never showed. I was worried about him, and when he never came back, I kept my eye on you. There was no need to interfere any further if you showed no signs of power. You'd been disrupted enough." He keeps his voice level, but there's an expression in his eyes I don't like.

"Do you know what happened to him?"

"No. I searched for him for months. I retraced his steps, spoke to people he spoke to, which wasn't all that many. We went up to the rings, and I found the leavings of an old spell. I thought that might be it, that he'd lost control of his power and hurt himself. I'd suspected he was Merlin's heir for some time, and that pretty much confirmed it."

"No. No, I was there when he did that. He called it a blood wish? Is that right?"

"That's dangerous magic!" Joth's eyes darken. "Especially for an untrained wizard."

"But it *didn't* hurt him. Nothing happened."

"Do you know what he wished for?"

"No..."

"What did *you* wish for?" Ren asks.

"I wished to see a faery... but it never came true." Joth and Ren both go grey. I stare at their faces with a growing sense of dread.

"You wished to see a faery?" Joth's voice is a whisper.

"But I never saw one," I insist.

"Oh yes, you did," Ren sits forward in his seat and hangs his elbows over his knees, "you've been seeing them for years."

"But I never—"

Joth holds up his long, twisted index finger for silence, which falls immediately. After a moment, he looks into my eyes. "It seems we weren't entirely right in our search for the heir. It's always been you, Merle. You were there when the first spell was cast, you were strong enough to bring the faeries through! You're the only one whose sanity they haven't robbed! My God, Marcus was never it, it's always been you."

I swallow, my mouth horribly dry. "No. He was obsessed with them, Merlin and Arthur, the rings. It must have been him first."

"But his wish didn't work, and yours did," Ren whispers.

"And that's why Mum can see the Shadows?" I offer cautiously. As difficult as it is to believe, their story makes sense. It explains everything, why Dad was so disappointed, and why he lost his mind. Why strange things happen around me when I don't intend them to? "I wished to see them and they came through? This is my fault?"

"Of course not," Ren snaps. The heat of his dark eyes draws me to him once again. "You were just a child and neither of you had any idea what magic like that could do! That it was even real?"

I study him for a second, and question what I've done to warrant such loyalty in such a short time. He doesn't drop his eyes and a blush creeps back into my cheeks. A strand of dark hair falls across his brow, and for a crazy moment, I want to reach out and brush it away. We look at each other for a little too long and Joth clears his throat. I snap out of my daze and turn back to the older man.

"Ren's right. Even if you had known, you couldn't have done anything."

"Why didn't you come then?"

"Because you were still a child, and it seemed the danger had passed. I didn't know about the Shadows. And you weren't old enough to decide whether you wanted to join us. There was no reason to upset you when you seemed happy. I didn't expect this to happen. For the fae to know who you were, to target you? No one could have expected that."

"You sent Ren, though. You say there was no reason to upset me, but everything's been the same for a long time. Why did you send him to find me now?"

"I already explained we have a duty to offer the heirs..."

"No," I cut him off. That explanation makes sense for Dad. Ten years ago, there was no Lux and Lore to protect. He would have been offered a place because of their strange traditions. Even with the limited information I have, it's easy to see that's not why I'm here now. It doesn't explain the desperation in Joth's eyes. "You've known about me all this time and done nothing. If you sent Ren to get me now, then you must have a reason."

Joth scrubs his hand through his beard and takes a long time to think before he answers. The quiet becomes so deep it's almost unbearable. "We're facing an attack from Morgwese."

"Who?" I know little of Arthurian legend, and this name rings no bells.

"She's an heir, and a powerful one, Arthur's half-sister.

Morgwese swore to take revenge on the Pendragon line after Uther Pendragon killed her father. She got too powerful and became such a threat that we had to banish her to the fae realm. When we banished her, the Templar was strong, and she was no match for us. Yet, over time, our numbers decreased. And she's been..." he pauses, looking for the right words, "not forgotten, but considered much less of a threat. Many of the knights think she's dead."

"But not you?"

He shakes his head. "We became complacent and stopped checking the faery rings as often as we used to. I thought we'd contained any threat that could have occurred from your father's stray magic. There have always been rumblings from the fae underworld, faeries slipping through the cracks. But six months ago our situation became much more dire. They killed one of our knights."

"I'm sorry." I drop my eyes, but Joth waves away the apology.

"Sir Tristen's daughter, Lila, was patrolling one of the bigger rings in their estate and she found a damaged circle. She was attacked, and the fae escaped. It's the first time they've made such a bold move. We doubled our patrols and found more tarnished rings, more than we're able to manage." He sighs and rubs his hands down his thighs. "I suspect Morgwese has finally built her army in the fae realm and restored her powers. She's planning to make a move, and we're on the cusp of war."

"War?" I gasp.

"I sent Ren because our time is up. We need a sorcerer, and we need one now. We can't contain them alone, and this is our last desperate attempt to save ourselves and the world as we know it."

His words hit me like a slap. It's hard for me to deny the existence of magic anymore, but there's still the question of whether I'm Merlin's heir. Whether I can do anything to save them, or to save myself.

"I'm telling you the truth," Joth says, responding to the apparent question on my face.

"And what about Mum? I can't just leave her!"

"We would never expect that. If you were to agree, then we would bring her too. She could get the care she needs."

"I need some time to think," I say. It seems too good to be true, an answer to all my problems. Knowing the Shadows are actually real might help Mum, and then Hazel wouldn't need to send her away. We could stay here, together. And I might be able to find out what happened to Dad.

"A little time we can give you," Joth nods. "But we'll need an answer soon."

I push my chair back and go to the door, Ren close on my heels. Hot, molten rivers run through my limbs. I want to go outside, to feel the cool air on my skin.

"I can show you around if you like?" Ren says. He's apprehensive. I can tell by the way he's slowed his pace, trying to stall my leaving. "Take you to meet Willow?"

"No." I shake my head. I want to go home, to take some time to think about what my options are.

"I know this is a lot."

"Do you?" I raise an eyebrow at him. This might have all been new to him too, a long time ago, but I think a small part of him must have forgotten.

"Will you come back?" I'm not sure if the hope in his voice is real, or part of my imagination. "I want you to, if that adds any weight to your decision." He steps forward, his hand outstretched as if he means to touch my shoulder, but then he pulls it back and looks away.

It adds more than I'd like to admit. For the first time in a long time, I think I've got a friend, an actual one. Someone who I can trust and rely on. I don't want to disappoint him, or any of them. I see the hope fading from his eyes and can barely stand to watch it. "I'll meet you again tomorrow."

"You will?"

"Yes. Just let me speak to Mum first."

The grin he wears lights up his face, adding colour to his cheeks and deepening the brown of his irises.

"I promised I'd meet Shelby in the morning, at the coffee shop. But after? Twelve o'clock at the park?"

"It's a date," he says.

On the short walk home, I have a lot to think about. After speaking with Joth and Ren, I feel the weight of responsibility bearing down on me. While they might have answered most of my questions, they've given me even more to be anxious about. The least of my worries should be Ren's comment about a 'date'. However, that's the thing I keep circling back to. Did he mean a date like a romantic date? I've seen him looking at me for too long; the flush of his skin when I don't turn away. But he can't possibly be interested in me like that, can he? He made it clear that they sent him to find me, that personal feelings weren't involved.

You want him to like you, though, don't you?

Stop it. There are more important things to worry about than whether a cute boy has a crush on me.

Albeit a very cute boy.

I roll my eyes and push through the kitchen door a little too forcefully. It slams into the shoe rack, sending our boots and trainers flying across the wooden floor.

"Damn it," I curse.

"Nice of you to finally join us," Aunt Hazel snaps from the sink. I squeal, my heart hammering in my chest.

"Sorry." I go to my knees and start to re-rack the shoes.

Hazel huffs and carries on with the dishes. I slink past her as soon as I'm able, and head upstairs to find Mum.

She's sitting in the armchair by her window, looking out over the fields. The day's fading sun sends shadows skittering across her pale cheeks. I grin and bend to hug her.

"Hi, Merlie. It's lovely to see you, darling!"

"You too, Mum!" She seems different, as if the trip's breathed some life back into her. "Did you have fun in the lakes?"

"Yes! I had the very best time." She nods but rubs the soft spot at her temple as if she has a headache. "It's been wonderful getting away. You should have come with us, love."

I wish I had gone with her. The last few days have been very confusing. It could have been avoided if I hadn't been so stubborn. "I had fun here."

"Well, that's great, sweetheart. Have you eaten tea yet? Maybe we could eat together? I'm feeling much better."

"Whatever you want, Mum."

I spend the next few hours in her room, and she tells me all about her adventure. Ali and Hazel come to join us, bringing up dinner on trays and filling in any details Mum might've missed. Surprisingly, it's very few. She remembers everything, even down to the name of her favourite otter, Tripp. It's fantastic and unnerving. I'm trying to enjoy it, but there's an uneasy feeling creeping over me. For the last ten years, she's done nothing but wander the halls of our house like an unrestful ghost, or cry in her sleep, and tell me about Shadows. It's troubling that she's so changed.

"*Be on your guard,*" Ren's voice echoes in my mind.

I bat the thought away. I'm being silly. Mum's feeling better; I should be pleased!

Around nine o'clock, Mum starts to get tired, and I know it's time for her to sleep. I kiss her on the cheek and tuck her covers to her chin. In the hallway, Hazel's waiting for me with arms folded, her black hair scraped firmly back in its usual bun.

"Did you have a nice trip?" I ask, breaking the silence.

"Yes. I'd still like to talk to you about what happens now."

"I'm tired..."

"Then I'll make you breakfast." She says, no room for argument in her voice. "Please Merle, this is already difficult enough."

Even though my heart aches at the thought of what to come, I give her a small nod. "Okay, I'll be awake for breakfast."

"Good." She turns on her heel and back down the stairs; to feed Alfie, I expect.

At that, a wave of sadness rolls through me. Alfie and I have never been on the best of terms, but over the last few days, we've bonded. He's become my friend, and now I've lost him to his mistress again.

Sometime later, when I've tossed and turned myself into a knot with worry, my door creaks open and a familiar weight clambers onto the bed. My friend is back after all, and with that knowledge, it's much easier to sleep.

7

The next morning, anxiety ripples through me as I descend the stairs to see Hazel. I don't want to go. I could just pull the covers over my head and go back to sleep. But no, this conversation is coming, whether I like it or not. I try to coax the dog to join me, but he's not budging. After momentarily opening an eye to assess the situation, he goes back to sleep, obviously not crazy about what he sees.

Hazel's staring out of the window from her seat at the table, her face a mask of doubt and sadness. She jumps when she hears me, a small smile spreading on her face.

I sit down at the table and help myself to some toast, waiting for her to speak. It seems now she's got me, she doesn't know what to say. It doesn't matter, we're both aware of how this conversation ends and I don't have the strength to fight. Maybe it's best if I start?

"I'm sorry, Aunty Hazel."

"What?" She looks at me, apparently startled.

"I'm sorry. I know I've been–" I let the silence spin for a moment. "I understand. I just don't want it to happen. I don't want everything to change."

Hazel reaches across the table and squeezes my fingers. "It's too much for us. It's too much for anyone. And we haven't decided on anything yet. We'll look at all the options, find somewhere nice, close by." She sinks back into her chair and pulls the plate of toast towards her. Then she sighs, apparently it's not over yet. "Look Merle, I know I'm sometimes hard on you, I know I didn't do everything right. But I do love you, and I only want the best for you, okay?"

"I love you too."

She meets my eyes for a moment, then a smile breaks over her face. "Good."

"Can I ask you something?" Hazel doesn't look up from buttering her toast, but inclines her head slightly, telling me to go on. "Did Dad ever tell you about a man called Joth?"

"Joth?" Her eyes cloud over, irises sliding up to the left, remembering. "I'm not sure. He worked with a lot of strange people, your dad."

I'm about to ask her what makes her think Joth is 'strange' when the oven timer rings shrilly, making me jump. Hazel gets up and removes a tray of sausages and bacon from the oven. She takes two sausages and two pieces of bacon for herself, putting them in a sandwich. I hear the familiar sound of thumping paws on the landing. Alfie searching for a treat.

"Joth, Joth, Joth," she mutters under her breath. "Now where have I heard that before?"

Alfie pokes his nose round the door, sniffing. Hazel doesn't notice him, but I know his game. He tips his head on one side as if he's asking what I intend to do. Deciding to continue to foster good relations with the enemy, I don't draw any attention to him. Instead, I turn back to my aunt.

"Oh, yes!" she says as she sits back down, her lips parting in a smile. "I remember that name, though it's been a long time since I've heard it. A couple of years before your father disappeared, he got a letter from a man named Joth. Wanted your dad to help him with some kind of history book, I think? He'd seen some of Marcus' drawings and wanted him to illustrate it."

"Do you know what kind of history book?" My heartbeat quickens.

She pauses again and rubs at the centre of her forehead with her first and second fingers. "Knights? Dragons? Something to do with mediaeval times? I can't remember. I know he decided not to do it at first. He already had quite a lot of freelance work. He was really popular then. It was just after he'd bought this place – clients begging for a Marcus Wilde original." She smiles at the memory. "I think Joth wanted him to work on quite an intensive schedule that wouldn't leave him much time for anything else, and they fell out over Marcus' fee."

It seems Dad did an excellent job of covering his tracks. "What do you mean 'at first'?"

"Well, a couple of years later, he got short on money. Your mum lost her job, and your dad's work wasn't selling nearly as well. Fickle like that, the art world," she says and gives me a pointed look, as if she knows everything about it. I resist the urge to roll my eyes. "Marcus wanted to reach out to this Joth character to see if the book still needed illustrations. I don't suppose he ever had time, though." Sadness creases the lines of her mouth. Her eyes are downcast, hands clasped together on the table.

"I met Joth yesterday." My voice is so quiet I'm not sure she heard. "He wants me to help him with a book, too. That's what he says, anyway."

"Surely he found someone else to do it after all this time?" There's suspicion in her voice. "And you don't draw."

"It's not the same book. He wants help with research. And he said they were friends." I get up from the table to put my plate in the sink so she can't see my face.

"And he's going to pay you for it, is he?"

"I guess."

Out of the corner of my eye, I notice Alfie lifting his front paws onto the kitchen worktop, stretching his brown snout as far as it'll go until he reaches his prize. With a lick of his tongue and a snap of his jaw, he's secured a sausage. As quickly as he came, he scampers out. It's an effort to keep my face straight.

"Well then, I don't see why not? It'd be good for you to have some money of your own seeing as—" Her cheeks flush pink and she pushes herself back from the table, taking her own plate to the sink.

I know that trick, having just used it myself. "Seeing as what, Aunty Hazel?"

She takes in a deep breath, which immediately puts me on red alert. I'm going to hate what she has to say. "We're selling the house, Merle." She averts her eyes, busying herself with the washing-up liquid. "It's the only thing left to do, really."

Words crowd up my throat and stay there, choking me.

"I know it's difficult, love, and we'll have to have a proper talk about it, but—" As she's babbling, she notices the missing sausage. "Alfie! That damn dog! Just wait until I get my hands on you!"

"Wait, you can't sell the house!"

"Alfie!" Hazel screeches and flaps into the hallway. "Well, we'll have to tell you about it. We've spoken to a lawyer and— oh, is that the time? I'm gonna be late for work, Merle." She doesn't even bother to look down at her watch. She pulls her coat off the hook and struggles into it. "Like I said, sweetie, we'll have a chat about it tonight when I get home. All right, have a good day, won't you? Love you." She's been talking as fast as she can while backing to the door. I just about stop myself from giving her the finger as it closes behind her.

I'm trembling with adrenaline. Sell the house? Spoken to a lawyer? No wonder she was so ready to forgive me! I stomp back up the stairs. I'm meeting Shelby in an hour and need to get ready, even though it's the last thing I want to do.

She won't get away with this, I think while glaring at myself in the mirror and scraping a brush through my tangled hair. *She can't.*

Alfie looks up from my bed and *humphs*.

"I'm glad you got that bloody sausage," I say to him. "Next time, nick the lot!"

Fifteen minutes later, I'm pulling on my boots and coat. It's still cold out, but not as bad as it's been the last few days, and I'm actually looking forward to the long walk into town. It'll give me time to clear my head and prepare for my meeting with Ren later. I'm only occasionally distracted by Hazel's bombshell. It's not even her house to sell, is it? I don't really know, but maybe Shelby or Nicky will.

As soon as I enter the Java Bean, the comforting smell calms me. Shelby's sitting at the counter, her long grey hair plaited around her head, which is bobbing up and down with laughter. When she hears the bell at the door, she spins in her seat, wiping her almond-coloured eyes, which are streaming. She pats the space beside her for me to sit.

"I didn't expect to see you, kid." Nicky raises his eyebrows and hands me a mug before I can order.

"She agreed to meet her favourite old bat for coffee," Shelby says, still grinning. There's a lot of colour in her cheeks, her eyes unusually dark.

Nicky shrugs and turns his back to us, probably restocking something or other. I take a sip of the hot, strong drink. Its bitter taste coats my tongue, followed by hints of chocolate and caramel. After a few seconds, I realise Shelby is staring at me. "What?"

"Something's different about you."

"How do you mean?" I wince at the sharpness in my voice, but I'm not in the mood to play strange guessing games.

"You're worried about something."

"It's nothing, Shelby."

"I don't believe you," she shakes her head. "Are you coming down with something? You looked a little peaky the other day, and you still look pale." She reaches her hand to my forehead.

"Honestly, I'm fine."

"Hmm." She purses her lips disapprovingly, but removes her hand. "How's your mum? Did she enjoy her trip?"

I talk for about half an hour. Now I'm back on steady conversational ground, I tell her about Mum's good turn and

Hazel's announcement. About halfway through Nicky sidles over, eavesdropping.

"I don't know if she can do that, can she?" I finally ask. "Dad left the house for Mum—"

"Hazel's got power of attorney though, doesn't she?" Shelby responds, biting her lip.

Nicky slides a piece of sponge cake into the space between us, which means it's bad, and I lower my head to the counter. As the only responsible adult, Hazel does have power of attorney.

"So she can do whatever she wants?" I mumble. "And where will Mum and I go if she gets her way?"

"It might not come to that." Nicky's heavy hand pats my head.

"And she certainly won't leave you with nothing! For all her faults, she's never been like that!" Shell adds. "Now come on and eat some of this, will you?"

I raise my head and take one of the shiny silver forks. The cake is excellent, full of sweet whipped cream and cherry jam. It makes me feel better and gives me a chance to calm down. "What about your family, Shell? Are they as crazy as mine?"

"I wouldn't know, darling."

"Tell me about them,"

She rolls her eyes but starts talking. "I have two sisters, Maureen and Elizabeth. Maureen lives in France, but I don't see her. We're estranged. We had a bit of a disagreement and could never reconcile."

"What did you disagree about?"

"Politics." She raises her thin eyebrows. "It can rip families apart, stuff like that. Elizabeth and I made friends again, though it took a while. Then there's Matthew, my son."

When she says his name, her face lights up. I think she's mentioned him before, although I'm not sure. "He's on an expedition. Somewhere in Europe last time we spoke. If you were a few years older, I'd introduce you!" I know from the twinkle in her eye she's thinking what a good pair we'd make.

"You'll be lucky to get her away from that other boy," Nicky chuckles and my face burns.

"Oh, the boy who keeps coming here? I did wonder—"

"Enough!" I say, rising to my feet.

"We were just teasing, sweetheart!" Shelby pats my hand. "Stay for another coffee?"

"I can't." It's almost eleven thirty, and I'll be meeting Ren soon. "But you should come to the house and see Mum before Hazel sells the place. I don't remember the last time you came over."

Or if she ever did, my mind whispers. I ignore it. Why am I suddenly so suspicious? I rub at my temples to chase away the small, dull ache forming there.

"We'll think of something, Merlie," she says.

Nicky sends me on my way with another coffee and I make it to the park with ten minutes to spare, finding my way to a bench, making sure I'm in a visible place from every path. Nerves flutter in my stomach again. After talking to real people in the real world, the story Joth and Ren told me seems very far-fetched.

Dad believed, I remind myself.

Yes, and look where that got him.

I snarl in frustration and shove the thought out of my head. Listening to things like that won't help anything.

The nicer weather means the park is quite full, the last warmth of the autumn before winter finally takes hold.

There's a family of four on the grass not too far away. One child walking a doll across a picnic blanket with Mum One, another being thrown up in the air giggling by Mum Two. Someone whizzes past me on a bike, and in the distance I see Ren, his hands shoved deep into the pockets of his jacket. About twenty feet in front of him is another man. He's dressed in a long black overcoat trailing to the floor, and a scarf pulled up around his mouth. The man's hair is so dark it has a blue tinge, his pale hooked nose shining with sweat.

He's looking right at me, and as I shift uncomfortably in my seat, he speeds up.

There's no way to get to Ren without passing him, and he's almost at my side. If I ignore him, he might just go away. He can't want anything to do with me. As the toes of his boots enter my peripheral vision, I'm hit by the sharp smell of old pennies. I glance upwards, unable to help myself.

The man's leering at me. His scarf has fallen, revealing blue lips pulled back against pointed incisors. I lurch to my left, meaning to put as much distance between us as possible, but his black-gloved hand snatches out at me, gripping my wrist and pulling me towards him.

"Hey!" I shout, trying to rip my arm from his fingers. They clench like a steel band, causing a sharp flare of pain in my wrist.

The man stares down at me. He has unsettling honey-coloured eyes, the pigment twisting around his pupils, moving like a whirlpool. Then the black of his pupils split, spilling out over the whites until I can see my reflection in the glossy surface. His hands go up to my throat. At first I think he means to choke me, but he's not, he's grabbing for the ring. I scramble for it, closing my fingers around his. He

97

snarls something at me in a low and guttural hiss. There's a burning sensation at my throat, an electric current zapping through my limbs. My vision goes grey and my legs collapse under me. The next and only thing I know is pain. Pain as my head hits the ground so hard it feels like it'll come detached from my shoulders. I moan and roll over. The man reaches for me again. The fingers of his gloves have split, showing long, milky claws.

Suddenly he's gone. Two white hands on his shoulders pull him backwards into the dirt. He falls, then Ren's pulling on my arms, willing me to get up. I'm too dizzy to move. None of my limbs obeying my command.

"Hey! Is everything all right?" It's a woman's voice, probably one of the Mums.

The man, the thing that I now suspect is a faery, snaps its head up to us, his face twisting in a sneer. Ren tenses and growls something under his breath, the same sound he made when he killed the faery at my house two nights ago. A flicker of fear crosses the thing's face. It moves back, jumps to its feet, and sprints back down the path.

"Merle?" Ren whispers, brushing my hair back from my face. His eyes widen as his fingers come away red with my blood. "Merle, are you all right?"

I don't have the energy to answer him or to do anything. The sight of the sticky crimson liquid on his hand makes my stomach turn. He calls my name again before my eyes slide closed.

I wake up to a cool grey light shining through the window. I groan and cover my eyes. There's a bandage on my forehead and the memories of earlier come flooding back. The man in the trench coat, his strange eyes, Ren's mouth forming a wide 'O', his fingers scarlet with blood. My blood. My stomach turns again at the memory and it's only when I'm certain I won't be sick, I sit up.

I'm in a room I don't recognise. The bedding is soft and plum coloured, gold thread stitched into it in ornate patterns. It's the most beautiful room I've ever seen, and I feel grubby by comparison. The canopy above me is open so I can see the bare stones of the ceiling. I swing my legs over the side and another wave of dizziness washes over me.

"Don't get up," a rough voice advises me. "You've had a nasty bump."

I stop trying to stand but look towards the sound. Joth's sitting in a chair by my bed. I must be at the Templar.

"What happened?"

"You were attacked in the park by what we believe was a faery," he says slowly, giving my throbbing head time to process his words.

The man's yellow eyes swim in my memory. I instinctively reach for the cord at my throat and relax a little as I realise the ring's still there. "I remember. I think he was trying to get this."

"Whatever he was trying to get, he gave you a pretty good shock. You've been asleep for a long time." He sighs. "I think it might be best to expedite the process of moving you and your mother here. I wanted to give you more time, but I don't think it's safe to wait."

"How long have I been asleep?" I ask, the rest of his words unimportant for the moment.

"A day at least."

"A day?" I assumed the half-light shining through the

window meant it was evening, not the next morning.

I immediately think of Mum and Hazel. They'll be worried about me. I've never ever stayed out a whole night before, certainly not without checking in. Panic runs through my veins. Any upset might be enough to ruin Mum's shaky progress. "I have to go, Joth."

"I'm not sure that's..."

Before he can finish his sentence, I'm up and looking for my boots. My head swims, but after a second, the pain fades to a dull ache. I find them at the end of the bed and pull them on.

Joth studies my face for a moment, then he nods. "Follow me."

We head down a hallway and an enormous set of stairs to the front door, which I remember from my previous trip. I reach out for the handle, but he shakes his head. "Wait, a moment. I'm going to send Ren with you, it isn't safe."

I nod and watch him turn down another hallway.

I wait for Ren for an entire minute. When I don't hear the sound of Joth's return, or any sound at all, I know I have to leave. Joth thinks it's dangerous enough for me to need backup, but Mum and my aunts might be home! If there is danger, they're not equipped to face it.

There's a woman making her way down the staircase. Her face tells me she's a little older than I am, even though she's built like a sparrow. All bones and sharp angles. Dirty-blonde hair trails around her face in thin wisps. Her eyes as pale and sharp as the rest of her, meet mine, and she grins. It's a strange grin, sly like a fox's might be.

"Tell them I've gone, will you?" I say. I don't wait for her response as I flee into the dawn.

By the time I'm shoving open the back door, my head is pounding. I'm sweating under my arms, breath burning as it rushes into my lungs. "Mum?" I shout, skidding into the kitchen. "Mum!"

"Merle!" She's sitting at the kitchen table, her red woollen cardigan pulled around her waist. The crescents under her eyes look darker. "I've been worried sick!"

I go and wrap my arms around her, squeezing tightly. "I'm so sorry! But it's okay, I'm here. I'm home."

8

Mum pulls me close for a second and then releases her grip. "You've been gone all night! What happened to your head?"

"I don't have time to explain now." I peer around the kitchen, looking for her shoes. Alfie's water bowl reminds me I better get him, too. "We need to go, it isn't safe here."

"Of course it is. All that stuff I said before, I was just confused. At least let's have breakfast first. I got stuff for waffles, your favourite, right?"

"No, Mum. We really have to go... where's Hazel? And Ali? They'll have to come too—"

"Don't be silly! There's always time for waffles!" She goes to the fridge, putting her hand on the door. There's something wrong with it. Mum's always been small and thin, with bony limbs and fingers, but the hands on the fridge are grotesquely elongated. The knuckles and joints are so pronounced they're skeletal. Her nails, usually short and bitten raw by nervous teeth, clink on the door's surface, drawing to a head in sharp points, glinting like pins.

"They've gone to work. Hazel thought you'd stormed off in a huff because she told you about the house. Now, do you want strawberries or syrup?"

"Neither!" I snap. At least I don't have to worry about getting my aunts out of the house. I can leave messages for them at work. "We have to go, now."

"Don't take that tone with me, Little One." Her reply is cold, and an uneasy feeling seeps into my blood. Mum stops moving, one of her disjointed hands freezing as it goes into the fridge. Then she sighs. It's an old sigh, like leaves rustling in the wind.

"I promise I'll explain everything when we get to the Templar! We need to pack a bag," I urge her. "And where's that damn dog?" For months she's been afraid of the house, *years!* How can she be so sure we're safe now? I desperately wish I'd waited for Ren.

"Oh, the Templar? And I suppose that's where you've been while I was worried sick?" Mum turns from the fridge and ducks beneath the counter to retrieve a big mixing bowl for the waffle batter. She doesn't meet my eyes and moves too quickly for me to see her face properly. Her voice has taken on a high, shrill tone I don't much care for.

"How do you know about the Templar?"

There's a low growl from the doorway. Alfie's there with his head lowered and back legs tense. He's ready to pounce, sharp white canines flashing in the light. He would never growl at Mum, *never.*

"I've always hated that place," she snaps and now doesn't

sound like Mum at all. "Those new friends of yours are just trying to scare you. Was it Joth filling your head with stories? Or maybe Ren Du Lac?" Her throat makes a nasty clicking sound on the hard 'C'.

I never told Mum Ren's name. I'm sure I didn't. Neither did I mention the Templar. My chest is tight, pulse thudding in my temples.

"Mum, how do you know Ren's name?"

"You told me, sweetheart."

"No. I didn't."

"How else would I know?"

"I didn't."

Mum puts one of her spindly, deformed hands to her forehead and then looks at me. Her entire face has changed. Her nose is much longer and pointed, her chin sharp and severe, cheekbones jutting from gaunt bluish skin. The colour is darkest around her features, grey deepening to cobalt. The tip of her nose and the sockets of her eyes glow with it. She stares me down, and in her gaze, there's nothing left of my mum. Instead of drained-blue irises, her whole eyeballs are black, like an insect. She tips her head to one side and smiles, revealing a set of pointed, needle-like teeth. Alfie barks, intermittently snarling and shaking his head from side to side. I know what she is now, just like that thing that attacked me, and the man in the park. A faery.

"Why are you so curious, Merlie?" the thing spits at me. It uses Mum's voice, but it's not her.

I push myself back from the table. "Where's Mum?"

"Why sweetie, I *am* your mum," the thing makes its way around the counter towards me, "or at least, what's left of her."

"What have you done to her?!"

"What she always wanted!" The thing is closer to me now, taller and horribly stretched, as if it's crawling out of Mum's skin and into its own feral body. "She was so easy to take in the end. Her mind so *fragile.* I was hoping I'd have more time before I had to kill you too!"

"*You can't let it, Merle,*" Dad's voice is so real and vital he could be standing behind me, whispering in my ear. "*Fight it, kill it!*"

As the thing advances, I stumble back. The pulse that was beating in my temples is now wracking my whole body. There's no air in the room, and my throat is closing up. My treacherous legs buckle beneath me. Two days ago, when the Shadow was in front of me, it wasn't like this, so solid and alive. I was scared then, but now I know what terror truly is. Choking screams and disobedient limbs. I'm about to hit the wall; out of options and nowhere to run. And this time, there's no Ren. Now I'm glad I didn't wait for him or put him in any danger. Even if it means I won't see tomorrow.

"Don't worry, Little One," it coos, "I promise it won't hurt a bit."

Use the magic inside of you, wake it up!

Alfie launches himself forward, snapping at the monster. Its long, spidery claws swipe at the air and hit the dog, sending him crashing over the counter and into the cupboards. That's enough to turn my fear into rage. Only one thought rips through my head like a blinding white light. *Kill it!*

We're both blown backwards by the force of my command.

My back hits the wall, knocking the wind from my lungs.

I slam forward onto my knees, sending a shooting pain through my shins before I fall onto my face. My ears are ringing and the darkness behind my eyes is pulsing with light. I'm wheezing, my lungs on fire, and I roll onto my back, trying to get my breath. After a few moments, I push myself into a sitting position, opening my eyes. A long blue leg protrudes from behind the counter. Its toes are pointed towards the ceiling, nails curled under. I steel myself for a moment, and then crawl forward. I don't want to see what's there, but still I have to look.

When I get to the body, there's no movement, no breath. I shuffle forward so I'm level with its face. Its head is thrown back in an agonised scream, mouth hanging open. There are rows of smaller teeth behind the first, all of them sharp and filed into lethal points. Its eyes are open, glossy black orbs rolled up to the ceiling. It's already flaking away like the one Ren killed. I know nothing about faeries, especially not enough to know whether this thing used to be my mother. Either way, it's definitely dead.

Used to be. The thought slips into my mind, and now it's there, it takes root. Panic rips through my body and I swallow down great whooping breaths as I crawl backwards, away from the awful, decaying form.

Gravel rattles against the kitchen door which crashes into the wall startling me. I fall backwards onto my hands.

"Merle?" Ren's voice is breathless, his face flushed, as if he's run the entire way. When he sees me, he lunges down and spins me around so we're on our knees, looking at each other. He searches every inch of my face, panic fading from his eyes.

"Joth told you to wait for me!" He shakes my shoulders.

"It could've killed you! Do you know how stupid it was to come here alone?!"

I stare at him, tears welling in my eyes and sobs crowding up my throat. I throw my own arms around his neck. He grips me tightly and rubs my back in slow, circular motions. "Are you all right? Did it hurt you?"

"No."

He brushes my hair off my face with tender fingers, then snatches his hand backwards as if he's suddenly become self-conscious. "Joth's on the way. I thought we might need him. You killed it?" His eyes are alight with wonder. "How did you do that?"

I shake my head.

He glances at my face, and what he sees there seems to unsettle him. He sighs and sits next to me, pushing his back against the wall. I take his hand when he offers it.

"Where's Alfie?" I ask, tears still running down my cheeks. There's a small yip from behind the table and my loyal companion limps over to us, resting his tired head on my thigh. At that, there's no chance of me controlling my tears, and by the time I hear Joth entering the kitchen, I'm blind with them.

"We're here," Ren calls.

Joth's brandishing a sword. It's curved along one edge, tassels hanging from its handle. Under other circumstances, it might be comical. He sees us both on the floor and nods his head, colour coming into his cheeks. Ren squeezes my fingers, getting up and pulling me to my feet.

"It was another attack, Joth. Another faery-"

"It was Mum," I say, the lump in my throat growing again. "Before it was that thing. It was Mum."

Joth nods and reaches down to pat me on the shoulder, following Ren's glance at the foot poking from behind the counter. He approaches the body and crouches beside it. After a few minutes, he comes back to my side. His navy-blue eyes are full of sorrow, and my knees tremble. He takes both of my hands.

"I'm sorry, Merle."

My mouth drops open. That thing wasn't my mum really, it was just something pretending to be her! It has to be! It can't be real.

"I killed Mum?" I whisper, unable to keep the tears from my voice.

"Never think that!" His eyes widen. "You killed a powerful faery! It will already have been too late to save her. I'm so sorry."

My knees tremble. I should never have tried to stand.

"Ren, maybe it would be best if you took Merle in the other room—"

"No. You aren't going to shove me out. When we can't even be sure that it's really her—"

The older man takes a couple of steps forwards and lowers his head a little so he's looking directly into my eyes. His voice is soft when he speaks, but firm. "I'm sorry, Merle, but I am sure. She's gone."

Joth holds me up while I cry. Eventually he hands me off to Ren, who takes me into the living room. I sit in silence for a long, long time. Every time I think I might say something, the words fall dead in my throat, useless in the current situation. What should I talk about? How can I pretend everything's all right? Ren hasn't left the room, although he's pacing around like a restless tiger, flicking strained glances in my direction. I think I'm scaring him. He keeps putting cups of tea into my hands and reassuring me it isn't my fault. Not that it matters.

Even if I didn't kill her, she's dead. She's never coming back. She'll never be here again. I will never see her wandering around the gardens in the sun. She'll never brush my hair while we watch TV. She'll never make me waffles, or wake me in the night so I can tuck her back into bed. My mum is gone, and I will never see her again. I blink tears from my eyes, but they don't stop coming.

"—is that okay?"

The end of Ren's question finally gets my attention, although I've no idea what I'm supposed to be approving. It's been hours since it happened and every fibre of my being aches with holding myself so rigid for so long.

"Joth called some of our knights to come and move—" he stops for a moment. I'm glad for it; the last thing I want to hear out loud is 'body'.

"Yes. Fine."

"And your aunt Hazel's on her way."

I've forgotten all about Hazel, and she'll be devastated. "What do I tell her? She doesn't know about any of this, she'll never understand."

"You don't have to tell her anything," Joth's voice sounds from behind me as he enters. "I can do it. We've dealt with situations like this in the past, although not for some time. It'll be easier that way anyway, especially if you're going to be coming with us."

Out of the corner of my eye, I see Ren wince, and he's right to do so. Whether or not Joth knows it, it's exactly the wrong thing to say. Anger replaces the grief in my blood.

"Because she's out of the way now, you mean?" I snap. "And do you really think for a single second that I'll be coming with you now she's dead? Whatever it is you've involved me in is the reason she's gone! I don't know if I could stand it!"

Joth stares at me. "You don't have a choice, you *must* stand it."

"Joth—" Ren tries to cut him off, but he's not quick enough.

"Must I?" I shoot to my feet, shaking all over. My mind is a black swirl of rage, whipping me into a frenzy. "Both of my parents are dead because of these ridiculous stories! And I'm the one who 'must stand it'?"

"I never meant—"

"I don't care what you meant!" I scream at him, the words ripping at my throat. "All that matters is that they're gone, and they aren't coming back whether or not I go. I couldn't save them and I can't save you!"

With that, I spin on my heel and race from the room. My first thought is to run into the garden, but I don't think I could face seeing that thing again. Instead, I fly up the stairs and into Dad's study. Everything's as I left it, even down to the footprints I made in the dust. That was only two days ago. It could be a hundred years. I crawl into the space under the desk, just as I would've done when I was small, and cover my eyes with my hands. Maybe if I'm quiet enough and still enough, I can make myself believe none of this is true. When I go back out there, time will have gone backwards. It'll be Tuesday afternoon again when Alfie and I still hadn't found Dad's secret note.

After a while, I calm myself down enough for some

semblance of rationality to seep back into my thoughts. Joth may have misspoken, but I can't stay here. Hazel will sell the house, and now Mum's gone, there's nothing to bind me to her. I've no other family, and no money to speak of. Maybe Nicky would take me in? Or I could live with Shelby?

The door creaks open and two black boots move into view. Then there's a gusty sigh. "I'm sorry Merle, I really am."

"You tried to warn me and I didn't listen!"

Ren sits down beside me and puts his hand on my shoulder and gently turns me to him. "I obviously didn't do a good enough job. I know what to look for, what to do, but you don't. I should have prepared you better."

"I wouldn't have listened, and I think you know it. It's all my fault!"

"None of this is your fault. But we know whose it is, we know exactly who sent that faery here, and exactly who killed your mother." His eyes are full of venom. "And if you'll still come to us, I'll do everything in my power to make sure that vile old witch pays for her crimes." He folds his legs beneath him so he's on his knees; it brings his face much closer to mine, and he's more serious than I've ever seen him. "She deserves to pay for what she's done, but only you can extract the punishment that's due."

"So many people are already dead."

"This will never happen again." Now he presses his forehead to mine. "I swear to you with my life that I will protect you." His eyes are so deep and sincere I'm overcome with emotion again. I close my eyes.

"You really have no doubt about me?"

"No doubt at all."

Ren tells me to nap. I don't think I'll sleep, but when I open my eyes again, it's almost three o'clock. Clouds have gathered around the house like a storm, the night rushing in on us. Time doesn't seem to stand still out there as it does inside the walls.

A few hours ago, I heard the door opening and closing and Hazel shrieking, but I wasn't awake long enough for it to register properly. The only company I've had is Alfie, whom I'm eternally grateful for. He's been snuggled beside me all afternoon, licking streams of tears from my face.

My head's so heavy and full when I sit up, I almost have to lie back down again, but I've spent enough time sitting on my own. I keep replaying the horrible event over in my head: the stretching of Mum's face and hands; the blue thing with rows of pointed teeth slashing at me. I shiver. As I push myself out of bed, my stomach rumbles, and my throat aches with the need for a drink. I hate that I need anything. Why should I be standing here with a beating heart, aching limbs, and a throbbing head? Why should I be feeling anything at all? I should be dead, not her.

Her loss stabs at me like a hot poker. No, I can't sit up here all night alone. I might drive myself insane. I shuffle into my slippers and pull a jumper over my head. It's Mum's, my favourite one of hers. I remember her wearing it when I was small, the teal bringing out the colour of her eyes.

As she's haunted my nights for years, she haunts me now. Still floating through the halls, casting spindly shadows on the walls. I bat the thought away. It's almost enough to send me back over the edge. I can't let myself get caught up in tears now, or I'll never get moving.

"Come on then, buddy," I say to Alfie. "Let's go down."

Joth and Hazel are sitting on the big couch, my aunt dabbing her eyes with a white cloth. Ren's sitting on the smaller one and he turns to look as he hears my footsteps on the wooden floor. There's a tenseness in his face that seems to drain out of it when he sees me. I try for a smile, but I can't make it sit properly on my face.

Hazel yelps and jumps to her feet, gathering me in a hug. I barely have the energy to hold myself together, and even though she needs the comfort, I don't know how long I can endure it. "Oh darling, you must be devastated!" She grips my arms just above the elbow so I can't squirm away. "I just can't believe it."

Over Hazel's shoulder, I see Ren get to his feet and gently extract Hazel's clinging arms from my shoulders. She's reluctant to let go, but he mutters something about 'shock' in her ear and she finally releases me. She goes back to her place beside Joth, who pats her hand lightly.

"Tea?" Ren whispers under his breath.

I don't really want tea, but neither do I want to stay here. I follow him through to the kitchen and sit at the table. There's no sign that anything happened here other than a smudge of wet paint on the wall where I must've hit it. Ren boils the kettle, shooting the occasional glance over his shoulder. I'd forgotten he knew where everything was from the other night. Finally, he puts a mug in my hands and sits across from me.

The tea makes me feel better, actually. It soothes my aching throat and gives my body some much needed hydration. Ren doesn't pressure me to speak or ask me questions. He brings me another cup of tea when I've finished the first, and then puts a sandwich under my nose half an hour after that. I protest by sliding the plate away, but he pushes it firmly back. "It's non-negotiable, Mer."

"That's the third time you've called me that."

"Do you mind?" He raises an eyebrow.

"No." I've had nicknames given to me by my parents, but never by a friend. I suppose I'll never hear the former again, only when their voices speak up in my head. "What are Joth and Hazel talking about?"

"He called her work as soon as you went to sleep. Obviously he didn't want her to come home and find—" he stops, wincing.

In truth, I'm glad Joth did it. Whatever differences lie between us, she loves Mum. Then the shock of her cause of death on top of it. I can't imagine what that would be like. At least I had some notice.

Some notice? You killed her. I drop my head into my hands for a moment, trying to compose myself. It wasn't her anymore.

"He told her everything, Merle. About who we are, how she was killed, who we believe you to be. I wasn't sure it was the right thing to do, but he said it was better to be honest with her."

"And how did she take it?" I sip at the hot drink and take a bite of the sandwich. It's cheese and pickle, my favourite. And it's good.

He shrugs. "About the same as you did at first. But I think he's convinced her now. He told her exactly what he knew about Marcus and when he went missing, about the Shadows. Now they're talking about funeral arrangements, I think."

I hadn't even thought about that. When Dad disappeared, we never had to. There was no body, and no definitive proof he was dead. My grandmother died when I was young and I certainly had nothing to do with the funeral planning. Another wave of guilt washes through me. I'm selfishly glad I don't have to be involved. My chest tightening again at the thought.

Ren reaches across the table and takes hold of my hand. "What Joth said earlier—"

"He was right," I cut him off. "You know that as well as I do. As awful as it sounds, I think it'll be a relief for Hazel, really. She's spent her entire life taking care of us. It's time for her to have a life of her own with Ali. I don't blame her for wanting that."

There's a muffled squeak from the doorway and I spin in my chair to see Hazel covering her mouth with her hands. For a moment I can't tell whether she's furious or not, but then she opens her arms and comes to hug me again. This time, I don't squirm or push her away. Instead, I let her cry into my shoulder.

Some time later, when we've both settled down again, she explains that Joth has offered to arrange a headstone at the local cemetery. If I agreed to it, we could have a small service next week.

"I want them to put Dad's name on there too," I whisper.

"I agree," Hazel nods, dabbing at her eyes again.

I feel like there should be more to say about it, but there isn't. There's no point continuing to pretend that he might come back. They're both gone, and they should be able to rest.

"You don't have to go, you know," Hazel suddenly blurts out. "I know we haven't always been on the best of terms, but I do love you, and I would never make you go with them if you don't want to. Ali and I will always take care of you."

"I know." I squeeze her fingers. She's got puffy eyes and the tip of her nose is red. "But I want to go, really I do."

"All right."

There's only a little talk after that. None of us really have anything more to say. I also don't want to be in the room when Ali comes home. I can't bear to see her cry.

"I better be going. I've got some arrangements to make," Joth decides at around half-past six, rubbing his hands down the front of his trousers as he stands. He takes hold of Hazel's hand one last time. "Again, I'm so sorry for your loss. I'll be in touch about the arrangements."

"I'll show you out." I push myself up from the sofa and follow him as he makes his way through the kitchen and out onto the step. Joth looks at Ren expectantly, waiting.

"Well, I'm not going anywhere," he snorts and stares at me defiantly. "That's absolutely out of the question."

"I'm fine," I say.

"I'm staying." His dark eyes don't leave mine; they're swirling with emotion. Stubbornness, anger, fear, and something else I can't quite place. Something dark and secret.

Joth nods and goes down the steps. As he's about to fade into the night, a wave of affection sweeps over me, and I step out onto the stone in my bare feet and jog after him. He must hear me because he turns, and I wrap my arms around him, squeezing just below his ribs. After a moment, his hand pats the space between my shoulder blades. He smells like musty old books and tea.

"Thank you."

"We'll be in touch with you too, about what happens now. But first you're to get some rest, all right?"

I nod and go back inside, watching a small smile creep over his face before pushing the door firmly shut and locking it. That leaves Ren and I alone in the kitchen again. As I'm about to speak, the front door opens and closes, Ali coming home. That means there's no time to spare in getting out of the way.

"Come on." I grab hold of his wrist and start pulling him towards the stairs. "There's something I need to show you."

9

I sneak Ren upstairs and back into Dad's study, leaving him there for a minute while I grab the books I found. It seems far too intimate to invite him into my room. First, I've only just met him. Second, I've never had a boy in there before, and the thought of him sitting on my old flowery sheets and judging my stripy pink-and-purple wallpaper is enough to make me nauseous.

Ren looks at Dad's books for a long time and I sit cross-legged in the chair, watching him. His expression alternates between concentration and fascination. The dull glow from the dirty lamps – that haven't been cleaned in a decade – cast shadows on his face, deepening the hollows of his cheeks. Thankfully, he's so engrossed in the book he doesn't see me staring again. When he unfolds the picture of the children, his eyes widen.

"That's Lux and Lore! Wow... they weren't even with us then! I can't believe it." He looks at me. "Your father was very talented, and apparently clairvoyant."

"The Pendragon twins? Arthur's kids?"

"Anna's great-great-great-great-grandchildren," he says, folding the paper and sliding it back into the musty red book as if the words that have just left his mouth make perfect sense. "They're good kids. Annoying sometimes, but aren't all ten-year-olds?"

"I wouldn't know."

"It fascinated them when we brought you to the Templar yesterday. It took all of Joth's persuasive techniques to get them to leave you alone."

"I never thanked you—"

"You shouldn't be thanking me for that." His voice is grave, cheeks flushing a dull red.

"You saved my life, *again*."

"Not before I endangered it."

"What?" I shake my head at him in disbelief. He can't be serious?

He gets to his feet and paces across the carpet. "I saw it, I saw it walking towards you, and I did nothing. I knew something was wrong. I could smell magic, I thought it was you." He flicks a look at me. "I just stood there! By the time I realised what was happening, it was almost too late."

"Don't be ridiculous."

"I'm supposed to protect you!" Ren grinds his fist into the palm of his hand. "If I'd been one second slower... and even then you got hurt! You were out cold for so long we didn't know if you were going to wake up. It would've been my fault!"

"Ren," I keep my voice level to calm him, "I know it's your duty to—"

"It isn't about duty." His dark eyes flash dangerously in the light. "The thought of something happening to you is—" he snaps his mouth shut and turns his back to me. "I should have been on my guard too, and I wasn't."

I sit up straight in my chair, wishing he'd finished his sentence. As I stare at his strained shoulders, I know it isn't the time to pursue it. He already looks tense enough to snap. Instead, I loop my necklace over my head and hold the ring in the palm of my hand. "I think he wanted this. Although, I can't be sure why."

He turns to me and I hold out the cord, dropping it into his outstretched hand. His eyes flicker for a moment and he starts to curl his fingers around it, then he shakes his head. "Who gave you this?"

"Dad."

"It's got magic in it."

"How can you tell?"

"Can't you feel it pulling?" He dangles it from the end of his fingers, holding it in front of his face. It sways towards me even though there's no breeze. "Do you know what it's supposed to be used for?" I stare at him blankly and he chuckles. "Stupid question, sorry. It could be a protection spell? It must do something if the faery wanted it."

"I might be wrong. Maybe he was just trying to strangle me."

Ren's face goes dark again, the joke much too soon.

"What's it like there? At the Templar?" I ask, changing the subject.

"Well, you've seen some of it. It's a nice place to live.

There's me, Joth, the Pendragons, and Willow. Then there's Mona, the housekeeper, Etta and her kitchen staff, and Benjamin, who helps with the grounds. Their families have been part of the Templar for hundreds of years. We wouldn't be able to run anything properly without them."

"Do you like it?"

"Yes," he smiles, "but I don't want to say anything to cloud your judgement. You might not want to stay once the danger has passed."

"You're no help at all."

He comes back over to me, leaning on the desk. "I can tell you all about the Templar, about Lux and Lore and the knights. But if you don't like it, you might resent me for it. That's the last thing I want." He has that look in his eyes again, the secret one, but he turns his head before I can decipher it.

"I'm not sure what I want."

"I know." Ren looks down at his hands, then back at me. "It's late, and you need to sleep. We can deal with everything in the morning." His dark-brown eyes are sincere and persuasive, and I *am* tired. I get to my feet and pull my jumper closer around me.

I feel I should say something, thank him for staying, for running to me when I needed him. Anything to break the silence as we get to the door of my room. Instead, I'm only aware of the heat of him, that he smells like soap, and the fine muscles of his cheek forming a smile. Then suddenly, his gaze is burning, Adam's apple bobbing in his throat. He raises his hand again, then when it's almost at my cheek, he stops, shaking his head, like he's waking from a dream.

Hoarsely he whispers, "Goodnight, Merlin's heir."

The next night is the worst of my life. Worse than when Dad disappeared; worse than the first day I saw a Shadow. Worse than anything I thought I could endure. Every time I close my eyes, I see Mum transforming into that thing, her skin stretching and ripping. The glossy eyes staring up at the ceiling, lifeless. I lay there, unable to bring myself to move, and unable to sleep.

As the sun rises, a glimmer of silver light flashes across the ceiling. It's the charm bracelet. I shoot to my feet and grab it from my dresser, holding it up to my eyes. Is this from them? The faeries? Something to mark Dad's passing; another of their murders. Will I get one for Mum now, too? I'm about to throw it across the room in a rage, then I think better of it. It might be useful if it *is* from them. Ren will know what to do with it. I slip it onto my wrist and get dressed.

Thankfully, when I poke my head into the hallway, there's no sound of anyone else being awake. I've listened to Hazel and Ali sobbing on and off all night. My ears ring with it, and I can't wait to be outside, if only for a little while. I wrap up in my coat and head to the backdoor to find my boots, when I notice a figure waiting outside.

When Ren sees me, he smiles, momentarily hiding the concern on his face. I can't deny the warmth that spreads through my body when I see him. That even in this sea of tumultuous grief and unknown nightmares, I'm not alone.

"I thought you might like some company," he says as I close the door behind me.

"I would."

"Did you sleep?"

I shake my head and fall into step beside him. "I keep seeing that thing, crawling out of her. I can't get it out of my mind."

"It will go though." He reaches out to squeeze my wrist, his fingers brushing the metal of the bracelet. "What's this?"

"I don't know. I got it from the Shadows—"

"*What?*" He stands still and gently pulls my arm towards his face, inspecting the bracelet.

"They bring the charms every year, on the anniversary of Dad's disappearance. I found it again this morning. Do you know what it is?"

"No," Ren says. He lets go of my hand and looks at me with wide eyes. "I've never seen anything like it."

"I think they're just taunting me," I whisper, on the edge of tears again. Is it not enough to have taken them both? To have robbed me of them?

"Someone at the Templar might know what it is," he grumbles. "But until then, you should wear it. Show them, the Shadows, the faeries underneath, that you aren't afraid of them."

I *am* a little afraid of them, though. Surely that much is obvious?

We've walked almost a full circuit of the field by now and my fingers are as cold as ice. I invite Ren inside for tea and he's helping with the milk and sugar when Hazel appears in the doorway.

"Will you be all right for a while today, sweetheart?" she asks. "I've got a few bits with the house to sort out, and—"

"I'll be fine," I say, waving away her concerns.

"And I'll stay." Ren shoots a smile at her and Hazel pats him fondly on the arm. She also accepts a cup of coffee and takes one upstairs for Ali. That leaves Ren and I alone again, but even the silence is nice. We spend most of the day in

Dad's study, sorting piles of old books into boxes. As the day slowly turns to night, Ren becomes more fidgety, probably anxious to get home.

"You can leave if you want," I say. "I really appreciate you being here, but I know you've got things to do."

He shifts uneasily in his seat. "It's not that, exactly."

Oh no, my mind panics. *Oh no, oh no—*

"I've got to go away for a few days," he says, his cheeks flushing red. "It's the worst possible timing! And I tried to get out of it, but there's been another fae attack and—"

"You have to go." I desperately don't want him to, but I understand why he should. And it's not my place to keep him here.

He grimaces. "Yes. And that's entirely the problem."

"I'll be okay."

"I know." Still, he doesn't look entirely convinced, torn between staying with me and doing his duty.

"Soon I'll be going with you," I say, trying to lighten the mood and he laughs.

"Soon, you'll be running the entire operation."

The next night isn't as bad as the first, but it's still awful. Every time the wind moves my curtains I jump, and I can't sleep for seeing shadows. Ali comes into my room at around lunchtime with a cup of tea and a cheese sandwich. Her eyes are puffy, blonde hair ruffled around her ears. She sits with me on my bed until I've eaten everything.

"Will you come down at any point, love? I think Hazel wants to talk about the f-f—" then she bursts into tears. I assume she was trying to say 'funeral', and at the thought of it, I burst into tears too. An hour later, when Ali hasn't reappeared, Hazel finds us huddled on the bed with watery eyes and red noses. Alfie even comes for a look, jumping up to snuggle with us.

"Just this once, eh?" Hazel allows, choking back her own tears and patting my head as if I'm the labradoodle rather than him.

We find a clumsy sort of peace between us as the days roll on. Ali comes in every morning to check on me and promises not to tell Hazel about Alfie being on my bed. She brings tea and toast, and we often just sit together, saying nothing. Hazel's done most of the planning for the funeral, inviting the few friends Mum had left. I called Nicky and Otto, who didn't know Mum very well, but might want to pay their respects. Really, I want them there for me. I give Nicky the details as he comforts me down the phone, and he promises he'll be at the small village church on Saturday morning.

"And tell Shelby, won't you?" I ask. "I'm sure she'll want to come. I've tried to ring but I can't get through."

He promises to do that, too.

Aunt Hazel spends the rest of the week talking me through the legalities of what will happen now, with the money that's left, with the house, with our things. She and Ali intend to go away for a while, six months to a year. Travelling like they've always wanted.

"You can come with us, you know? We'd love to have you," Hazel says, and I think she genuinely means it.

I consider it for a long time – all there is, it seems, is time – and I swing back and forth between going with my aunts, or chasing after Ren and Joth, and their promise of magic and adventure.

I know what my heart's telling me to do.

"And that's the only thing you can ever really trust, Wild'un," Dad's voice reassures me.

It's Saturday morning, as we're leaving for the church, when I realise I haven't heard from either Ren or Joth in at least five days. I know Ren said he had to go away for a bit, but to hear nothing at all from anyone is still unnerving. The spike of anger that jolts me like a lightning bolt is a welcome distraction from the sadness I've barely been holding at bay.

Where are they? I thought they wanted me to help them? If they've appeared in my life just to turn it upside down, and then disappear again, I really will lose my mind. Ren said I could go with them! Have they decided against it? Realised I'm not who they want?

"It's time to go, love." Ali pokes her head around my door, cutting off my internal rant.

Mistaking my fury for grief, she rushes over and pulls me into a hug. Then she quickly ushers us downstairs to find Hazel, who's waiting for us outside beside a huge black car. We all pile in wordlessly.

The service is nice. The vicar talks slowly and respectfully about Mum's life, how much she loved Dad and I, and what an integral part of the community she was in her younger years. There are lots of people here to say Mum hasn't really interacted with anyone in five or six years. I recognise Mrs Alvez from the post office, and Lizzie from the café where we used to go every week for lunch. Nicky, Otto, and even Marnie huddle together at the back, dabbing their tearful eyes with handkerchiefs. I notice as I look around that Shelby's not here. I can't see her anywhere in the church, and Nicky promised he'd tell her. It's strange she wouldn't come.

She was Mum's friend long before I can even remember.

When the funeral's over and Mum's coffin has been lowered into the ground, we all make our way back home. It's easier somehow, knowing she's not in there. That doesn't mean I'm not weak with grief. Hazel's holding my hand so tightly my fingers are numb, and Ali's weighing on the other shoulder like an anchor. It's a wonder we make it back at all. The wake's being held in our house, which is certainly big enough for the twenty people that follow us up. It's a relief when Nicky and Otto finally get there, though the only person I really want to see is Shelby.

Well, that's a complete lie, my internal voice whispers.

Maybe so, but I'm too angry with Ren and Joth right now to admit that, even to myself.

"I'm so sorry, kid," Nicky says as he throws his arms around me. "I can't believe it. How are you holding up?"

I shrug, hopefully conveying my exhaustion at answering this question repeatedly. "Thank you for coming."

"Of course."

"How's the shop?"

"I don't want to bother you with all that," he says with a little wince.

"Well, move over then." Otto pushes past him, taking my hand in his and giving it a squeeze. "How about you make this old man a cuppa, and I'll tell you all the gossip?"

"Coming right up." After spending a week doing nothing but crying, and thinking, and worrying about what will happen next, I'm glad Otto's had the brains to realise I need a distraction. Hearing about the normal goings on in the world is a welcome break.

At about five o'clock, we wrap everything up. There's lots

of hugging and kissing on cheeks, as people I haven't seen since childhood give me their final condolences. Nicky and Otto linger longest, and I know exactly why. I've told them about Hazel and Ali going away, and that I'll be moving in with my 'uncle', so I can't work at the shop anymore. None of us want to say goodbye, and I don't know when I'll see them again, even though I've promised it'll be soon.

Half an hour later, there's just the four of us left, including the dog. He's behaved well and I grab him some ham-sandwich leftovers, feeding him under the table. Hazel and Ali bring us more tea and sit down across from me, holding hands.

"You've got some news?" I ask.

"Yes," Hazel proceeds cautiously. "We've got a buyer for the house, Merle. It's not quite final in writing yet, but I'm confident the sale will go through."

"Oh." The word comes out of my mouth a little crestfallen, but I immediately right myself. The three of us have talked about this, and I've already agreed to all the terms. "That's great news, Aunt Hazel, really."

"And you're sure about us going so soon?" Ali's green eyes meet mine.

"Yes." I've insisted they leave as soon as possible. They've been waiting for this for almost a decade, and it's unfair to keep them any longer. They wanted to stay for another month at least, but what's the point when I'm supposed to go to the Templar any day now?

Unless they've forgotten all about me. It certainly seems that way.

"And you're all set?" Hazel asks.

"Yes," I lie.

She eyes me suspiciously and then lets it go. "Well, the papers and everything should be here on Monday. And of course we'll leave you the contact details for all our stops."

My aunts have told me all this at least a thousand times. I want them to go, mostly so that they can enjoy themselves and I can start a new life, but also because I couldn't stand to sit around here for much longer and mope, tearing up every time I see something that reminds me of Mum.

I don't sleep very well that night, or the night after. Even with Alfie snuggled up beside me on the bed. I lay awake, restlessly worrying about Ren and why he hasn't been in touch. When I wake up on Monday morning I have stinging eyes and an awful headache from crying all night. I shrug on my dressing gown and my slippers, and make the descent to my last breakfast with Hazel and Ali. We eat toast and eggs and drink many cups of tea. This is the first time in my whole adult life that I've enjoyed my aunts to the point where I can't imagine them being gone. And now, they're packing their bags to leave.

Ali's the first to get in the car after she hugs me tight. "We'll call as soon as we land, all right?"

"Okay," I sniffle and reluctantly let her go.

That leaves Aunt Hazel and I standing in the cold.

"I guess this is it then, Merlie." She puts both hands on my shoulders and looks straight into my eyes. "Now, Joth promised he'd take good care of you and that you wouldn't need anything other than yourself and your things. There's some money from the house sale, and from your dad. You know where to find it?"

"Yes."

"All right, good. And these came this morning." She

reaches into her handbag and gives me a brown paper envelope. "This is the paperwork you'll need to keep safe until we get back."

"I'll look after it."

"Well, that's it then. Be careful, won't you? And don't do anything too dangerous!"

I laugh through my tears. "I'll try not to. Make sure you have a good time, though. Don't worry."

"I'm always going to worry, sweetheart. I love you, Merlie." She grabs me in a big bear hug.

"I love you too," I choke out, even though it hurts my throat to talk.

After a long moment, she pushes herself back, laughing a little. "Think of how silly we're all being! We'll see you again in six months!"

I can only nod.

"I'll give you a minute with the dog, shall I? Just got to nip to the loo, anyway." She kisses my cheek, still wiping streaming tears from her eyes, and runs back inside.

A minute with the dog? My slow brain repeats Aunt Hazel's words, taking a while to figure out what she means.

Oh no. Oh no, no, no.

I've not even considered Alfie. For some reason, I'd assumed he'd be staying with the house as if he was part of the furniture. The dog in question trots to my feet, looks up at me and barks once. I can already feel more tears waiting behind my eyeballs. Is it stupid to talk to a dog? Will he even know what I'm saying?

"Well, I guess this is goodbye then, Alf." I crouch so I'm at his eye level, putting the brown envelope on the ground beside me. "Have a good holiday, right?"

He yips.

"Make sure you look after those two."

Alfie cocks his head on one side.

I roll my eyes. "And I suppose I'll forgive you for all those times you got me into trouble. You've been a huge help these last few weeks."

"*He's not your secretary, Merle. He's a bloody dog,*" Mum's voice sounds in my head, and I can't help but laugh.

"Friends?" I say and hold out my hand.

Alfie considers me for a minute, then pounces forward, knocking me to the gravel and licking my face. There's a wail from behind us. I tilt my head back and see Hazel sobbing and laughing at the same time. When Alfie finally lets me up, she gives me one more cuddle, and I give Alfie a final pat on the head. "I'll miss you, you stupid mutt."

He sneezes in my face in return. Well, I guess that serves me right.

Then they pile into the car and are gone with one last wave, grey smoke streaming from the exhaust. I keep it together until they get to the end of the driveway, then I start bawling. It takes me a while to calm down, long enough for my fingers to have turned to icicles. Picking up the letter off the gravel, I stumble back inside, wiping tears off my face as I close the door behind me. I promised my aunts I'd make sure everything's ready and clean for the buyers, so that's what I spend my morning doing, checking all the rooms to ensure nothing's left behind. They've really done a terrific job. Not a speck of dust anywhere.

In the afternoon, I double check the items I've packed. A few bits of clothing, jeans, leggings, an array of t-shirts. Then the books with Dad's notes and the drawings, which don't fit in my rucksack but are definitely essential. I place them in a canvas tote, along with a last addition of woolly socks and two thick jumpers. It's almost winter, after all. I can't think of anything else I'll need. Now I just have to wait for Joth's call.

At five o'clock, when there's nothing left to do, I sit at the table and nibble at the food my aunts left me, everything else packed or thrown away. After minutes of staring at the wall, I decide to look in the envelope Aunt Hazel left behind. The first few pages are the itinerary of Hazel and Ali's trip and the address of their first hotel. Behind that is the deed for the house. I skim the document, curious about the name of the new owners more than anything.

Merle Wilde is typed in the box.

"Got to be a mistake," I huff to myself, nerves jolting in my stomach. I'll have to call them. As if I haven't had a bad enough morning, now I have to ring the solicitor and sort out this mess. I'm not even a proper grown-up yet. I take a few minutes to find the number and explain my situation to Oliver The Receptionist, and then Minnie The Lawyer.

"Oh no, that's not a mistake," she says finally. "The buyer wanted to gift it to you, the house. Didn't anybody tell you?"

"My aunt's been very busy," I say, a little defensively. "Could you tell me who the buyer was? I'd like to send a note."

"One moment."

I'm sure I already know who bought the house. There's really only one person, or group of people, who would.

"Er, all I can seem to find is Joth. Didn't give a last name."

"That's great, Minnie. You've been a big help."

I don't wait for her to respond before I put the phone down. After a moment of trying to compose myself, gripping the edge of the counter and clenching my jaw, I let out a cry of frustration.

How dare they?! I growl internally. *Turning up at my work, telling me the most ridiculous bloody story, then nothing! Absolutely nothing! For days! Complete silence! Then they bought me a house! My house!* I turn on my heel and storm to the back door. Shoving my feet into my boots, I march into the field, furious. How dare they leave me hanging for so long? Not a single word or instruction for almost a week. And then this! I don't *want* gestures. I want stability, comfort, and the family I've so recently lost.

By the time I get to the Templar, I'm freezing cold, and my boots are covered in sludge. I'm shivering with rage and still trying to wrap my head around what the hell's going on. How can people be so forthright one minute and so distant the next?

I don't knock at the front door, or when I get to Joth's office. Instead, I push it open to find him sitting at his desk with fingers steepled in front of him. He raises his head, surprise registering in his eyes. "Merle—"

"What the hell is this?" I slap the brown envelope down on the table in front of him.

He takes the envelope, pulls out the contact and skims through it, a smile breaking out on his face. "We bought the house! I knew your aunt wanted to sell and—"

"Why? Why did you?" I snap, the smile fading from his face. "And you didn't think about asking me? And why would you, when I haven't heard from you at all? I'm supposed to be coming here to live with you, and do whatever job it is you want me to do, and instead of making sure everyone knows what's going on, you're buying run-down houses and not telling anyone!" The hairs on the back of my neck stand up, a tingle prickling down my spine. I assume that means Ren's standing behind me.

"Well, don't you want the house?" Joth says.

Ren groans.

"That's not the point!" I'm on the verge of tears again. "The point is, you left me there, on my own, with no word or messages or instructions or anything! You promised you'd take care of me. That's what I want, not a stupid house!" With that, I turn around and storm back out, trying not to look at Ren. From a little way down the corridor I hear his voice:

"Well, that was exactly the wrong thing to say." Then: "Merle, wait!"

I will wait, but not inside. Instead, I run back through the hall and into the half light, over the grass, ducking back through the hole in the fence Ren showed me from our last visit. I'm almost through when he finally catches up.

"Merle—"

"And you!" I turn on him. "You're just as bad! Where have you been?! A few days, you said, but then you never came back! Everyone's gone! Hazel and Ali went this morning, and Shelby didn't even show up at all! Even Alfie had to go. You said—!" My voice cracks, tears overtaking the words. Then I'm crying again, overwhelmed by it all.

"I know what I said." Ren steps forward, and I'm not quite distraught enough to ignore the elegance of his movements. "You're right, I'm sorry."

"What?" I sniff. Did he just say I'm right?

He sighs and puts his hands on my shoulders. "I'm sorry, and Joth's sorry. It took me longer than I expected, but that isn't an excuse. We should've been more thoughtful."

"Yes, you should've," I nod decisively.

He looks down at me, taking in my watery eyes, wet cheeks, and trembling mouth. I try to take deep breaths to calm myself, but it's obviously not working. Realisation dawns on Ren's handsome face, that I really thought they were leaving me behind, and how terrifying that's been – and it has been! – and it sets me off again.

"It's all right." Now he pulls me to him fully, squeezing me hard. "It's going to be all right."

I feel better after I've cried for a bit, and Ren doesn't grumble or tell me to stop. After ten minutes, I finally slow the stream. "Sorry."

He shakes his head. "Don't be."

"What now?"

"Now?" He raises an eyebrow. "Now you get your stuff, you come back over here and settle in, I guess?"

"Okay." Even though I don't feel like crying anymore, I'm deflated and empty. My throat throbs, my words raw and aching.

"Come on," Ren swings his arm around my shoulders and guides me back across the field, "I'll make tea."

10

I leave Ren in the kitchen while I run upstairs to get my things. The house looks exactly the same, even though it feels empty, as if all the life's been sucked out of it. No Mum wandering around, neither of my aunts fussing over laundry or the state of the carpet. Not even Alfie waiting to report my misbehaviour. I smile at the memory of him and my throat burns. Who'd've thought he'd be the one I miss so desperately?

My arms prickle with goosebumps as I go into my room and pick up my battered old rucksack. Even though the house is still mine, I feel like this chapter of my life is closing. The walls are to be left to themselves. Only the ghosts that rest here making use of them, stuck forever in the warmth of memory and wishes. I think about having a final glance into Mum's room but decide against it; not seeing her tucked into bed is more than I can bear. Slinging the rucksack over one shoulder and the tote bag over the other, I go back down to the kitchen.

Ren's sitting at the table staring out of the window. "You didn't have any milk."

Of course we don't. Hazel emptied everything perishable out of the fridge before she left.

"Are you ready?"

I nod. I give Ren one bag to hold while I check all the doors are locked, and he insists on carrying it back to the Templar.

"You've already got one, it's only fair," he says.

We cross back over the fields and through the fence, the enormous front doors still standing open from our earlier stormy exit.

"Your room's this way."

I wearily follow him up the stairs, but even with my tiredness I can't miss the ornate décor. The walls are panelled with dark wood and stern portraits, dark shadows cast on the floors by the flickering lamps. It's like going back in time. The further I enter the less real the outside world feels. As we reach the second floor, Ren finally slows down. The hall he takes me to is full of large, dark archways.

"This is my room," he motions to the second door on the right. "The twins have a bigger one on the next level up because they share. I don't think they've ever been separated in their lives."

"How old are they?"

"Ten, they'll be eleven in the spring." A light, almost paternal shine comes into his eyes, then he shakes his head and points across the hall. "That's your room. You might not remember, it's the same one from when you were here before."

"I remember."

"It's pretty bare at the moment, but it's yours, so you can change it," he shrugs. "I could take you on a tour if you want? Show you the Knights' Hall?"

As interesting as that sounds, I'm too tired to consider it. The last few sleepless nights have really taken it out of me. The only thing I want to do is curl up on my new bed and rest. "Maybe tomorrow, is that okay? I just need to..."

"Tomorrow it is. You know where to find me if you need anything." He smiles at me and then ducks into his doorway. I let out a long sigh. It's unfair that someone so handsome can also move like a dancer. He's so graceful, every action like a river that knows exactly where it's supposed to flow.

I turn back to the archway and open the heavy, dark wooden door, noticing as I go that it bears the same iron filigree as the front doors. When I enter the room, I'm hit with a strong smell of lavender. I like lavender; it helps me sleep and keeps me calm. But surely Ren or Joth couldn't have known about that? I throw my backpack down and inspect the furniture. There's a set of drawers and a wardrobe in the same wood as the door, a running theme, it seems. As I'm laying out the meagre amount of items I've brought with me, I have time to wonder about the strange scenario I now find myself in.

I'm a witch, although I've really got no control over my powers. I'm employed by the Knights Templar, an organisation that's existed for millennia, although I've got no idea what it is they really want me to do. My last living family is gone, either dead or away, and I barely know the people my life is now entrusted to, although I do trust them. I flick off my shoes and lay back on the bed. I keep waiting for anxiety to kick in, but it never does.

"*Because you're finally where you're meant to be, sweetheart,*" Dad's voice echoes.

I'm bone-tired and want to sleep, so I wriggle out of my jeans and crawl under the covers. The bed is so soft and warm. I breathe in lavender and close my eyes.

When I open them again, I'm standing in my kitchen. The light makes strange dappled patterns on the tile floor. A steaming kettle sits on the table, next to the sugar and a plate of biscuits. There's a rustling sound from behind me and I turn to see Mum. My heart jumps, the warmth of happiness flooding through my core, right to the tips of my fingers. She grins at me, eyes sparkling with joy, her usually pale cheeks pink with blush. Then she holds out her arms, and I can do nothing other than fall into them. What wonderful magic is this? Somehow she's come back to me, and she can stay here with us at the Templar, all back together again!

The surge of delight in my chest dampens, an icy river cutting through it like a blade. No, that can't be right. Mum is dead. She might not know she's dead – that's clear with the smile on her face – but I do. I've spent days in bed weeping over her loss, wishing I could've prevented her passing. She can't be pottering around the kitchen as if everything is as it was. She *can't* be here.

"Hi, Merlie," she whispers into my hair.

"Mum!" I whimper. I know she can't stay, but I can't let her go. "I love you."

"Yes, I know you do." Her fingers, so soft a moment ago, dig into my back, her knuckles like tree knots, nails ripping into my shirt. "Can I make you some waffles, Merlie?"

I freeze in her embrace. She might not realise she's dead, but she knows she isn't my mother. I disentangle myself and step back from her at least three paces, and once again, I face the deformed fae. It looms over me, black eyes and terrible claws bearing down. This time, in my heart, I know there's no magic. It was a one time thing. I'm not who they think I am, and I can't stop the faery again. I cover my eyes as it advances, and when I feel hands on my shoulders, I scream.

"It's all right," whispers a small soft voice I don't recognise.

I bite down on my lip to stop myself from shrieking again. It's a girl's voice, and with two deep breaths, I remember where I am. Not at home in the kitchen, but here in the Templar, safe. I brush a trembling hand through my hair, moving the sticky clumps from my forehead. A small hand squeezes my wrist, encouraging me to open my eyes. The most beautiful child I've ever seen is sitting beside me. She has the face of an angel, perfectly symmetrical, with rosy cheeks and pale skin. So pale and dewy that she's almost translucent, humming with her own internal glow. The child's eyes are grey, the colour of storms and rain clouds. Ash-blonde hair is braided around her head like a crown, and I recognise her instantly. Ren was right when he said that Dad's drawings were eerily accurate. Even if I didn't have those to go by, she's unmistakable. A queen.

"Are you okay?" she whispers.

"Yes." I push myself into a sitting position. "I'm sorry if I scared you."

"You didn't," Lore Pendragon smiles, showing her perfectly white and even teeth. "I'm not supposed to be here.

Joth told me to let you sleep, but I wanted to see you! All Ren has done for the last two weeks is blah, blah, blah." She raises her hand in front of her face and opens and closes her fingers while sticking out her tongue. I imagine Ren pulling the face and laugh. "You were having a nightmare when I came in, but I could only see a bit of it."

"You could *see* it?"

Her fine eyebrows knit together, puzzled by my puzzlement. "Sometimes. Joth says I take after our great-great-grandmother more than the Pendragons. I can do special things with magic," she grins, "like you."

"We don't know that for sure," I sigh and swing my legs out of bed. I need a shower and some food. My stomach growls as if to enunciate the point. "What time is it?"

"Late! Almost eleven o'clock!"

"And past your bedtime, I imagine." I smile at her and she blushes. "Come on, show me where your room is, I'll take you back."

"Do we *have* to go back? I can take you to the kitchen, there's cake." Her mouth turns down at the corners. I should definitely take her back to bed, but with her sad face and huge puppy-dog eyes, I'm not sure I can go through with it.

"Yes, Lore," a voice from the doorway makes me jump. I didn't even hear the door open. Where Ren's concerned, I suppose I'll have to get used to it.

The little girl screws her face up in a scowl, hops down off the bed and takes Ren's hand. She stares up at him, covering a yawn with her palm. "I'm not even tired."

The picture of them together, bathed in the soft light, washes away any of my anxiety about the nightmare. They are beautiful.

"You good?" Ren asks.

I nod, ignoring the lump in my throat I can't seem to swallow. I'm growing too attached to them already. What if I don't want this new life? What if I can't bear the responsibility? It's already obvious I've got no control over my powers. I might hurt them, or fail to stop something else from hurting them.

"Go back to sleep."

"But she's hungry," Lore seems to have perked up again, "are you going to let her starve to death?"

I laugh at the genuine concern in her voice, and Ren rolls his eyes. "And I suppose you think you can fix that? All right then, but after you've got to go straight back to bed."

"Deal!" Lore grins up at him and then runs to me. I get up at her insistent pull on my arm. Ren winks at me, leaving as silently as he arrived.

Lore leads me through a maze of dimly-lit passages and dark staircases. Severe eyes peer down at us from lofty portraits, probably wondering how someone such as I dare walk these halls. The little girl doesn't once falter, though, her slippered feet whispering on the thick rugs. After a left at a particularly gruesome painting – an ogre devouring a knight, it looks like – we make it to the kitchen. It's a vast room, all the surfaces shiny and silver, the array of pots and pans showing my reflection at distorted angles. When we reach the fridge, Lore climbs onto the counter. She struggles for a second, her feet slipping on the metal. I reach out to help her, but then she gets it, swivelling around, so she's facing me.

"This one has stuff for sandwiches."

"I remember there being some mention of cake?" I raise

147

my eyebrow at her conspiratorially.

"Bottom shelf."

I can barely believe the amount of cake there is. There's a chocolate one with dark swirls of icing, one which I assume is carrot because of the piped-orange vegetables on its surface, and a Victoria sponge stuffed with cream and jam.

"Are you sure we can eat this?" It looks like they've been prepared for a party, and I don't want to get in trouble less than twelve hours after my arrival.

Lore rolls her eyes at me in exasperation. "Etta won't mind. She enjoys making cakes. And there's more in the other fridge. Can I have the carrot?"

"Sure." Shrugging, I pull it out of the fridge. I'm glad to see slices already missing. I carve two pieces and open cupboards until I find plates, then I jump up on the counter next to Lore. She's already made a good start on the wedge. There are crumbs down the front of her pyjamas and icing all around her mouth, but I still beat her in finishing it. Lore giggles as I lick the last of the icing off my fingers.

"I knew this was a good idea! Ren never lets me have a midnight snack. Well, sometimes... but not enough! And Lux is a baby. He won't ever sneak out with me!"

"He sounds well behaved."

"Boring!"

I laugh at her screwed-up nose and stuck-out tongue. I love her already. When she finishes her cake, I help her down off the side and follow her back up the stairs. Ren's waiting at the doorway of his room and Lore goes to him, obviously tired.

"Do you never sleep?" I ask.

"It's like eleven-thirty," he smiles, "and time for bed for

you, Princess."

"And you better remember it." Lore jabs him twice in the ribs playfully. "Now escort me back to my room!"

He grins at her and then shoots his hands to her midsection, tickling her until she's giggling uncontrollably. When she's regained her composure, she gives me a hug goodnight and wraps her arms around my waist.

"Don't worry about the nightmares, you won't have anymore tonight, promise," she smiles, then turns and skips off towards her room. Ren raises one quizzical eyebrow at me, to which I respond with a shrug.

"I'll get you for breakfast," he says, then he turns and follows her shadow down the hall.

The next morning, I've already been awake for about an hour, staring up at the ceiling, trying to imagine what my days might look like now I'm here, (now I'm Merlin's heir rather than Merle Wilde), when there's a light tapping on the door.

"Hello?"

"It's me," Ren says. "Breakfast's in ten minutes. Do you need me to wait?"

"No, I can find my way."

"If you say so." His dark chuckle and soft pad of footsteps signal his retreat.

I push the covers back and take stock of my new surroundings. There's a dresser opposite the bed with a mirror balanced on it. The rim of the mirror is decorated with beautiful, ornate patterns. I think they're flowers, maybe roses. The glass reflects my pale face. High cheekbones, now much too pointed against my taught and sallow skin. Over the last week or so, since I killed the faery, I've not been eating nearly enough, and it's painfully obvious. Only my hazel eyes still look bright; a flicker of my old self. Sighing, I brush out my hair with my fingers and then give up on trying to make it lie flat, twisting it into a bun on the top of my head and securing it with a band. It won't stay where I put it anyway.

When I'm dressed, I creep out into the hall and go back the way I remember from last night. As I get to the staircase, I realise I've reached the limits of my geographical knowledge of the Templar. So that's why Ren was laughing. This place is like a rabbit warren. Even after spending a hundred years here, I wouldn't be able to navigate my way around. I start left through another arch and come face to face with the gruesome ogre painting from the night before. I can't be too far from the kitchen then, maybe if I take a—

A short tinkling laugh echoes from somewhere in front of me, and while I've had little experience with Lore Pendragon, it sounds like her. Following her voice, and smells I recognise – eggs, toast, and pastries – I finally locate the dining room.

"I was about to send out a search party." Ren grins, patting the empty seat beside him.

"You'll get the hang of it." Joth pushes a plate in front of me, loaded with various breakfast items. My stomach growls appreciatively. I can barely wait to tuck in. It seems Joth has other plans, though, as he clears his throat and casts his eyes to the back of the room. Waiting there with arms clasped at their backs are two women and one man. They must be the staff Ren told me about. "I thought we'd take a moment for introductions."

"Hello," I say, casting off my seat and going to them. "I'm

Merle."

"Etta." The older woman takes my hand and gives it a rough, warm squeeze. The cook. Not only did Lore mention her, but her apron smells faintly of onions. "I hear you enjoyed my carrot cake?"

There are snorts from behind me and heat runs into my cheeks, but Etta's smiling, her round face creased with wrinkles. "Very much so, probably the best cake I've ever had."

"*Such* flattery." She rolls her eyes and waves me off, but I can tell she's pleased.

Next is the young man; tall, very tall. Towering over me, and probably both Ren and Joth. He has a bush of curly hair on his head and is dressed in green overalls. "I'm Benjamin, Miss. Or Benji, or Ben. Help out with the garden's 'n that."

"Nice to meet you." I shake his hand too, then turn to the last. I recognise this woman as the one I saw on the stairs and asked to tell the others I was going. That I just couldn't wait to get to Mum. Even though by then it was already too late, the faery already had her and was wearing her skin like a suit, *already dead—*

"Mona," she says, gripping my hand tightly, aware I'm going somewhere I shouldn't in my mind. "Nice t' see ye again. I'll be 'elpin' y'get y'self around." Her accent is so broad I can barely understand her. I nod my thanks and she gives me a wolfish grin.

With those introductions finished, it's time to turn to the one remaining at the table. Across from where I sit with Ren is Lore, who's frantically trying to get my attention, and a boy peering at me suspiciously. Lux is even paler than his sister, with the same angelic face and tiny smudges of pink on his cheeks. His eyes are lighter than Lore's by two shades, ash-blonde hair sticking up in rumpled clumps. Much like his twin, he seems to glow.

"I hear you met Lore last night." Joth raises his eyebrows at the girl, and she flushes. He's smiling, so I know she's not in trouble. "This is Lux."

"Hi, Lux."

"Hello," the boy grumbles, narrowing his pale eyes at me. "Are you the witch they've been looking for? You don't look much like a witch."

"I'm just Merle."

He studies me for another second, assessing me. I can't help the smile that breaks out on my face, and Ren laughs.

"Let's just get through breakfast first before we start the interrogation process, shall we?" Joth says.

"What would you know about witches, anyway?" Lore turns to her brother. "All you're bothered about is boring old knights."

"Who are you calling boring?" Ren interjects, and Lore's cheeks turn pink. Lux smirks into his eggs.

After we've all finished and the plates have been cleared and replaced with tea and coffee, Joth turns to address the twins. "Can I trust you to behave while I show Merle around?"

Both of them sit straight in their seats, devoting their full attention to his words, nodding vigorously.

"In that case, I suppose you can go and play—"

"For the entire morning?" Lore blurts out. The twins' faces are alight with anticipation.

"For the entire day." Joth leans in conspiratorially and the kids whoop with laughter. "But if I hear you've caused any trouble—"

"We won't!" Lux shakes his head vigorously. "We promise we won't!"

Joth gets to his feet and motions for us all to do the same. The twins join hands and wait to be excused. They look like I imagine Hansel and Gretel would on their way to the forest. Joth gives them the signal and they run off into the rabbit warren, laughing. That leaves the three of us.

"We've a lot to talk about, some history to run through, and you need to know about the task ahead of you," Joth sighs wearily. "And I think it's time for you to meet Willow."

"The historian?"

"Yes, she'll be in the library, but doesn't allow hot drinks in there. We'll finish our coffee through here." Joth points in the opposite direction to the twins. I refill my drink and follow him, with Ren close on my heels.

The sitting room is as ornate as the bedrooms. Along one wall is a stone fireplace that's stacked with logs. Above it hangs a painting that must be King Arthur. He's radiating light and pulling a sword from a mountain of stone. There's no carpet in the room, but there are a handful of woven rugs scattered around, all red and gold and green. Ren goes to one of the two couches and Joth sits on the other. I plant myself beside Ren.

Joth coughs to clear his throat. "How's your head?"

"Better." I feel along my hairline and find the scab that sits there. In truth, I'd forgotten all about it.

"I owe you another apology. We knew there was a threat, and we still weren't vigilant enough."

"It isn't your fault."

"That attack in the park shouldn't have happened. Your

mother's death shouldn't have happened. We moved too slowly. I had no idea the fae would be so bold. We've never dealt with anything like this before." Joth always appears so controlled and sure, but the man before me now is afraid, eyes darting back and forth, wringing his hands in his lap.

I sit forward in my chair. I can't deny magic exists and that I'm sometimes able to wield it. However, there's still the question of whether I'm actually the heir of Merlin, or something else. The question of whether I'll be enough to strengthen the Templar and somehow save them from this threat. They've both said they're sure it's me, but how can they be?

"What happens now? Do I have to do a test or something?" I say, half joking, but Joth's face drops, flushing a dull red.

"I'd hoped to give you more time to acclimatise before dropping all of this on you, but time is against us." His blue eyes meet mine. "Yes, there is a test of sorts."

I swallow and put down my cup. As much as I enjoy caffeine, it'll do nothing to help the nervous energy running through my veins. Ren shifts beside me uneasily.

"And when can I take it, this test? What do I have to do?" I turn my gaze from Ren to Joth and back again. "And why do you look so worried?"

"I'll explain it all to you, I promise." Joth finishes his drink and puts the empty cup on the table next to him. No coaster. Aunt Hazel would go spare. "But later, after you've met Willow."

"All right. And?"

Joth grimaces. "Honestly, Merle, no one's ever passed this test, no one else has ever tried."

"That doesn't mean anything," Ren blurts out before I can respond. "We still have time to fix everything. We believe you can, that you'll be able to undo the damage we've caused."

I'm terrified, I want to tell him. *I'm terrified that you're wrong and I can't do this. That you waited too long, and I'm not the person you think I am.*

Instead, I bite my lip, holding the words in. If the situation is as bad as they say, then my doubts won't help. Joth breaks the silence.

"I've done enough talking. Come on, let's find Willow. Hopefully she can give you reassurance as to why we brought you here."

11

Joth ushers us through another door and into part of the Templar I haven't yet had the chance to explore. At the end of one corridor, a set of stone steps lead down, a metal railing guiding them. At the other end is a huge and high arch with double doors that are easily ten feet high. A long bar runs across their front, holding them shut. I want to ask what they're guarding, but the others are way ahead, and I don't want to get lost. I might never find my way out again.

Joth turns left onto a thin staircase. The walls, instead of stone, are lined with panels of wood and a series of portraits of old men with grey beards and severe glares.

"They're the knights," Joth says as if he has read my mind, "well, the old knights."

"From the Round Table?" I ask.

"No, not nearly as old as that! They're the

grandfathers of most of the knights that form the Templar now."

He points to the painting by the top of my head. The man in it stares out with scathing blue eyes, his lips pursed in a sneer. He's one of the few knights who still has a full head of black hair, fading from his temples in a widow's peak.

"That's Jonathan Geraint, a descendant of Sir Geraint and Lady Enid. His daughter now sits in his seat. He was, to put it mildly..."

"A crazy old bastard," Ren interjects, "like the rest of his line. Well, Lydia's all right. The original Geraint was so convinced Enid was having an affair, he made her go through a ton of trials and tests to prove her love."

"Insecurity is never pretty," I sigh. Then I ask, "Women can be knights too?"

"Of course! We might be descendants of a line that started in the dark ages, but we aren't stuck there! Heirs can be of any gender; my job is to offer every rightful candidate a place at the table." He pauses, "There's Lydia Geraint and Asher Gaheris. They come from the Templars a little further North. There's also Amalie and Aurora Percival, but they live in France, so you won't meet them yet. But I'll explain all that later. Willow has more than enough to show you now."

At the top of the stairs, Ren takes a sharp right towards another set of double doors. "This is the library, where Willow spends most, well, all of her time." He pushes the doors open and then steps back to let me admire the view.

He's right to do so. I've always loved books, and spent more happy times in Dad's study – pretending to read when I was small, and actually reading when I was able – than I can count. The library in front of me is like nothing I've ever seen.

There are rows and rows of volumes, worn spines standing to attention, bound with leather and cloth. They smell of old paper and ink. It's one of my favourite smells, so calming and comfortable. A chandelier hangs down in the centre of the room, bathing everything in a soft peach glow. It's beautiful.

"Go on." I can see Ren smiling out of the corner of my eye.

I move forward with almost comical slowness, as if my limbs are pushing through water or treacle. It doesn't even bother me that my mouth is hanging slightly open.

"Willow should be upstairs." Joth breezes past me and points towards a wooden ladder. "She's expecting you."

"You aren't coming?"

"I'm far too old to climb that rickety thing, and I need to check on the twins. Who knows what mischief they're getting into?"

I go to the ladder, reach for the highest rung I can, and pull myself up. It's a quick climb, and when I swing my legs over the bannister, I'm further surrounded by books.

"Willow's 'office' is through the space between the second and third bookshelves," Ren's voice sounds from below me. "I'll be up in a minute."

Following his instructions, I manoeuvre my way around the piles of books on the floor until I reach the opening. There's a woman standing at the desk, her long brown hair pooling on the table she's leant over. She has brown skin, and brown eyes which sparkle behind her glasses. She's older than me by a few years, maybe in her mid-twenties. Willow puts down her pen and comes around the front of the desk, offering me her hand. Her high cheekbones catch the light, pointed chin emphasising her heart-shaped face.

"Hello, I'm Willow."

"Merle."

"Yes, Joth said you were coming. I've got a bit of family tree to show you, although I've not had time to make the amendments yet. Tracing the history of the knights and the Templar is difficult, but the bloodline of Merlin," she breaks off with a slight shudder.

I purse my lips against a grin. Willow goes back around her desk, which is piled high with stacks of paper, open books with hand-drawn pages, and scrolls in different shades of brown. I assume I'm supposed to follow and watch as she unfurls the papers with gloved fingers. She reaches into a tub beside her and hands me a pair of white latex gloves.

"You can touch, but put these on. Some of this stuff is thousands of years old. I don't want to ruin it."

"Always with the gloves." Ren's shadow falls across the paper in front of us.

"What are you doing here? You hate history." Willow raises an eyebrow at him and crosses her arms over her chest.

"Yes, but only when it's my own."

She shrugs and turns to me. "It's best if I start from the beginning if you're ready? Depending on which historians you read, Monmouth, Nennigan, Malory, it changes. I've done my best to piece together what I can. Arthurian legend spans much farther than Merlin's, you know? And half of those things aren't even true." Her hands go to her hips, long brown fingers squeezing slightly. "Can you imagine the trouble I've had figuring out what's fact and what's fiction?"

"I can't," I say. I'm completely serious. It's beyond me how she's done any of this, but Ren bursts out laughing.

"So immature," Willow sniffs, but she's smiling. "The

grail stories alone are enough to drive anyone insane, but Merlin didn't play a massive part in those." She lifts one of the enormous books off the top of a pile. Its cover is red and worn, woven with great letters that seem to move across the page. They're all straight lines and angles, but I'm sure I can make out words. Before she's got a chance to open it, I reach forward to run my fingers across it.

"*In linea regum*," I say slowly, not sure I'm pronouncing any of the words correctly. "Is that right?"

When I glance back up, Willow's staring at me with her mouth open.

"Well, we'd really have no idea," Ren answers, a smug smile on his lips, dark eyes full of fire. "The inside's all Latin, but that's Merlin's script, and no one's ever been able to decode it."

Heat creeps into my cheeks, and I clear my throat. "What does it mean?"

"'The Line of Kings'," Willow whispers. There's a shiny look in her eyes, as if I'm some kind of rare creature, a unicorn.

"Don't worry," Ren says. "She's just coming to terms with all the new things she can learn now she's got someone who can read it."

"Well, just think of all the things we can know! All those volumes that I've never been able to translate, hundreds of them—!" Willow starts, but then cuts off as she registers the smirk on Ren's face. "But all that can come later, we've got other fish to fry first."

Even though the thought of getting my hands on the books Willow mentioned has made my heartbeat quicken, I want to know about the history Joth promised. Willow opens the cover again and smooths out the first pages. One side is thick with rows of looping text, the other portrays a crimson demon looming over a blonde-haired woman. Her mouth is a wide 'O' cupped by fretful hands.

"An Incubus demon and a human woman sired Merlin," Willow begins. "The legend says the demon seduced the woman, intending to create one of the most powerful men in history. We don't know for certain who his mother was, but Merlin's half-demon side is the reason he had powers. Some say he stayed with his mother, who raised him. Others say he lived in the woods, a wild man who could talk to animals. Either way, he learned his powers of sorcery from the earth, how to grow things, mould things, build. The earth doesn't teach the power to destroy, only to create..."

"Like growing plants?" I butt in.

"Yeah, I guess. Why?"

"I can do that, well, kind of. Mum says I have a green thumb." Too slowly, my brain realises I've misspoken. Not *says* but *said*, not here but gone. I clamp my teeth together. It's the only way to stop myself from crying, and even then, it's not a sure thing.

"Interesting," Willow muses, oblivious, but Ren reaches behind her and squeezes my arm just above the elbow. "Anyway, word of him spread to the towns. A boy with no parents and potentially full of magic. Obviously he caused a stir." She turns the pages of the book to reveal an oil painting of a young man enrobed in a cape of leaves. Around him are words in swooping swirls. I reach forward to touch it and Willow flinches, but doesn't stop me. The paint's rough beneath my gloved fingers, and his looming golden eyes seem to follow their movement across the page.

"Is that him?" I've seen that face before; it's the same as the one in Dad's sketches.

"A version of him," Willow nods. "Sometimes he's pictured as a nobleman, but I think the wild man's more accurate. Someone born of the earth wouldn't end up as some wizened old man with a horrible old beard. And the stories that depict him as civilised?"

"Nobody wants to hear a story about Merlin's social development, Willow. Get to the good bit," Ren says.

She narrows her eyes at him but continues. "Merlin became the advisor to King Vortigern and later to Uther Pendragon, but that's a story for another day. Their rise to power and the birth of Arthur is great, though. I'll lend you a book about it." She brushes her long dark hair behind her ears. "Merlin took Arthur from Uther and Igraine and raised him with Sir Antor to be a good and wise man. They did it away from the court, so politics or wealth wouldn't mar him. When Uther died, Merlin took Arthur to draw the sword from the stone and be recognised as the true King of England. He advised Arthur for a time, then he took on Arthur's three half sisters as apprentices, the strongest of the three being Morgwese."

"The bad one?"

"And that's putting it mildly!" Willow huffs. "After he trained them to do as much as their skills could manage, he travelled around Europe. Sometimes with Arthur and the knights, mostly without. Then he fell in love with Nimue, the Lady of the Lake, not to be confused with Vivienne, the Lady of the Lake who raised Lancelot. Anyway, Nimue didn't truly return Merlin's affections. She told him she could never be with him, afraid of his demon half and the darkness that lurked in his soul. So, he bartered a deal with the fledgling sorceress. He would teach her all the magic at his disposal in return for her love. Nimue couldn't refuse, and love him she did, for a time." Willow has a small half smile on her face. She's a natural storyteller, building suspense with breathless ease. She turns the page to reveal another exquisite painting. Merlin looks older, but is still handsome. There's a beautiful woman beside him with long auburn hair and a stream of magic running from her fingertips. "Nimue bore Merlin a child, Sybil. Then when she'd learned enough magic to overpower him, she entombed him in rock. After, she moved to the king's court with Morgana Le Fae and Sybil so they'd be safe."

"Always the women," Ren mutters under his breath.

"That's where his body still is, we think. In the enchanted forest of Broceliande, waiting for his heir to inherit his magic." Willow's enormous eyes brim with excitement. "That's you!"

"We don't know for definite," I say.

"Well, no. First, you have to convince the knights, go into the cave, and claim the magic." Her eyes are still shining, but nerves jolt in my stomach. I've heard nothing about convincing. I'm only just convinced myself.

"But we can't do any of that if Merle doesn't know her line." Ren's voice is low.

"Right, sorry, it's all just so exciting!" Willow continues, "It's reported that Sybil had a few illegitimate children. Most of them were stillborn or didn't survive through infancy. I could only trace two, Caelia and Clarion. Clarion died in his quest to join the knights, who would never have accepted him as one of their own, even if he had found them. Caelia, however, a beautiful princess, half human and half demon like her grandfather, left the court with her beloved, Ider. They had five children, two of which I traced, Clarine and Evalac. I'm working on their lines," she sighs. "We have about ten generations pinned down, leaving four hazy ones in the middle."

"Ren's told me a little about how the heirs work," I say. "I don't really understand."

A sparkle shines in Willow's eyes. I've seen it happen with Shelby when I want to know more about something she's passionate about. "What do you want to know?"

"As much as you can tell me."

"The abridged version though, please." Ren squeezes the bridge of his nose in mock exasperation.

"Well, I imagine Ren told you the descendants of the knights behave strangely?"

I nod.

"According to the documents the Templar has, there were twelve knights who sat with Arthur at his table. Those were the ones he trusted more than others. In some stories, there are hundreds of different knights. Joth though, who's part of one of the few families that weren't 'lost', told me to trace those twelve lines."

"Lost?"

"Like Merlin's line and Lancelot's. Sir Kay, for example, has always been a part of the Templar. He grew up in this world, as did Gawain and Bedivere, although you shouldn't worry about them just yet." She pats my hand. "After Arthur died, the Knights of the Round Table mostly went their separate ways, and that's when the trouble started."

"Because no one kept proper records?"

"Exactly!" She beams. "As you'll know from basic history lessons, there was a lot of war, famine, destruction... but what's *absolutely* miraculous is that not a single one of these twelve lines ever died out. The strange thing about it, though, is that there's only one heir for each generation that produced offspring. Well there's one case that doesn't fit the pattern, Sir Percival's, but I can explain all that later. If we look at Sir Kay, his grandfather Simon had three siblings, but two of them perished before having children, and his sister wasn't able. Simon had two sons, but only the eldest, Kay's father, could produce an heir."

I must pull a face because some enthusiasm drains from Willow's. "How about I try to show you?"

"Oh, here we go!" Ren huffs.

Willow crouches under her desk and comes back up with another binder. This one has many tabs of rainbow colours sticking from the side. She flips through it, stopping at a blue tab, then she lays the open folder in front of me. "This is the latter part of Sir Kay's family tree."

On one stark white page are several names, linked by thick black lines. I trace upwards from the last row. *Andy Kay* is in bold, while *Rebecca Kay* is marked as deceased. Above, their parents, John and Maria, a brother Marc listed on John's side, but with no offspring. Rows of names and red Xs. And one clear line down the centre, one path leading back generations.

"Do you see how there's only one line? Always the oldest child, and always only one heir."

I trace my fingers over the lines. I *do* see that. Even when there's been a marriage or the children lived to adulthood, there's only one true heir.

"It's the same for everyone, although it's harder to track those of you who went gallivanting off out of Arthur's court." She flicks a long, dark strand of hair behind her ear.

"How did you find all this?"

"With great difficulty. I'm in the process of drawing out a family tree, but until I have all the parts, it's mostly fruitless work. Every time I think I have someone nailed down, someone else pops up with an illegitimate heir or a sister that wasn't there before. Believe it or not, one of the easiest lines to trace was that of the Pendragons. It's common knowledge that Arthur's father was Uther Pendragon, and Lux and Lore are descendants of his union with Igraine. I suspect they're the great-great-great-great..." she pauses. "For the sake of my vocal cords, just know when I say great, I mean fourteen or fifteen generations, okay? So, they are the great-grandchildren of Arthur's full sister, Anna Pendragon."

"How can you be sure about them?"

"They had papers," Ren adds lazily.

"Papers? Like pedigree dogs?"

He laughs at the shocked expression on my face. "Surely you don't think the secret descendants of Arthur come *without* papers?"

"Well, everyone else was so organised..."

"What he means is," Willow cuts Ren off before he can open his mouth again, "Lux and Lore came with a document signed by King Arthur himself. One of only two copies of his signature, the first being what Lux and Lore brought. A note explaining the carrier of the document was his true heir."

"And the second?"

"Queen Guinevere's death warrant," Willow whispers, and my stomach lurches. I know she was freed in the end, but still. "I authenticated the paper and the ink and matched the signatures. It was over a thousand years old, and they came with all sorts of relics."

"Like what?"

Ren and Willow share a look, as if it's some secret between them. It frustrates me to the point of anger. I'm already on emotionally thin ice, my nerves frayed to breaking point. Ren shutting Willow up about me having to 'claim' Merlin's magic, whatever that means, gave me an uneasy feeling. Surely they want me to know all the information they have before I face my task? Instead, it looks like they're trying to hide something from me. I peel off my gloves and throw them on top of the book.

"When you decide to let me in on the secrets you have, you can come and find me. I came here because you asked." I point my index finger at Ren. "If all you're going to do is give me confusing history lessons, I want no part of it."

"Merle..." Ren starts, but I don't hear the rest of his sentence.

I stomp back through the line of books and swing my legs over the bannister, sliding down to the floor and marching out of the library, thankful not to hear Ren's footsteps behind me.

How can they hide things if they want me to trust them? After storming through the doors I swing a left. Frustration burns like hot metal in my throat as I pace, choking me. There's a set of twisting spiral stairs carved into the bare stone of the back wall. I start towards them and look up; they seem to go on forever into some kind of tower. The steps differ from those of the grand wooden staircases I've already climbed. They mirror the ones I saw earlier, though those trailed down instead of up.

It takes a long while to reach the top, and by the time I do, I'm breathing hard. The reward of fresh cold air on my face is worth it. Through the archway is a circular room with wide open slits in the stone. Above my head are rafters full of wooden boxes and remnants of dusty hay. My guess is that I'm about fifty feet up, and from this height, the view is beautiful. I can see for miles, right to the farthest edge of the woods and the rolling hills behind them. In the other direction is the winding road that leads to Little Oulmarsh's centre. I can't quite see the shape of the Java Bean, although I know it's there, the remains of my old life. I tuck myself onto a stone ledge, not quite brave enough to swing my legs over the edge. *Am I being too hard on them?*

With everything going on, I'm not in complete control of my thoughts and feelings. Just as I've had these strangers thrust into my life, they've had me thrust upon theirs. They have their secrets, thousands of years of them, and they don't know if they can trust me. Even if they think I'm the true heir, currently nothing cements my position. If I decide to leave, to go back to Hazel, Ali and Alfie, then I've lost nothing, really. They, however, would be sending a stranger out into the world with some of their deepest secrets. The thought of my aunts and Alfie makes my heart twinge painfully. I miss them, all of them, including Mum and Dad. If my parents were here, maybe they could help me figure everything out.

"*But they aren't,*" a stern voice, possibly my own, sounds inside my head. "*Whether or not you like it, you trust Ren, and you might even trust Joth. And you certainly don't want anything to happen to the Pendragons!*"

No, I don't. They're the most beautiful of treasures, and

I couldn't live with myself if I put them in jeopardy. Already I'm connected to them. Ren saved my life. He came the second I needed him; Joth too. Really, they've been good to me. They've welcomed me into their home with no resistance, and even though some of their actions have been questionable, their hearts have always been in the right place. I can really be a part of this, if I want it. There's no point throwing that away over papers and relics.

Now I'm calm. I've got the task of trying to find my way back to civilisation. I slip off the stone ledge and out of the corner of my eye I see movement at the front gates. My whole body relaxes with relief as I see a grey head bobbing up and down, a body enrobed in pastel blues and pinks.

"Shelby!" I call as I race back to lean over the edge. "Shelby!"

The figure twists round and then waves her arms over her head. It *is* her, she's not forgotten me after all! I wave wildly back and bolt for the stairs, worried she might soon disappear in a cloud of grey smoke.

It takes me a surprisingly short amount of time to find the front doors. I made one wrong turn, but when I recognised my bedroom door, I knew I could find my way out. I race down the path, realising only then I'm not wearing any shoes.

Shelby's still waving at me, tens of delicate bangles jangling on her wrists; a heavy amber necklace winking in the autumn sun. The gates are closed but I don't think they're locked, and usually she isn't so polite as to wait for an invitation. Maybe the immense house is too intimidating?

"Oh, sweetheart!" Shelby cries when I get close enough. There are tears in her eyes and she's holding her arms out wide. "Come out here and give this silly old woman a hug!"

As soon as I'm through the gates, she throws her arms around me and kisses me on both cheeks. "You haven't been eating enough! And you've got no shoes on! You'll catch your death! Who are these people? Don't they take care of you?" She tucks a stray strand of hair behind my ear. The familiar action is comforting and reinforces how much I've missed her.

"I'm fine, Shell," I smile. "I'm just glad you're here."

"Of course, darling." She pats my cheek with her palm, running her other hand down the length of my arm. Her fingers stop at the bracelet hanging on my wrist, and I feel her fingers exploring it. She mumbles something under her breath.

"What was that?" My heart leaps into my throat. I would swear she said '*you're missing one.*'

"Cotton wool in your ears, darling? Usually charm bracelets have an even number of charms, for balance you see, Yours doesn't, that's all."

I nod, the uneasy feeling passing. Trust Shelby to know an obscure fact like that.

"I'm so sorry about the funeral." She coos and rubs my arm. "I was struck with an awful sickness bug. Did the boys tell you?"

By the boys, I assume she means Nicky and Otto, and they didn't tell me, but she's here now, at least that's something.

"And then I thought, 'oh, I'll walk over and give my lovely girl a surprise!' But that didn't work out either. I couldn't get through the gates!" She removes her hand from my cheek and taps her own forehead. *Scatterbrain*, that movement's supposed to say. Instead, it says *'lie'* in big red letters. The gates weren't locked, so I don't know what she means by 'couldn't get in'. She just saw me open them easily. I control my facial expression, making sure the smile stays plastered there.

"Don't worry, Shell. It's nice to see you."

"And how've you been?"

"I'm doing okay," I shrug. I don't really have anything to say now, a horrible anxiety creeping over me. Why would she lie to me? And what else has she been lying about? "Do you want some tea?"

"Darling, I'm so sorry, but I can't stay! I just popped by to bring you a few things." She shoves the wicker basket she's been holding in my direction. "Oils, plants, some protective crystals. I doubt you remembered to bring any of those!" Her voice is light, but underneath that is deception.

"Shelby, is everything okay? You seem a little... off."

"Oh! Look at you!" Her eyes fill with tears. "After all you've been through, still worrying about an old woman like me! That's why you've always been my favourite!"

I stare at her intently and her hazel eyes meet mine, unwavering. "I guess I'll see you soon then?"

"Yes, darling. Why don't you come for coffee? Tomorrow or the day after? Yes?"

"Yes—" I start, but I'm cut off by a shout from behind me.

"Merle?" Ren's striding towards us, suspicious eyes darting between Shelby and I.

"Oh, he is handsome, isn't he?" Shelby gushes. "I best not keep you from him another second."

"No, Shell, wait..." I reach for her arm, but she evades me

with much quicker movements than her elderly frame suggests possible.

"Oh, don't be silly, sweetheart! Go on, go inside. I'll see you soon." She's already hurrying away from the gates. "I love you!"

"I ah... I love you too, Shell," I whisper, but she's already out of earshot. When I turn, Ren's waiting with his eyebrows raised.

"She didn't want to come in?"

"No." I'm hurt and confused that she'd miss the funeral and then refuse to come inside. She's supposed to be my friend. Ren shrugs and swings on the gates to open them. He takes the basket out of my hand without my asking and slides it into the crook of his elbow. "Is everything okay?"

"Yes," Ren nods. "Lore said you were talking to a strange lady at the gates. I just thought I'd come and check... I didn't realise she meant Shelby."

I'm flattered he cares enough to check up on me, although I suppose at this point it shouldn't surprise me. He has my back, it seems, where even my oldest friends don't. "I'm sorry about earlier."

He tilts his head to one side, and his nose furrows a little. "Sorry for what?"

"For freaking out! I shouldn't have stormed off like that."

"You don't have to be sorry for freaking out, Mer. You've been through a lot in such a short amount of time, I'd be more worried if you *weren't* freaking out a little." At the use of the nickname, a small shiver of pleasure runs through me. He bumps me on the shoulder with his own. "It's time for lunch, then you can go back and see Willow. She enjoyed talking your ear off."

I tug on his wrist as we make it into the entrance hall; he stops and slowly rotates so he's facing me. I lean forward and kiss him on the cheek, pressing my cool lips to his hot skin. When I step back, his eyes are wide, searching my face as if he thinks I'm playing some kind of joke. "Thank you, Ren. For everything."

He nods, clearing his throat, face flushing a dull red. Then he lets out a small sigh and leads me through to the kitchen for lunch.

12

After soup and sandwiches, I go back to the library. Ren makes his excuses, the twins want to play outside for a while and he needs to supervise.

"I'll come up later," he assures me as the kids drag him out of the door.

Eventually, I make it back to the library and climb up the ladder to find Willow, who's sitting where I left her. Around her head is a strange band, like the torches miners wear. Instead of a light, there's a series of magnifying glasses, each smaller than the last. When I clear my throat, she lets out a small scream as she scrambles to pull the contraption off her face. I can't help but laugh.

"Sorry, I didn't expect anyone, especially not someone magnified a hundred times." The grin is wide on her face as she waves me forward, then her eyes narrow a little and she plucks something from my hair. In the tips of her fingers, she holds a tiny white feather. "I see you found the Mews."

As if the others let me walk around with that in my hair all this time, I think, then, "Mews?"

"Where the birds used to live, when there were birds here. We still get a few pigeons sometimes."

"I love the outdoors."

"I know." She blows the feather off the tip of her fingers and it floats in the sun for a moment before settling on a pile of books. "It isn't surprising."

"It isn't?"

"No. I'm no expert in magic, but from what I've read of Merlin, most stories agree he was raised in the woods. He could speak to animals, grow things, create things using the power of the earth, and you've already said you can do that. And we'll know about the animals when you get your familiar."

"My what?"

"Most witches and wizards get one, an animal companion. But I'm jumping the gun a little."

The mention of an animal makes me think of Alfie and how good it'd be to have him back.

"As for Merlin, as far as I can see, his mastery of other forms of magic came later. Your connection to the outdoors, to light and trees and stuff, could be down to the fact that earth magic is your fledgling magic."

"But I wasn't outside when I killed that faery."

"In times of extreme danger or panic, your magic becomes 'unlocked', so to speak. But if you learn, you'll probably start with earth magic. You've already shown some aptitude for stronger powers."

"You mean the blood wish?"

"Hmm," Willow nods, "will you tell me about it?"

I close my eyes, taking a second to think. The musty smell of old books meets my nose, calming me. "The first time I went with Dad, he told me we would wish and then he cut his finger with a penknife. I copied and wished to see a faery. I thought it hadn't come true. The ground shook a bit, but nothing like what happened last time."

"That's because you were still a child! There are thousands of legends about blood wishes, but they're too entwined with sacrifice and weird demonic summoning to make sense. What about last time?"

"I had a dream about Dad. He was at the faery rings, so I went there. I sat in the same circle and made my wish. Then the grass sucked up my blood. First it went red and then black, then the mushrooms burst and I ran."

"Did your dad seem normal in the dream? Did he say anything?"

"No... I don't know if he looked normal, I haven't seen him for a long time."

"Do you dream about him a lot?"

"I guess I do. He opened his mouth to say something, but black water came out instead. It was horrible."

"Maybe somebody's been messing with you, and they might've known you're Merlin's heir as long as we have."

"What do you mean?" I'm glad I'm already sitting because my legs begin to shake.

"When you made the wish all those years ago, it's plausible that something got through. Something powerful. It probably followed you and your father back to your house and kept watch. It'd take time for a fae, even a powerful one, to take on a convincing human form. They can't exist in our world for very long unaided." She moves to a shelf and pulls off another brown book, this one she opens in the middle and hands it to me. There's a picture of a faery, clawed hands reaching out towards us. Deep-blue features, high and proud on its face, black eyes peering out, ethereal in its distaste. "Is that what you saw?"

"Yes! That's it! That's what I killed!" Although my one wasn't nearly as beautiful.

"A Royal." Her eyes light up. "Wow. I've never met anybody who's seen one! There might not be anyone alive who has! Nothing as grand as a king or queen, but certainly in the family—"

"Willow," a wave of nausea washes over me, "it killed my mother."

Her cheeks flush. "I'm sorry. I got carried away, but it might help explain some things."

"What do you mean 'Royal'?"

"Just like humans, faeries have political systems. As far as we know, a monarch still controls their realm." She flips to another page, showing an illustration of a bewitching creature on a throne. Her skin is a deep shade of violet, long silver hair running over her shoulders, glowing with celestial light. Gossamer wings extend high above her shoulders, glittering with dew. To complete the picture, a crown sits on her noble head, so fine it could be spun from a spider's web. "Queen Solena, the last queen we know of before the fae circles were closed, although we suspect Morgwese is queen now. Royal is short for someone of high standing in the fae court. They're powerful. If one got through, it could have followed you to your house all those years ago. It would explain your father's disappearance, all the shadows, and the strange dreams. It was goading you, forcing you to go back to the rings and give it more blood, to open the door again."

Fury runs through me, a hot flash, almost unbearable. Does that mean the pull of the rings is a lie then? The comforting sense of home when I'm in them a trick? Not mine and Dad's place, but theirs. Stolen from us. Ruined. I can't even bring myself to speak, burning, hateful tears forming in my eyes.

"These faeries are powerful," Willow continues, oblivious. "They must've known about you and your mother, and they could've been manipulating you for years! You had no information, no way to protect yourself!" She looks away and shakes her head. "We should have come sooner! There was no reason to disrupt you when you seemed happy. There was no imminent threat..."

"It isn't your fault either, Willow."

"No," she agrees, "but with this information, I can make sure we get a handle on this before it gets any worse. Did you tell anyone about the dreams? About the Shadows?"

"Only Hazel and Ali."

"Sure?"

"And Shelby." For a moment, I thought about holding her name back, and I'm not sure why. "Shelby Lewis, she knew my parents before. She's my friend."

"Okay." Willow nods. Her mind's already somewhere else. The cloudiness in her eyes tells me so. It's time to make myself scarce.

"Can I borrow that book you mentioned about history? I'd like to read it."

"Sure!" Her face brightens. "It's more of a journal, all the notes I took when I was doing my degree."

She moves to the table and pulls out a ring-binder larger than my waist. There are lots of little slips of paper sticking out at odd angles, bloated pages so fat they push the binder to its limits. When she puts it in my arms, it's so heavy I almost drop it.

"Thanks."

"You're welcome. Nobody else ever wants to look at it." She smiles. "On the other side of the library, there's a sofa. Make yourself at home."

With great difficulty I negotiate my way back down the ladder and across to the other side of the library. There's an opening in the bookshelves overlooked by a large bay window, a battered red chair full of mismatched cushions and a spider plant hanging in the alcove. Its long green spines trail over the edge of a cream pot, twisting around each other like vines. Instead of taking the chair, I pick off some cushions and pile them onto the window seat, making myself comfortable by balancing the folder on my knees. On the first page is a picture of the Round Table. On the second, writing, some typed, some handwritten.

The legend of Merlin has been told over centuries. There are many versions of his life story. However, this is my understanding of the truth.

Willow's signed her name – *W. A. Jhaveri* – with a tiny heart above the I.

King Constans, the ruling king of England at the time of Merlin's boyhood, was a devoutly religious young man. He wished to become a monk and had no taste for power. While many of his advisors spoke against it, his most trusted advisor, Vortigern, commended the decision. He put everything in place so the young king could abdicate his throne for a life of prayer. Vortigern settled himself in Constans' court, as neither of the king's younger brothers were of an age to rule.

Vortigern intended to take the throne for himself, building power and friends who would fight for him. Unknown to Constans, the evil advisor paid Pict mercenaries to assassinate the young king while he travelled to the monastery. When he was killed on the road, Vortigern took power. Loyal Templar knights sent the younger brothers of Constans— Uther and Aurelius—to France, safe from Vortigern while unrest raged throughout the kingdom.

Uther's name is underlined in red. It's the only name I've heard before. As for Constans and Aurelius, I wouldn't know them if they walked over and shook my hand.

King Vortigern allowed the Saxons to settle in Britain and married a young Saxon princess. They had many children, and Vortigern gave many great powers to his father-in-law. Eventually, the Saxon king invaded and Vortigern, having given away many of his forces to the invading king, was defenceless. He fled to Wales and tried to build a magnificent castle, in which to hide. But every night after they had completed work, the walls fell. The king went through tens of advisors, charging them with figuring out the problem, all of them worse than the last. One soothsayer advised that to keep the wall standing, he needed to spill the blood of a boy with no father on the foundation. The advisor knew of such a boy and sent knights to apprehend him. They brought him Merlin Wyllt, a wanderer who had lived in the woods near the castle grounds since he was born. There had always been whispers of him, legends of his young mother and demon father.

Before Vortigern could slit Merlin's throat and spill his blood, the wizard delivered a prophecy. He told the king that a river ran under the fortress, and beneath two dragons raged. It was not magic that kept pulling down the walls, nor would magic keep them up. As long as the fortress trapped the dragons underground, their constant fighting would topple the walls every night. The following night, they released the dragons from their tomb, and for the first time, the castle wall stood. Vortigern banished all the advisors who existed before Merlin, and the wizard became the king's most trusted second.

Britain really is in tatters, I think to myself. Overrun by Saxons. A cowardly king, and a boy wizard who's skating on thin ice with Vortigern.

I turn the page. Pushed inside a plastic wallet is a drawing of an enormous castle on fire, the flames licking the stone. In the top window of the tallest tower, a pale face looks out, its mouth in a wide black 'O' as if it's screaming.

Aurelius and Uther returned from France to overthrow the Saxons and kill Vortigern. They were the true and rightful heirs to the throne and intended to take it back, no matter the cost. Vortigern fled to his castle and was trapped by the brothers. They defeated his remaining army and set the castle alight, burning him to death in his fortress. When the wrongful king had been removed from the throne, Aurelius and Uther vowed to rid the kingdom of Saxons, aided by Merlin. However, one night on the battlefield, Merlin and Uther saw comets flying across the night sky, all of their tails in the shape of mighty dragons. Merlin received another vision in which Aurelius was slain, and he bestowed on Uther the name Pendragon and the title of king.

Uther defeated the Saxons, driving them from his kingdom, reclaiming his castle and settling there. To celebrate his victory, he held a party for the greatest of his knights. Sir Garlois, the bravest of his captains, came to the ball with his beautiful wife, the Lady Igraine and Uther fell madly in love. He demanded her hand, and upon rejection, he decided to go to battle with Sir Garlois.

"Jesus," I whisper to myself.

"Just got to the bit about Uther starting wars over women?"

I'm unable to stop the surprised croak that jumps from my throat, and I whip my head around so fast my neck burns. Ren's leaning on the bookcase closest to me with a huge grin on his face.

"You're a jerk!" I snap, but he dazzles me with his white-toothed grin.

"Well, what do you expect, with our ancestors behaving as they do? I'm a result of adultery, you the result of trickery and bribery. We were destined to be messed up." He comes to sit by me. The space is small, so he sits close, and the heat of his thigh on mine is distracting to say the least.

"Yeah," I nod and shift a little in my seat to look at him. He trains his deep-brown eyes on mine.

"What is it?"

For a moment I don't intend to tell him, to keep all of my anxieties in, but then, "What if I'm no good as an adviser? What if I can't do magic? If I have to leave and I know a ton of secrets..."

"We already know you can do magic."

"Not necessarily."

Ren rolls his eyes.

"No, I mean, I *know* I've done some magic, but never on purpose."

"Try then." He has a small smile on his face, one that oozes confidence.

I wish I felt the way his smile looks. I've never tried intentionally, and now the moment seems to be upon me. I don't want to. Right now, everyone believes I'm a powerful witch, and that cements my place here. If I prove them wrong, I don't know what will happen.

"Just try. Joth doesn't think you'll have proper powers until later, anyway. What harm can it do?"

A lot, probably, I think but don't say. Instead, I close my eyes and try to call upon the sweet tingling feeling that's always accompanied my magic. I focus my energy on the bookshelves, specifically a red hardback book that caught my eye.

Come to me, I command with my mind.

Is there a slight rush at my fingertips, or have I imagined it? When I open my eyes, the book hasn't moved an inch. I sigh audibly and scrub my hand through my hair, pulling at the dark tendrils.

"It didn't work."

"I don't know what you were trying to do." To my surprise, Ren's grinning. "But something happened."

He points to the hanging plant. The spines that were flowing over the side of the pot now reach the floor, tripled in size.

"Oh wonderful, I'll just photosynthesise the faeries to death."

Ren laughs, the deep, throaty chuckle echoing off the stone. There's a dimple in his cheek, which makes my heartbeat quicken. "Don't be so hard on yourself."

"You really aren't worried?"

"About what?"

"That I'm going to mess this up?"

"So far, we've all messed up! Right now, you're the only one who hasn't! Before you came here, we had no witch, no adviser, but with you..." he trails off, and I am sure he's blushing. "We have a chance at both things."

"Okay."

He smiles again, takes the folder off my lap, then closes it.

"I wasn't finished."

"I'll tell it. I've read the thing at least a hundred times. Get comfy."

I shuffle so my back's against the wall, and Ren begins.

"After Uther decided he *had* to have the Lady Igraine, and Garlois' obvious refusal, there was nothing to stop the king's rage. The war went on for months, a bloody massacre that killed hundreds of soldiers. Uther's forces pushed Garlois back to his castle; out of men and supplies, he bartered for a truce, and Uther agreed to meet him. The king asked Merlin to transform him into an image of Garlois, so he might sneak into the castle and seduce Igraine. Merlin agreed to do so if Uther promised to call off the war and leave Garlois and Igraine alone. Uther agreed. At the meeting, they killed Sir Garlois. Igraine was widowed and her three children left fatherless."

"Really? Merlin helped him do that? He *let* him do that?"

"Merlin was under the king's command, and he believed Uther wouldn't kill Garlois, but Uther lied," Ren shrugs.

"He sounds like a piece of work."

"Have you ever heard of a king that wasn't? Uther moved the family into his castle and took Igraine as his wife, who soon became pregnant. Merlin demanded that when the baby was born, Uther was to give him up, as he wasn't fit to raise a child. Merlin, who'd had faith in the young king was disgusted by his actions. He wanted the heir to the throne to be better. Uther and Igraine agreed, and nine months later,

Igraine gave birth to a baby boy, Arthur Pendragon."

"What happened to Igraine?"

"She lived, and later gave birth to another baby, a little girl called Anna. She was raised with her three stepsisters in the castle."

"The sisters Willow mentioned?"

"Yes, and you've heard of Morgana Le Fae? They demonised her in the later legend, but she's a good witch."

"And where's she?"

"France, in her everlasting Cave of Wonders, or so the legend says. Morgana's super powerful! Even more so now she's had hundreds of years to perfect her craft... there're whispers she can even bring people back from the dead." His eyes are wide. "But I don't think it's true. Then there's Elaine. She died many, many years ago. She didn't want to be immortal like her sisters."

"And then there's Morgwese," I say, already the name sends shivers down my spine.

"The eldest sister. She saw everything that happened on the night of Garlois' death, and she never forgave anyone involved. Her powers allowed her to see Uther's true form that night, and she tried to warn her mother, but Igraine didn't listen. She hated them all for it. Uther for the murder, her mother for being so easily manipulated, and her full sisters for accepting their new life. Even Anna, for being the spawn of an immoral union. Arthur didn't appear at court until he was much older, but Merlin was a familiar face. He was the wizard who'd allowed it to happen, and Morgwese vowed to destroy everything he held dear. When Arthur grew older and Merlin's services were needed less, he taught the sisters almost everything he knew. Made them into amazing witches."

"I thought Morgwese hated him?"

"Yes, but she wasn't stupid! And Merlin didn't know about the resentment until later. Morgwese thought, being the oldest child, she would be the heir to the throne. When she realised she wasn't—" Ren raises his eyebrows. "What better way to get revenge than to learn magic and try to overthrow everyone with it?"

"Did she?"

"She never got the chance. Even though Morgwese was by far the strongest on her own, Morgana and Elaine together were more than an equal match. They trapped her in the fae underworld, and she's been safely locked there for three hundred years. But then something happened."

He drops his eyes from me, but I know what he means; *I* happened. All those years ago when I opened the first ring, and then again when I opened the second one.

"Can she get through?"

"Not yet, but she will." When he sees my face he adds, "She would have anyway, Mer. The plan was never to keep her there forever. It was to find a way to get rid of her. Morgana won't help us, and Elaine is dead. That's why there's been such a scramble to assemble the knights and find the remaining heirs. And you're the last one. That's why Morgwese has to be stopped. She's coming for all of us, especially the Pendragons."

"But they're her blood!"

"She doesn't feel that way. In her mind, any line of Uther and Igraine is illegitimate. She wanted the crown instead of Arthur."

"And that's what she wants now?"

Ren sighs. "We don't know exactly. She feels she's owed the crown as compensation for what happened to her family. The only way for her to take back the throne in Avalon would be to destroy everything left of Arthur. But she wasn't, and isn't, the heir. It's Lux and Lore's birthright when they turn fifteen. They're supposed to go to Avalon and watch over it, to make sure the people there are happy. Those with magic can use it without consequences to this world, humans and fae together. Like in Arthurian times, when faeries and humans coexisted, not always peacefully, but sometimes. We think she wants to reclaim this world for herself. It means she has to get rid of Lux and Lore, the last protectors of Avalon and the true king's line."

I let my mind chew over this information. "Ren, what will happen if I'm not Merlin's heir?"

"I already told you..."

"No," I stop him. "I mean, what will happen if I do everything you and Joth are asking, if I do what I'm supposed to do, and I'm just *not?*"

His face goes blank, and he stares down at the folder in his lap. "If you're not, then we're out of options. Without Merlin's magic, Morgwese will claim her place as queen. Our defences will fall, and everything we know will be gone. She'll destroy us, the Templar and the Pendragons. Avalon will burn, and chaos will reign." He looks at me with a terrible fear in his eyes. "We've run out of time, Merle, and if you *aren't* the heir, then all of us will endure her wrath. You're the only chance we've got, the most sure we've ever been. If we're wrong, there's no hope we can win. None at all."

13

After my conversation with Ren, and the eventful day I've had, I excuse myself from the library and go back to my room to take a shower.

While I'm washing my hair, teasing out its horrible, matted tangles, I've got time to reflect on all the new things I've learned. The most troubling thing is this 'task' that no one seems to want to talk about, what Willow called 'claiming the magic'. Joth must plan to tell me about it at some point, and soon. If the situation's really as bad as Ren thinks, then there's no time to waste.

When I've scrubbed enough so that my skin is singing all over, I get out of the shower and change. On my bed is the basket that Shelby brought for me. I see she's brought some of my plants from the Java Bean. My aloe vera looks sad and deflated, the collection of succulents a little shrivelled.

I put them on my windowsill to get some sunlight. Ren comes into my room to find me whispering to them, encouraging them to grow.

"Joth wants to see us."

"Okay." I smooth my hands down my own ratty t-shirt. For some reason, I feel I should be smartly dressed for a meeting with Joth. As if I'm a candidate for a job interview I'm not entirely qualified for, which I guess isn't far from the truth. He's an important man, though, at least I think he is.

As we head to Joth's office, my stomach flips nervously. I've enjoyed meeting Willow, but there's still too many missing pieces. It's all well and good knowing the past, but that doesn't help me if I can't see my future. According to Ren, Joth has the answers to most of my questions, and if he doesn't know, nobody does, which isn't a comforting idea. We go into Joth's office, which has the same warm décor as the other rooms. He's sitting reading a book in a chair by the fire. When he hears us enter, he jolts and rubs his eyes, pushing his glasses back on top of his head.

"Come in, come in. How was your visit with Willow?"

"Interesting. I have some questions."

"I bet," he says, grinning and gesturing to the seats beside him. "Well hopefully I'll be able to answer them, it's time to tell you what I know. You've done more than enough to show you're Merlin's heir, and what Willow has found of the bloodline has proved true. She's amazing at what she does, and has traced many of the heirs all by herself, including the Pendragons." Joth's smile falters. "The knights are usually thorough and like to stick to protocol—"

"They'd let the Templar burn down around their ears if protocol told them to," Ren grumbles.

Joth glares at him. "There have been cases where we've expedited proceedings, and we might have again if you were the heir of a lesser knight. But you aren't. You're *Merlin's heir*, which makes things even more complicated. They want to be convinced, thoroughly, that you're who I say you are. We're protecting a great treasure and inviting just anyone in... it could ruin us." His bushy eyebrows crease together.

"So, how do I convince them? I can't control what I can do. I hardly know anything about it."

"Once we have full proof of your bloodline, not even the most uptight among us will deny you. Most of the knights are sticklers for the rules and they won't break them, no matter how much some of them might want to."

Why would anybody want to? They asked me here, didn't they? Surely they want me to succeed?

"But?" I ask.

"But it might take Willow more time to finish her research, and time is exactly what we're running out of. Underneath this Templar is a series of tunnels, buried in the heart of the catacombs, is Merlin's 'tomb'. A magic cave in which all of his secret magic, his scrolls, his potions, his books, are supposedly hidden."

My face sours. Surely they don't want me to go into a tomb with Merlin's corpse.

"Oh, his body isn't there," Joth says, reading my expression. "Nobody really knows where that is, but it's besides the point. Like only the true king could pull the sword from the stone, only Merlin's true heir can open the cave. Most of us have seen the entrance, those of us that have served long enough may do so, but no one's ever been inside."

"And that's what you expect me to do?"

"It's what you're going to do," Ren says.

"How?" I search their eyes. Joth's cool blue ones, and Ren's supportive dark embers.

"We don't know. Nobody does, it's been sealed for centuries, only Merlin himself and his heirs can enter. Not only do you have to open the cave, but you have to find it. There's a maze of tunnels under our feet. People have gotten lost down there for days and never laid eyes on the thing."

I sigh, exasperated. "And I suppose I'm not allowed any help?"

"No, no help."

Ren's face darkens. But I've got another question. "You keep saying, 'if the knights agree' or 'if I can convince them'. I don't know what you mean."

"He means that like any other democratic function that used to work, the system we've got to make sure everything's 'fair'," Ren brings the index and second finger on both his hands to the side of his face, curling them in air quotes, "only really slows us down."

"We have a voting system, in which a knight from each house will cast a vote either in favour or against an action, and the majority wins." Joth shoots a glare at Ren. "I don't get to vote, as I'm a Guardian rather than a knight, but the other twelve representatives will. They get to decide, *fairly*, whether you can attempt to find the cave."

"Unless my bloodline's been proven?"

"Exactly," he nods. "As time is of the essence, that's what's going to happen three days from now. We have a party of knights arriving in the morning, and on the evening before the vote, we'll host a ball. I intend to use it as an opportunity to win everyone's favour."

"Because some people don't want me here?"

Joth grimaces. "Unfortunately, some believe I'm fabricating a threat. That I'm creating danger to get more power for myself, and you're an unfortunate pawn in that."

Rage stabs through my chest. Both my parents have been killed while unknowingly protecting the Templar. It's no fabrication, no lie. "Then we must convince them."

A look of pride dawns on Ren's face, so intense that heat creeps up my cheeks and shivers run down my spine.

"And you're ready?" Joth asks.

"I am." I owe it to them, to repay their loyalty, to prove I'm who they think I am. And I owe it to my parents, so that their sacrifice might mean something. "What will happen at this party?"

"We have people coming to visit from the other Templars. Only the twelve true children of the Templar knights have any say in what happens, but they want to meet you."

"It's no big deal." Ren looks at me, his face still flushed. "We have parties all the time. We'll wander around a bit, say hello, nothing to worry about."

"Okay." I'm not sure I believe him, but I'll let it go for now. "In the meantime, can I see it?"

Joth shakes his head. "The cave? I'm afraid not. Like I said, it's strictly forbidden for those who haven't been knighted. But the Templar is an old, old building. If you were to be exploring and stumbled upon them, well, I'm only one man. I don't have the time to keep an eye on everything that goes on. Especially with a party to prepare for." He drops a wink at me and stands up. "The rest of the day is yours, then tomorrow afternoon, I'll coach you for the party. To make sure that you know who everyone is and what they'll expect from you. Go on now, we all have work to do."

I bound out of Joth's study; he's not given me direct permission, but indirect is enough for now. I tug on Ren's arm. "Show me."

"Absolutely not." Even though he's smiling, there's a serious undertone to his voice. "If they catch you down there, they'll give you a slap on the wrist. If they catch me, someone who's still waiting to come into their very own knighthood, they could exile me."

"Really?" It seems harsh for someone doing a little exploring.

"Really." He puts both of his hands firmly on my shoulders. "They take things seriously, Merle. There are so many ancient rules and regulations no one remembers, you're probably breaking four eating breakfast. I can be exiled, Joth could be too. Willow would lose her job..."

There are two people left, by my count, who can't be sent away. So valuable to the Templar, the knights will fight a war for them. "I understand."

"You do?" His eyes widen a little at the corners, as if he senses my deception.

"Sure. Exile, rules, boring old knights," I count the reasons off on my fingers and then shrug. "I get it. But I'm still going to go exploring, so it's best if you don't follow me."

He smirks. "I've never been into the catacombs. I don't know what it's like down there, so be careful."

"I will." I take his hands from my shoulders, then I leave him standing in the hall as I try to figure out which turn will lead me to the Pendragon bedroom.

After what seems like hours of searching, I find a staircase that reaches the top floor of the house. At the end of the corridor, there's a set of double doors with heavy ring handles. Pasted on one side is a picture of a dragon locked in battle with a knight. The dragon sends licks of orange and yellow flame pouring from its snout, the knight's armoured chest blazing with a red cross. Pinned to the other door is a scribbled note that reads: *No girls allowed.* Next to it is another: *Except Lore.* I grin and knock; I'm not Lore, but I'm sure they'll make an exception.

The door swings open, and the little girl in question stands in front of me. She has her golden hair down around her face, her jeans ripped at the knees. She crosses her arms over her chest, the holes in the sleeves of her shirt tucked around her thumbs. When she recognises me, her face brightens. "Hi!"

"Hi Lore."

She untangles her arms from around her middle and breathes a sigh of relief. "I was worried you were Joth coming to get me for lessons."

"No, but I need your help with something."

"You do?"

"I need to get into the catacombs underneath the Templar."

"Really?!" she grins and twirls on her toes. "I *love* going into the catacombs. Joth and Ren never let me go."

"You know how to get in?"

"Sure!" she nods enthusiastically. "I only go a little way in. If I got lost, everyone would be so mad."

Lore takes my hand and leads me back down the stairs, giddy with excitement. When we get to the dining room, she stops to check the coast is clear, and when she's sure it's safe, she tiptoes down the hall. She stops at the grandfather clock on the back wall, something I've not noticed before. It stands at least a head taller than me and is just as wide. Rather than being split into numbers, the face is divided into twelve coats of arms. The artwork is exquisite; each of the drawings has a name above it. Where twelve would be is Pendragon, next is Lancelot, then Tristen, Percival, Lamorak, a few more I can't make out.

"It doesn't work," Lore whispers.

"Then why are we here?"

"Twist the big hand until it lands on Pendragon, the little one to Lancelot, you'll see."

I reach for the spindly metal, my hands shaking. I don't feel comfortable playing with such an ancient and no doubt expensive relic.

"Quick! If someone catches us, I'll never be able to sneak in again!"

The hands make tiny clicking sounds as they turn; when they're in place, there's a loud snap. I swallow a startled gasp, sure I've broken it. When I look at Lore's face, however, she's smiling. She hooks her fingers into the body of the clock and pulls on the door. Behind it is a deep black hole.

"You first," she nudges my leg. "I have to go last to shut it so we won't be locked in. There's two steps down and then it's flat."

Crouching low to fit through the small hole, I squeeze my way into the dark, edging forward so there's enough room for Lore to follow. She fumbles with the lock, and then the light shining in from outside is gone. It's so dark I can't even see my fingers when I hold them up to my face. Lore shuffles past me and I hear her rummaging around on the floor before she puts a cold metal tube in my hand.

"Torch," she whispers. "I brought a spare one for Lux but he won't come, he's *such* a baby."

"I guess it really is forbidden then, huh?"

"Yeah. There's another entrance in the Knights' Hall. It's much bigger. I tried to use it before, but Joth checks that one. He saw me once and takes special care now. I got in *big* trouble, but they can't send me or Lux away," she huffs. "But Lux wants to be king when he's old enough. So he never breaks the rules. It's annoying, but I guess I'm proud of him."

"Do you want to be queen?"

"No," she looks over her shoulder at me and shakes her head. "I could, but I want to learn magic."

"Is that why you're helping me?"

"Yes, but not *only* that. I like you, and Ren and Joth like you." She pauses. "I guess you want to go to the wall with the writing?"

"What?"

Her voice takes on the exasperated tone reserved for children who think adults are being intentionally difficult. "You want to see the cave before the knights come tomorrow? It might not be the right place, but I can take us to the wall with the writing. I can't read it, I don't even think it's actual words, but it's the only place I can think of."

"You're the boss, Lore," I smile at her, and she giggles.

I follow her further down the passage. When we come to breaks and turns, she doesn't even hesitate before choosing our path. Somehow I know the way too. There's a pull in my heart, a familiar beat, drawing me further into the dark. I'm not afraid, though. That hum, high and sweet, is the undeniable tug of coming home. Joth said Lore has some magic. Maybe that's how we can both feel our way with ease.

The tunnel widens until we can walk side by side, then we enter a room of solid white rock. There are veins of colour running through it, some pale pink, some brown and grey. Carved into the far wall is the outline of a door. It has a high arch and the etching of a keyhole; a shallow circle waiting for the object that fits it. I put my palms flat against it, the stone cool and smooth under them. On the door itself are a series of symbols. They're strange, all angles and sharp lines, but not unreadable. The words swim in and out of my mind, burning with a dull pink glow. They're exactly the same as on the front of Willow's book.

"Is this what you meant, Lore?"

"Yes, but it's gibberish."

"No." My fingers familiarise themselves with the symbols. I can't read the words with my eyes, but I can see them in my mind. "No, it isn't."

"What does it say?" Lore's grey eyes are full of excitement, her smile so wide I can see most of her teeth.

I run my hands over it again. "*Here is Merlin, Cave of Magiks, blood may pass.*"

On the way back, Lore grips my hand tightly, swinging my arm like a pendulum. Her excitement is contagious, and I know I've gained a huge advantage by sneaking down here and seeing the cave for myself. When we reach the door, Lore packs up the torches so she can find them again later.

"How do we get out if there are people on the other side?" I whisper.

"I don't know, I usually come at night." She climbs into

the opening. After a few seconds of complete silence, she says, "Let's go; if there is someone, we'll make something up."

I think that's quite a big task, seeing as Lore and I will be crawling out of a clock, but I don't have a better idea. The door clicks and light pours into the space, so bright I have to squint. Lore shimmies out of the hole and I follow. As soon as my feet are on the floor, footsteps sound from the hallway. Lore stares at me, her eyes wide. I push the door closed, then I take Lore's shoulders and spin her so she's looking at the clock.

"What are those?" I ask, pointing at the clock face, hoping she catches my drift.

"Ah..." she murmurs. I'm not sure she's following. That doesn't matter now though, it's too late to explain. The echoing footsteps come to a halt.

"What are you looking at?" Ren's voice.

"Lore was showing me the clock." I glance at him through my lashes. He purses his lips, trying to hide his smile, and plucks something out of my hair. A silvery strand of a cobweb hangs from his fingers.

"Are you dusting it, too?"

"That, Renwick, is none of your concern." Lore's voice is so sharp it startles a laugh from me. She sounds like a queen conducting her jesters. I suppose that's exactly what she is.

"Renwick?"

He glares at me, daring me to laugh. "Dinner's ready, come on."

Lore smiles at me and winks slyly in my direction before taking my hand. We follow Ren through the door into the dining room. The table is full of food, all of which smells wonderful and I thank Etta as she scurries between us, loading food onto the twins' plates. The sweet aroma of basil mixes with the sharpness of tomatoes. There's pasta of different shapes and sizes, bowls of grated cheese, and luscious green salad. I take my place beside Ren and he hands me a bowl and then pushes a dish of shell-shaped pasta towards me.

"Not those," Lore shakes her head, "she likes the bows."

I snap my head up; it's true; I do. I like to flatten the ridges on my tongue. Ren shrugs and passes me those instead. I pile so many on my plate there's barely any room for salad and sauce and cheese. The food is so good; I help myself to more, and when I'm so full my stomach aches, I push myself back from the table. Lore is sleepily trailing her fork across her plate, her eyelids fluttering open and closed.

"What time is it?" I ask Ren.

"How should I know? You're the clock expert."

"Time for bed, I imagine," Joth speaks from the end of the table. "We have an early morning tomorrow. The knights will be arriving throughout the day and everything needs to be ready."

The twins get up from the table and don't even argue about bedtime. Ren and I follow them along the winding hallways and stairs and make sure they're tucked in before heading to our own rooms. I'm bone-tired; however, it seems sleep isn't in the cards for me right now. Ren glides past me into my room and dumps himself on my bed, folding his long legs beneath him.

"I take it you want something?"

"Your plants look a lot better. I guess talking to them does work." He's not looking at me, his comment a lame effort to avoid my question. I roll my eyes and he sighs. "Why were you really looking at that clock?"

"You didn't want to know, Ren, it's best you don't ask."

"Did you find something?"

"Lore's very adventurous," I say, pursing my lips to suppress a smile. "Knows about lots of hidden tunnels and places that she shouldn't. I could feel it pulling me along, the magic."

Ren leaps to his feet and grasps me in a hard hug, the heat of him wonderful against my chest. "I knew you could find it."

"Well, you have been the only one who's believed this whole time."

His face becomes serious, a reaction I wasn't expecting. "I don't know how you can't feel it, the electricity baking off you, the magic, the legend. Somehow you still don't understand that you are *Merlin Wyllt's* heir! You, in your blood, hold the key to all the mysteries of the universe. To endless ability, to more power than either of us can ever imagine." He pauses, reaching down and taking my hand. "I knew it was you the second I walked into that coffee shop. I could feel it in my *own* blood. It was like finding something I didn't know I was missing, the calm in a storm."

I felt it too. I *feel* it.

"The sooner you start believing, the better for all of us." He takes his hands from mine as if to leave, pauses for a moment, then kisses me on the forehead. "Goodnight, Mer."

"Goodnight," I stammer, alternating waves of hot and cold running through my body. I climb into bed, still shaking. *More power than either of us can ever imagine.* The words are as exhilarating as they are haunting.

The sleep that was promised only minutes ago escapes

me now as I lie in bed thinking of him. The heat of his eyes when they meet mine, the touch of his lips on my forehead, and how I wish he might kiss me again, and give me proper time to respond.

14

"Are you excited to see your girlfriend?" Lux jibes at Ren across the table.

The morning's breakfast has been uneventful up to this point, and I've been daydreaming about the cave, of going back down there to explore properly, but now my ears prick up. Ren shoots a dark stare in Lux's direction, making him laugh harder.

"Laina isn't my girlfriend, she's an ambassador from Avalon."

"Oh Laina, give me a kiss..." Lux raises the pitch of his voice and makes comical smacking noises with his lips.

Ren picks up a bread roll and throws it at his head. He dives under the table to dodge it, hysterical laughter rising from beneath the wood.

"She is pretty," Lore muses.

"Pretty schmitty." Ren gets up, his face

flushed, and drags Lux out from his hiding place, tickling the boy until his face is red and tears stream from his eyes.

I try to laugh with them, but it's strained. I don't want to think about this 'girlfriend', but the words pound behind my ribs like a heartbeat. Jealousy isn't a feeling I'm used to, nor do I like it.

"Have you got anything to wear tomorrow?" Lore asks me, ignoring the boys on the floor.

"Anything to wear?"

"For the party?" Lore sighs in the tone she seems to use for things she finds ridiculous. It's endearing that she doesn't know how highbrow she sounds.

"I don't," I say, my heart sinking. In the last ten years, I haven't even attended a birthday party, never mind a ball. "I might see if Willow can lend me something."

"Or we could buy something?" Her eyes light up, and she jumps down from her seat, scurrying to my side of the table. "Joth says we can't go out without a reason, and I love going to the shops. Can we? Please!"

"Sure, I guess." I wouldn't mind going out, and I want to visit the Java Bean to clear things up with Shelby. Yesterday, she left me with an uneasy feeling and I like that about as much as I like this newfound jealous streak.

"Let's go!"

"We'll ask Joth first, I don't want him to think you've abdicated."

Lore wrinkles her nose at me, oblivious to the awful joke. I laugh to myself and get up. Ren glances at me from the floor, giving Lux a moment to catch his breath.

"Do you want some company?"

"Looks to me like you've got your hands full, Renwick."

Lux bursts into fresh gales of laughter, and Ren's glare scorches me as I chase after Lore.

Joth approves our impromptu trip but gives me strict instructions to never take my eyes off Lore, and to stray no further than the high street. Lore rolls her eyes at the rules like any normal ten-year-old, but I take them dead seriously. It's clear she doesn't understand how special she is, and what might happen to *me* if I let anything happen to *her.*

"You'll need this too," Joth says, handing me a shiny black card.

I raise my eyebrows at him.

"It's a Templar expense, the outfit, and whatever Lore wants. Although," he looks at her, "you aren't to go too crazy, okay? And bring something back for your brother."

"Okay." Lore stands dutifully still while Joth does up her coat, and then plants a kiss on his cheek.

"Get whatever you need for the evening and please spare no expense." Joth turns his attention back to me. "We've only got one go at this, one first impression. Mostly you'll be judged on your character, but—"

"It won't hurt to look pretty. I got it." I grin at him and tuck the card safely in my pocket. Even though I think the decision about whether I'm allowed to open the cave should be based entirely on merit, I'd be lying if I said I wasn't excited to dress up. With one last check we've got everything, we're out of the door.

Lore drags me around a few shops, looking at toys and sweets. She buys some for herself and her brother with the generous stipend Joth's given us. Her particular favourite is a small stuffed dog with grey fur. Its head is almost twice the size of its body, and long curls cover the button eyes. Lore names it David, and hugs it to her chest as we wander through the streets.

Finally, she chooses a boutique for me to complete my errands. She makes me try on dress after dress, all bright colours that don't match my pale complexion. I wince as the choices get progressively worse. Eventually, the shop assistant steps in, his heart-shaped face showing obvious signs of distress. He ushers us away from the neons and over into the more neutral colours. At first, he hands me black dresses, but then he measures up my outfit and changes his mind.

"I think you should try this." Julian, who after Lore's fifth dress choice, told me his name and offered me some strong coffee, hands me a dark plum-coloured gown with a low neckline and spaghetti straps that cross over the back. The bodice has applique flowers stitched into it, leading into a flowing a-line skirt that will end just above my ankles, and a slit up the side running all the way to the middle of my thigh. It's much more risqué than something I'd usually buy, and the thought of wearing it in public makes my stomach do nervous flips. Julian doesn't seem to share my concerns and ushers me into the changing room. The dress fits me beautifully, hugging my waist and my hips, the cut exaggerating my curves. The dark colour also complements my brown eyes and hair, making them deep and rich.

I love it. When I walk out of the changing room, Julian clasps his hands in front of his chest. Even though Lore's choices had been completely different, a smile appears on her face.

"You look beautiful, Merle!"

"Thank you." I blush and twirl around. "Is this the one?"

She nods violently, and Julian winks as I step back into the fitting room. Changing back into my tatty jeans is deflating after the soft material of the dress. When I come back out Lore stands up, David's already scruffy left paw dragging on the wooden floor. I hand the dress back to Julian, reluctant to let it go, but he bags it up and puts it through the till. On Joth's orders, I put a pair of black heels on the counter and a beautiful pearl bracelet.

"We've got one more stop to make if that's okay?" I can tell Lore's restless to go home now, but there's still something I need to do.

She nods. "To see Shelby."

I've not told her that, but apparently, she's seen it flickering on and off in my mind like a flame. Another show of her gifts. Sometimes it's unnerving that she can pluck things out of my brain so easily and doesn't know she shouldn't pry. She takes my hand and we walk towards the Java Bean.

Five minutes later, I push the door open and wave at Nicky as he rushes round the counter to meet us, throwing his arms around me and squeezing tight.

"I didn't expect to see you so soon, kid!" He kisses my forehead.

"Hi, Nick." Hugging him makes me realise just how much I've missed this place, how much it's felt like home.

"And hello to you too!" Nicky peers down at Lore. "What's your name?"

"Lore."

"What a lovely name." He holds out his hand for her to shake, and she does. "Well, Lore, you're looking a little thirsty.

Do you want to come and help me make a drink while Merle goes to sit with Shelby?"

Lore looks to me for approval, and when I nod, a huge grin breaks on her face and she follows Nicky behind the counter. Shelby's been waiting patiently in our usual seat, and when I'm free, she stands up and throws her arms around my neck.

"Hello sweetheart, I'm so glad you're here!"

The comfort of her arms washes away all my anxieties about yesterday's strange events. She kisses my cheek and takes both of my hands as I sit down. I can tell from the look in her eyes that she's about to say something about Mum again, how sorry she is, how sad, but I can't think about it. Every time I do, it's like I'm suffocating, the grief far too overwhelming for one person to deal with.

"Don't, Shell, I know you mean well, but I can't."

She nods her head. "Are all the plants all right? All the crystals? I was worried I didn't pack you the right ones."

"They're fine. Gave them a bit of water and they seem to have perked up."

There's something different between us, and she knows it. For most of my teen years, she's been like the grandma I lost at a young age. But in the last two weeks, she's been acting strangely. It was so out of character for her to miss the funeral, and to not want to come inside the Templar and meet everyone.

"Look, let me say darling, I really am sorry about the funeral, and that I didn't check in. I knew you'd be having a rough time and I just— well, I don't have an excuse," she says as if she's read my mind. "Everything seemed to happen so quickly."

I pause for a moment, considering her words. In some senses, she's right. I left without warning, and I never spoke to her directly about the funeral. She's been my friend for long enough that I can forgive her for this, even if I don't forget it. "I'm sorry too, Shell, I didn't think—"

Shelby snorts through her nose. "You're eighteen, Merle, you're not supposed to think! You're supposed to act impulsively and do things someone my age wouldn't even dare to think of. It's why I was half suspicious you'd run off with that boy."

My cheeks burn and I stare down at my hands. "I wouldn't quite call it running off."

Shelby raises her eyebrows in a way it seems only older women can master. "I'm glad you went with him. If I was twenty, I'd run off with him too!"

"Not just him." I shake my head and motion towards the little girl bobbing towards us.

"I can see that. Who's she?"

"Lore."

Shelby smiles as Lore gets closer, and her eyes light up. I know Shelby has a son, but he lives far away. Maybe Lore reminds her of him? As Lore approaches, Shelby holds out her hand to shake, then the little girl pulls her chair closer to mine before jumping up. She's not reacting as I expected her to. I thought she'd like Shelby, maybe even grow to love her as I do.

Shelby's still staring, that glint in her eyes not leaving. She reaches out to touch Lore's back, and my instinct is to pull her away. There's something wrong that I can't put my finger on. The strange way Lore's acting, the greedy look in Shelby's eyes. When Lore edges closer to me in her seat,

Shelby takes the hint and moves her hands back, curling her fingers in. They seem extraordinarily long in the light. She peers at me with sad hazel eyes and I can only shrug. Eventually, the tension passes, and Shelby asks me what I intend to do now.

"I'm going to try this..." I pause as my mind fumbles for the words. I don't know what I should call my new job role, "...apprenticeship, and see how that goes."

Shelby nods. "And you're sure you can trust these people?"

"They've done nothing to suggest I can't."

"Why shouldn't she trust us?" Lore pipes up, not angry but inquisitive. A smile breaks over Shelby's face, happy that Lore finally wants to play.

"Would you like to see a neat trick?" she asks, expertly avoiding the question.

"Sure."

Shelby drinks the dregs of her tea, leaving a teaspoon of liquid in the bottom, then she hands the cup to Lore.

"I want you to close your eyes. Now think of a question you want the answer to. Anything you like." She pauses for a moment. "Do you have it?"

"Mm-hm."

Shell reaches forward and takes the cup back, tipping it upside down onto the table. The water dribbles out, a few bubbles tumbling over each other before bursting on the wood. After a moment, Shelby flips it back over. Clumps of leaves litter the bottom of the cup and I roll my eyes, holding back a smile. This is an old trick of Shelby's, one she's pulled out for me and various other customers and employees in the past. I've yet to see it work properly. All she ever does is spout bad omens and black clouds. The mystic in question holds out the cup to Lore again.

"Tell me what shapes are in there."

Lore squints at the cup, her small nose wrinkling down the bridge. After a full minute of consideration, she grins at Shelby. "I guess that could be a line, then next to it a circle? Or a cat? I like cats, but not as much as dogs... and a cloud, a rain cloud."

She smiles at me over her shoulder, as if she's looking for my approval. I smile back, but it's soon wiped off my face when I notice Shelby's expression. She's gone pale and her lips are pinched, a thin line under her nose. She meets my eyes, hers wide and watery, then she turns the cup to face her.

"What does it mean?" Lore asks, oblivious to the change in mood.

"Well, a line could be an altar." Shelby's treading carefully. That's clear in the tone of her voice. "It means sacrifice, or giving up something you like."

"Like sweets?"

"Yes," Shell nods. "Then the circle, the circle is a lovely sign, it means success, that whatever question you asked will come out in your favour."

Lore looks at me, not sure what she means.

"It means you'll get what you want," I say, butterflies in my stomach, alarm bells in my ears.

"Really?" Lore grins. "What about if it's a cat?"

Shelby licks her tongue round her teeth. "The cat can mean someone isn't being truthful, or they're hiding something."

I don't like where this is going. When Shelby read my tea leaves, she did the same thing, finding death notes and worry in everything. I didn't believe in magic then, but now I've seen things that change everything. These leaves really could tell the future, and I don't want her to scare Lore.

"What about the cloud?" I ask.

"Rain clouds mean trouble." There's no emotion in Shelby's voice. It's flat and lifeless. "It isn't a nice cup, trouble, and lies, and sacrifice."

These last words she mutters so quietly they're almost inaudible. Then she turns her attention back to Lore, whose lower lip is trembling, "But what do I know? I'm just a silly old woman. You shouldn't pay any attention to me. Merle never does!"

"She's right." I smile, but it's sour on my face.

I trust Shelby with everything and have done for as long as I can remember, but now unease uncurls in my stomach like a snake waiting to strike. She's been acting oddly, adding a sharp edge to her teasing and avoiding me at the house. The mean look in her eyes, something that looks an awful lot like pleasure, is really what's getting to me now. She could have lied about the cup. She's done it before. Instead, she scared Lore, and as I look at her, I know she did it on purpose.

Anger crackles in me like static. Not only at her actions, but because I don't understand them. Why would she? What's happened to her? My gut tells me it's time to go before I do something I regret. I push back from the table and pull Lore with me.

"I think this one's hungry." My voice sounds fake and lame to my own ears. "Can I take this to go, Nick?"

"Sure, sure," he smiles and goes to grab a paper cup.

"Are you sure you can't stay?" Shelby asks. "I've missed you."

That's a lie and we both know it. Now tears burn at the back of my eyes. I thought Shelby was my friend, someone I could rely on. I can't figure out what's changed, or why she would suddenly become so cold.

"I'll come back another day."

"All right," Shelby nods.

Nicky comes over with a large cup and a brown paper bag. "Food for the road."

I thank him and add the bag to my collection. As we're about to leave, Nicky throws his arms around us both again, and when he steps back, there are tears in his eyes. It hits me that this is probably goodbye. I'll never open up this place again, or see Marnie finish her novel, or rib Otto about his tea drinking. My old life is over and Nicky knew it, it seems, long before I did. He takes us in for a second and then plants a huge, wet kiss on my forehead.

"I love you, kid,"

"I love you too, Nick. Thanks for everything."

We head for the door. As much as I want to, I don't look back.

Lore's not said a word the entire walk back, and I still can't get Shelby's face out of my mind. That horrible hungry stare.

"What's going on, Lore?"

"I'm tired," she whines, evading my stare.

"Yes, but what else?"

She looks up at me, struggling with it, and then rolls her eyes. "I couldn't see her."

"What do you mean?"

"You know how I can do things? Like with your dream. Sometimes I can see pictures or words, sometimes colours. I know I shouldn't! Joth tells me not to look all the time, but when I meet new people..." she shrugs. "Like Nicky, he really loves you, and he really enjoys making coffee! But Shelby... It was like staring into a black hole. There was nothing there."

"Has it happened before?"

She shakes her head.

"Lore, what question did you ask?" I wouldn't usually pry, but if it was something silly I might be able to explain the omens away, put her mind at ease.

She stops dead in her tracks and looks over her shoulder, her bottom lip trembling. "I wanted to know whether you'd get the magic, whether you'd stay? And what she said, it means no, right?"

"I'm staying, Lore," I say, crouching down to her height so we're at eye level. "I promise you I'm not going anywhere, everything's going to be okay."

"Do you really think that?"

"Yes. You're my family now. We take care of each other."

She stares me down, checking my face, and probably my mind, for any glimmer of a lie. When she finds none, she nods and turns back to the house. We walk up the path hand in hand. Lux is sitting on the step. When we get close enough, he tips his head comically to one side.

"Ren wants you."

"Nice to see you too, Lux."

"He's grumpy, so don't wait too long." The boy offers his hand to his sister. "There's a special lunch. I promised we'd be good at the party if Joth got pizza. Come on."

Perking up at the sound of food, Lore takes Lux's hand and they make their way inside. "Is it the good kind, with extra cheese?" she questions as they pass out of my field of vision.

Before I find Ren, I need to go up to my room and drop off the dress and accessories that Lore and Julian talked me into. After I've carefully put everything away, I go to find Ren across the hall, rapping my knuckles on his bedroom door.

"Come in."

I've never been in Ren's room before, but it's very similar to mine. He has the same bed and furniture, but rather than purple walls, his are painted green. There's also a coat of arms hanging above his bed, a striped red-and-white shield with matching feathers, topped by a shiny silver helmet. He's sitting on his bed, a book resting across his stomach.

"Lux said you were looking for me?"

"Ah, yeah." He sits up, brushing a stray hair from his forehead. "You've been gone a while. I was wondering if he'd seen you come back."

"Worried about me?" I ask, hoping the raise of my eyebrows will convey my sarcasm.

"Yes," he says, completely serious. "Obviously. I wouldn't let you out of my sight if I didn't have to. I still don't think you understand how important you are." He cocks his head to the right, those dark eyes once again piercing straight into my soul.

"I-ah-I—" My mouth is completely dry and all my words fail me. I don't turn away from his gaze, but heat floods my cheeks. "Lore and I went to the Java Bean, I wanted to see Shelby."

"To find out why she was acting so strangely?" Ren's voice is husky, his gaze still burning into mine.

"Yeah. I wanted to say goodbye. When we went in, Lore was all over Nicky, but with Shell? I truly thought it'd be fine, but Shelby started acting weird."

"Weird how?" He swings his legs over the side of the bed and pats the space beside him. I sit down and clasp my hands in my lap, everything inside tingling.

"I'm not sure, but it was something about the way she was looking at Lore, it creeped me out. She tried to cheer Lore up by doing some trick she does with tea leaves."

"Like reading them?"

"Yeah, and it wasn't good, a lot of stuff about lying and sacrifice, bad omens. Shelby scared her."

Ren frowns. "You can't put any stock in tea leaves."

"Not even when they say I'm not who you think I am?" I don't dare look at him. He stiffens beside me for a second, then he lets the tension out in a chuckle.

"Luckily for you, I'm never wrong." He squeezes my wrist briefly, the action sending a hot spike through my body. "Like you said, it's an old trick and there's no way of telling shapes or divining meaning, even if you can do magic, not really. You know that, right?" His tone is kind, but it still makes me feel stupid.

"I don't! Two weeks ago I would have agreed with you, but since then I made a blood wish that worked, I killed a faery, and now I've found out that I'm a— whatever I am! So no, Ren, in terms of magic and crazy tea leaves, I don't know."

"Merle," he laughs, "you've been through a lot this last week. There's a chance that you're a little uneasy about everything. I would be."

"So you think it was nothing?" I bite the inside of my lip.

"I think she's a crazy old lady who sees you slipping away and is trying to stop it. If you're worried we can figure it out, we've done well enough so far."

"I guess."

He grins. "What I'm trying to say is that we know to trust your gut. Now you have to figure out whether you trust Shelby."

I consider him, and the question. Like the tea leaves, a week ago I would've said yes. Today I just don't know. It's horrible and confusing. I love her, but I suppose where trust is concerned, like or love doesn't come into it.

"You don't have to worry about it right now. Just relax for once. We can deal with it tomorrow."

"I know how to relax!"

"No, you don't," he chuckles, "and that's one thing I like most about you. Nothing ever gets boring."

"Well, thanks," I say, rolling my eyes.

"Let's just get through your coaching with Joth and the party. Then we'll tackle Shelby." A hot, dark blush creeps into his cheeks. "We can go together if you like? To the party."

"Yes," I say, not even trying to hold back my enthusiasm.

"Great." His smile is easier now, like a weight's been lifted from his shoulders.

"I better find Joth, then. You coming?"

"Always." He gets up too and follows me into the hall. "You'd never make it without me."

15

"Right then," Joth says as we take seats opposite him at his dark wooden desk. "Did you find everything you needed on your trip?"

"Yes."

"And Lore wasn't any trouble?"

"Good as gold."

He raises one bushy grey eyebrow. "Good. Now, before tomorrow, I've got a lot of information to give you. Who the knights are, what they'll expect—"

"How the voting works," Ren adds.

"And what's going on with the cave," I finish.

Joth smiles down at me. "As for that, I'll tell you what I know, but it's all shrouded in mystery. There're only rumours about what's in there or what might happen. And we might be best saving that for another day."

"But—!"

"I know it's what you want. But you won't get to set foot in the tunnels if you can't bring the knights on side."

"Unless Willow finds a full bloodline," Ren says.

"Yes. But as she's only got twenty-four hours until the party, we won't hold our breath. Now, it's best we start with the knights—"

"Let's start with you. I've got a general idea of what you do here, but," I shrug.

Joth flushes a little. "All right. Well, as you know, my title is Templar Guardian. I look after general day to day goings on, make sure the twins don't get into too much trouble. There are a few others, like me, who aren't knights themselves, but are connected to us in some way, that run various Templars all over Europe. There's Meredith Bowen in Wales, Rab MacGavin in Scotland, Fia Wolfe in Ireland, and Lady Cassandra in France. They oversee their own little band of knights and handle the acts of their respective Templars. The twelve knights don't answer to us exactly, but we mediate discussions and try to make things fair."

"They do answer to *you* though." Ren points his index finger at Joth's chest. F

The flush on Joth's cheeks gets even deeper. As he's about to answer, the door creaks open and Etta bustles in with a tray of tea, cakes, and sandwiches. "Thought you might be hungry, seeing as you missed lunch."

In fact, I'm starving and I help myself to a scone loaded with jam and cream as soon as she sets the tray down.

"Not being nosey, Etta?" Ren asks, raising an eyebrow and reaching for a sandwich. She swats at his hand with the tea towel.

"You've already had yours. Leave them for someone

else."

"I'm still growing."

"Yes, outwards not upwards though, eh?" She winks at me, her ruddy cheeks glowing, and I snort into my teacup.

When she's gone, Joth pours himself some tea and then continues. "My family have been Guardians of this Templar for over seven hundred years, and that kind of loyalty comes with certain benefits. The other Guardians come to me with issues they can't resolve on their own, and the knights answer to me if their behaviour becomes unsavoury. I don't get to vote on things, I won't have a say on what the knights decide to do with you, Merle. But I can influence the vote by stating my intentions, I can remove knights from their position, and I can appoint them. That's only in very special circumstances. I decide which knights get which land, and what their responsibilities will be. I also have guardianship of the relics and artefacts we've saved over the years."

"And the Pendragons?"

"Yes." A broad grin splits his face, showing slightly uneven front teeth. "I'm responsible for them until they reach the age of fifteen, then they'll be crowned and run everything themselves."

"In Avalon?"

"Yes. In a nutshell, I take care of the big picture, of liaising between Templars and keeping the peace, and I make sure the knights are behaving themselves and punish them if they aren't. Somebody fair, with the crown's best interests at heart, has to keep everything in check."

"Basically, everything a monarch would do if there was one," Ren clarifies.

"Okay." I take in a deep breath, trying to make sure my

brain has absorbed all the information about Joth's role before we move on. "Will I meet any of the other Guardians at the party?"

"Good God, no!" Joth exclaims. "The knights will be enough for now, I think. I love them all dearly, but Fia has quite a temper, and Merry Bowen might cause a ruckus. No. They're excellent at keeping things in check, but this vote is too important to be marred by their opinions."

"Because you think they'd vote against me?" I hate the note of panic in my voice, but it rings out regardless. Ren tenses in his chair, his face going blank.

Joth sighs. "It's certainly a possibility. A lot of the knights don't believe in magic anymore. They've been so long without it, most of them have never seen it. Your existence is a problem for them—"

"Great."

"What he means is," Ren says, rising to Joth's defence, "they don't believe in Morgwese, or that she's a threat to us. They've got their heads buried in the sand, and if you have magic—"

"And not just any magic, *Merlin's* magic," Joth adds.

"Then they can't deny the possibility anymore. They'll have to act, and it scares them."

I stare between their faces and see no lies. The steady throb of panic is now hammering in my blood like a war drum. How can I hope to convince twelve people that I don't know, in only one evening, that they can trust me with something so powerful?

"It's not all that bad," Joth reassures me. "On this, Ren will vote, and like I said, I have influence. Asher Gaheris is thrilled that you'll be shaking things up a bit. She's agreed to act as a chaperone for you at the party, introduce you to everyone."

"Okay."

"While we're on the subject of a vote," Ren presses on cautiously, "why don't you explain how it works?"

"It really is as simple as it sounds in premise." Joth rubs gnarled and knotted fingers across his brow. "Someone puts forward a request, 'can Percival extend the perimeter of his land?' 'can we have more money for food?'—"

"Can we go into the forbidden tunnels and give a random girl off the streets devastating magic that may or may not end in all of our deaths?" I purse my lips and raise my eyebrows. "I get the premise."

Ren chuckles under his breath.

"Whatever the request is," Joth continues, "the knights will listen to the case presented, and then take a vote. If it's an even split, a representative from Avalon will cast the deciding vote."

"Laina," Ren and I say at the same time.

"Yes," Joth looks between us suspiciously, "she's a half human, half fae ambassador, very little magic, one of the hybrids that's allowed to cross between here and the fae realm."

I cock an eyebrow. It doesn't sound very secure to me.

"There's a small portal in Avalon, between here and the faery realm," Joth continues. "It takes special magic to open it and no one of full faery blood can pass through. It's an age old tradition, to have someone who can cross between and serve us both. Laina has been vetted extensively, and she's never let us down over the years, always fair. I have an arrangement with an old friend."

"Where is it, Avalon?" I have many questions, particularly about this 'arrangement', but my curiosity about the magical kingdom is too great.

Joth grins. "All over the world there are places where ley lines meet. Ley lines are rivers of power that run along the earth's surface, and where they cross, the river turns into a sea. Sometimes only two might meet, maybe three, but Avalon is situated where thirteen of the lines converge. It is—" he shakes his head, unable to find the words. "One day you'll see it for yourself."

I lean back in my chair, satisfied for the time being.

"Now, I always attend the voting sessions, because as simple as it sounds, it never usually is. They like to argue a lot. There's a lot of rules and regulations passed down from Arthur's time. Some of us believe we can take traditions with a pinch of salt, others think we should follow them to the letter."

"So two days from now, each knight will get a vote, and if they like me enough, they'll let me find the wall with—" I stop myself, having almost given Lore away. "Merlin's cave. If they don't, they'll deny me. Then what?"

"As I've told you, I'm sure you're the heir. It's only a matter of time until Willow finds the missing links and then you'll be able to go regardless," Joth answers. "But time is of the essence, and the more time you've got to get used to your powers, the better for all of us."

Oh yes, another thing to add to the seemingly endless list of responsibilities.

"That's not what I asked."

Joth brings his ice-blue eyes to mine. "If they deny you, then we'll have to wait until they change their minds, or

Willow has a breakthrough."

"And you can't overrule them?"

"Not on this matter."

My mind is already running with the secret knowledge I hold. I could go against them all and try to take the magic anyway. Lore would show me the way again. But doing that could damage the trust between us irreparably, no matter how dire the situation. No, for now at least, it's best to do it their way.

"Now, your major problems will be Sir Kay, Sir Lucan, and possibly Monty Percival, although he could go either way—"

Over the course of the next few hours, Joth's voice grows hoarse and turns into a monotonous drone as he explains what he knows about the knights. I try my best to keep track of everything, but it's a tough thing. What it boils down to is the fact that there are some people who are already on our side, some on the fence, and some who won't be swayed. My focus should be on those in the middle: Pelleas, Gawain, Lamorak, and Bedivere. If I can get three of them to side with us, we'll win the vote. The rest of it is just hot air. Things they expect the twins to do when they rule, how likely they are to bend from their ideals, and what it might take to bribe them.

We eat dinner late, the remains of the pizza the twins were so excited about earlier. I nibble a few crusts, but mainly sip at my cola. My mind's occupied, thinking about Joth's words. I excuse myself before dessert and head upstairs to my room. I shower and change into my pyjamas, clean ones waiting for me on the bed. Mona's handiwork, I assume. I'm at the dresser, brushing out my hair when the first of the taps start on my door.

I'd expected that; Ren. Although it's taken him longer than I thought.

"What is it, Mer?" he asks, once again making himself at home on my pristine sheets.

I sigh and put down the brush. I'm not exactly sure how to explain it, the strange, heavy weight that's been pulling on my mind. He says nothing, waiting. Eventually I look up and meet his eyes in the mirror, dark with questions.

"It's something Joth said about bribing them," well 'making small promises in return for their votes' is how he put it.

"What about it?"

"I know it's what I'm supposed to do. Convince them to let me go down there. I want to. I want to be Merlin's heir, and I want that magic." I pause. Saying it out loud, after all this time, feels amazing. "But it's wrong to do it that way."

Ren says nothing.

"It's wrong to make promises on the twins' behalf for my advancement. If my role is to advise them when they're crowned, I can't be fair if old promises are always in the back of my mind. There's no integrity in it."

Because what Joth asked me to do doesn't sound like *convincing*, it sounds like *corruption*.

"So what will you do?" Ren's face is pensive, but I can tell he's nervous about my answer.

"I'll put the facts of the situation before them and then they can vote as they see fit," I say. "If they vote against me, then we'll come up with a new plan."

One that might involve me sneaking into the catacombs.

A wide grin splits Ren's face. Not what I was expecting, but apparently the right answer. "Good."

"Okay then."

He gets up from his position and strides to the door, stopping as he opens it. He takes in a breath and looks into my face. It's almost as if I can see the words on his lips, bubbling over. Then he lets out a whoosh of air and is gone.

Confusion settles in my stomach, hot and thick like molten lava. Sometimes he seems so close, as if I could reach out and brush his cheeks with my fingers. Close enough that he might let down his guard entirely. Then he's gone again. Closed. It's too much to worry about amongst everything else, and maybe something not worth worrying about at all.

"If it's meant to be sweetheart, it'll happen," Dad whispers in my ear. *"Fate has a funny way of putting you exactly where you need to be."*

I'm about to switch off my light at around ten thirty when there's a tap on my door. It certainly isn't Ren, as he would've let himself straight in. Maybe Lore? When I open it, I find Mona on the other side, holding a porcelain plate with a huge slice of carrot cake atop it. Her thin lips are peeled back in a smile that could be a grimace. I can never tell with her.

"Canna come in?" I swing the door open for her and she brushes past me, placing the cake on the dresser. "Etta said y'dint eat much. Though' you'd like this."

"Thanks."

She puts her hands on her hips. She's got something to say then.

"Surely that's obvious, Merle," Dad's voice whispers. *"She wouldn't have come all this way just to bring you cake. You barely know each other."*

"I know you've no' asked for mi advice," she starts, "bu'

233

I've to gerit off mi ches'. The knights tha'are comin' tomorrow. Most of um are old men. Most of um are comfy wi the way things are. They'd be blind to trouble if it knocked um on't 'ead." Her pale-blue eyes meet mine. They're serious and stark. "Bu' there *is* trouble. You've sin it, yer 'ere 'cause of it. Don' lettum make you doubt."

"Joth said—"

"I know wha' he said." Those eyes bore into me again. Then she grins, the same wicked grin I can never work out. "Bu' he's an old man too. A good one, mind. Be careful is all I'm sayin'."

"Okay, Mona. Thank you." A quiet understanding passes between us, or so I think. One that cements my worries of corruption and cowardice.

"Now, enough from me. You've gorra big day tomorrow. Eat ye cake and ge' some shut eye." She bustles past me. "I'll be back in't afternoon to help you dress."

I sleep in late the next day, not getting up until I can no longer bear the noise from the commotion outside. Cars pulling up, one by one, bringing the knights and their staff and squires. I stay in my room, pacing and trying to remember everything I learned from Joth, wishing I paid more attention. At around four o'clock, I shower again and tease the tangles from my hair. When I come out of the bathroom, Mona's sitting patiently on my bed, small feral grin on her face. She gives me an appraising look then says, "We'd bes' ge' going, no' much time nah."

There's very little talk after that and I'm glad of the quiet. Mona's busy concentrating on my hair and makeup, and we've nothing to say to each other, anyway. It takes a while for her spindly fingers to get to grips with the thickness of my hair. But after several attempts, a sleek swirl of French braid is rolling over my shoulder, full of sparkling diamond pins.

"Suppose' t've been Guinevere's," she whispers with obvious reverence.

Next, she moves on to makeup. She starts with the palest cream in the eyeshadow pallet, dabbing at the corner of my eye and sweeping it across my lid. She adds darker shades of brown and nude, putting a deep-chocolate colour in the crease. Finally, she paints on black liner and mascara. The effect deepens the brown of my eyes and highlights the tiny flecks of gold and green. She brushes on powder, and then a little blush in the hollows of my cheekbones. I've never been one to use lots of makeup. It makes my skin itch and my eyes run with tears after a while. On special occasions, though, it's nice. Something different. Something that makes me feel beautiful and fresh. Mona's expert hands do exactly that, and with a final touch of shimmery lip gloss, I'm finished. I look like a much more sophisticated and adult version of myself, like I really might be able to advise a king and queen if it came down to it. I open the wardrobe door to reveal the dress hanging there, and I'm still taken aback by its beauty. I start to pull it out, but Mona gives a little cry and moves me away. Obviously not as regal as I thought. She helps me step into the silk skirt and pull it over my hips, then shuffle the straps over my shoulders. At least I'm allowed to put on my own shoes. I unclip the charm bracelet, meaning to take it off and replace it with the jewellery I purchased, but Mona shakes her head.

"Don' change a thing. Ye look lovely."

"Only because you helped!" I say, and in the mirror my

cheeks turn pink.

"Maybe so," she shrugs. She's about to leave me to it, with one foot out of the door when she turns back. "An' you'll remember wha' I said t' ye? Abou' the knights?"

"I'll remember."

With a harsh nod, she closes the door behind her.

After that, all there is to do is wait for Ren, flipping through the pages of the books Dad left for me. I still haven't shown them to Willow, and I make a mental note to take it to her first thing in the morning after this whole debacle is over. A knock at the door snaps me from my thoughts. I get up, smooth my hands down my front and answer.

Ren's leaning against the frame, the inky-black tunic and stark contrast of the white shirt underneath make him ethereal. His hair is swept back from his brow, dark eyes in mine. At first I think he looks startled, but that emotion clears quickly from his face. When he smiles at me, a full-watt smile that reaches all the way into his eyes, brushing me like the rising sun, I let out a dry breath.

"You look beautiful," Ren says. "Are you ready?"

"Yes," I whisper, unable to say anything else.

When we get to the top of the stairs, the noise of the guests laughing floats up to us, and my stomach fills with butterflies. Ren stops us and turns me to him.

"I need to warn you—"

"You said it'd be fine!"

"It will be," his brow crinkles in the middle as he pulls an apologetic face, "but I may have been slightly underplaying the situation."

I smack his shoulder. "You could've said!"

"I'm saying now."

I hope my glare delivers the rest of the punch I can't follow through on.

"You're the heir of Merlin Wyllt, and everybody wants to see what you're made of." He puts his hands on my shoulders, the warmth of his fingers melting into my bare skin.

I want to kiss him then, looking into his eyes, with his body so close to mine. And I might have, if not for the opening of the doors at the bottom of the stairs and the flood of music that accompanies it. Instead, I draw back, pulling at the end of my plait. "You're infuriating."

"Are you ready?" he grins. This time he doesn't offer me his arm but his hand.

"Seriously, one day I *will* get you back for this."

"I don't doubt that for a second."

16

hen we go into the hall, the music doesn't stop, but every single pair of eyes turns to us. They pass over Ren, some of them lingering for a few seconds, and then they're on me, the main attraction of this particular circus. Some guests are even whispering behind their hands.

"Ren," I say out of the side of my mouth, trying to keep my smile intact, "Ren, this is worse, so much worse."

"Just smile and follow my lead."

I nod, wishing I could kick him in the shins and follow him through the crowd. He leads us towards Joth, who's with the Pendragons. They're lovely in their matching outfits, both wearing the same skinny-leg black trousers and long white shirts. Lore has her hair in braids while Lux's is slicked back against his temples. Lore grins at me and waves, silver bangles twinkling on her wrist. Joth is talking to the most beautiful woman I've ever seen. I know before I'm told that it's Laina. '*Pretty schmitty*,' Ren said. Yet another situation he's 'underplayed'.

Laina has the same glowing, translucent skin as Lux and Lore, but with more colour in her cheeks; a pink so perfect it must be natural. She has huge, wide eyes, the honey shade of toasted almonds with swirls of darker brown.

I know those eyes.

I start with shock and Ren squeezes my fingers reassuringly. I know them, I've seen them before, I just don't know where.

Laina's heart-shaped face is framed by auburn tendrils of hair that fall to her thighs like a waterfall. Her dress is made of beautiful, delicate leaves. A green bodice running into the colours of autumn, stitched together into a flowing gown. Laina holds out her hand to me. Her fingers aren't like claws, but they're elongated, as if she has an extra phalange attached to each digit. The faery's palm is as soft as I expect it to be like worn leather, although her grip is like iron.

"Hello Merle, I'm Laina." Her voice is sweet and melodious.

"Hi, Laina." If there's something between them, her and Ren, then I'm no competition for it. Aside from Ren leaning in my doorway, she's the most beautiful thing I've ever seen. Although, the more I look at her, the more familiar she seems. Could I have met her somewhere before?

She looks me up and down appraisingly, still holding my wrist. Then her eyes widen. "You have an *Armilla*?"

"A what?"

She pulls my wrist up to her face, inspecting each of the

silver charms that hang from the delicate chain. Her teeth click together when she turns over the last. The sun merged with the moon. "Faery Charms. My mother had one just like this. I wanted it, begged for it, in fact, but she left it to my sister, her favourite." Her tone is bitter and full of spite. "Where did you get it?"

"It was a gift." The words are an effort to get out. Faery Charms. Of course they are, the Shadows left them after all. I'm so hot I think I'm going to faint. Willow said someone might've been following, toying with me like a cat toying with its food.

"Wherever you got it, it's beautiful." Laina digs her nails into my skin, as if she's sensed I'm about to fall. It does the intended, bringing me back into the room.

"Thanks," I whisper, drawing my hand away, wanting her eyes off the bracelet. Not that I need to worry about that; her attention is already gone.

"Ren. It's nice to see you again," she tips her head at him, giving him the full wattage of her smile. If I'd been under her gaze, I would've melted like an icicle in the sun. Ren doesn't bat so much as an eyelash as he shakes her hand.

"Laina's a representative from Avalon. She's come to visit with you, to advise the knights on the next course of action," Joth adds, making me jump. I'd forgotten he was there.

Laina nods, still staring at Ren. She has the same greedy look in her eye that Shelby had with Lore, the same as the fae had when it attacked me.

"Merle, there are some people I'd like you to meet," Joth offers me his arm, "the knights who I think will be agreeable to vote in your favour."

"Okay," I smile. Ren squeezes my fingers again and then

lets go of my hand. I want to take him with me, but Laina's already replacing the empty space beside him, handing over a crystal glass.

Joth leads me through the crowd, expertly avoiding people who are trying to get his attention as we pass. Benjamin is waiting by the doors in a three-piece suit. He looks much older, and gives me a small salute when I meet his eyes. We stop when we reach a trio of two men and a young woman all dressed in tunics with different shields on the breast pocket. The men's shields are violet, with white crosses surrounding a bright-yellow lion with a red tongue lolling from its mouth. The woman's tunic is lilac, a great golden bird with two protruding heads embroidered into her pocket. Purple, it seems, is the colour of the evening.

"Merle, I'd like you to meet Sir Lawrence Lamorak, Owen Lamorak, and Lady Asher Gaheris."

As the three of them turn to me, the family resemblance between the two men is obvious. They're both tall, with broad shoulders and square jaws. The elder Lamorak has thin greying hair at his temples, and chin covered with stubble. The younger has blonde hair that curls around his collar, tumbling into his eyes. They share the same long, straight nose and square jaw. Owen looks as if he's my age, maybe a little younger. He's handsome, but in a sweet, innocent way, rather than Ren's stormy darkness. I shake their offered hands.

Asher has long, thick braids flat to her head. They fall to her waist in intricate, twisting plaits. She has sharp cheekbones and a smooth brow. We don't shake, but she grins widely at me instead and rolls her eyes at my empty hands. "Shall we get a drink?"

"Sure," I say as Joth gives me a reassuring nod.

"The bar's over there, let's go."

Asher and I weave through the crowd until we get to a table full of different bottles. Mona's stationed at one end in a crisp white apron. When she catches my eye, she smiles and tips her head at me before melting into the crowd with a tray of champagne flutes. Asher hands me a similar-looking glass and I take a sip. The drink is fizzy and fruity, the bubbles popping across my tongue.

"I know the old man introduced me, but I'm not into this 'lord' and 'lady' business. Asher is fine. Maybe I'm still getting used to it, being the latest recruit—"

"You're new?"

"Not *new*. But I'm the most recent of Willow's finds. Five years ago I was an accountant."

I nod. It would've been nice to have someone to share this journey with. Five years is a long time to acclimatise.

"What I mean is, I remember what this was like, being paraded around. Awful, I hated every second. But worth it. Do you know I can shoot a bow and arrow now? I've got land up North, Eyrie's set for life. Eyrie's my little sister," she adds when she sees my quizzical look. "It's the best thing that ever happened to me, even with the fae making noise."

"I hope you know they're doing a lot more than that."

She meets my eyes. "Yes. The sooner we act, the sooner it'll be over. Which is why it's in my best interests to help you."

"I need all the help I can get."

"Yeah, that isn't surprising. I mean, Joth always does his best to explain what's going on to new finds, and Ren is pretty good although... easily distracted," she sends a pointed glance his way. I follow it and see him holding a very full glass of clear liquid, his arm clasped around Laina's waist. A flash of jealousy runs through me, my green-eyed monster sneering at them. "But the other knights? They like to keep you on your toes."

"Why?" I scowl. "I have something to prove here. I get that, and I'm more than willing to prove it. I want this life, whatever it is, I don't want to go back to..."

"Normal?" Asher grins knowingly. "They don't like change, especially with us being women, and extra especially in my case being a black woman. All Arthur's knights were men, and all of them white... I mean, black people didn't exist in Mediaeval England, right? Not to mention all the women that were instrumental in our history." She flashes a wicked smile at me. "So they like to keep it 'traditional'. But they won't argue with bloodlines."

"So, they're going to make things difficult because I'm a girl?"

"Yes, but mostly because you're *Merlin's* heir. The most powerful person in this room in practice, and only second to the Pendragons in reputation. You could cause a lot of upset."

"That's what Joth said too."

"Yeah, he's not bad for an old timer. He understands things have moved on. Still, it doesn't negate the fact that you're going to have to perform like a show pony to get in."

"What are my chances?"

She winces. "Some believe and some don't. I do, for the record. I've heard the stories."

"Stories?"

"Killing faeries and opening portals." She grips my elbow gently and steers me through the crowd. "You can fill me in later. Right now, we've got a lot of work to do. Do you want to start with the worst or the best?"

"Worst, while I've still got some energy."

"Come on, then. Okay, Monty Percival, not a bad guy, but a little set in his ways."

She tugs at my arm again and pulls me back into the swell of the party. It's helpful to have her with me. As we move between the various knights, she feeds me bits of information and the angles to play with each of them. Sir Bedivere, loyal to a fault, only has concern for the well-being of the twins. Sir Matthew of Gawain's line wants assurance that, as adviser to Lux and Lore, I'll make sure they know of social issues. That they'll be generous to the poor and fair in delivering justice. Each of the knights has their own idea of who and what the Pendragons should be, and while I'm fond of some, others, I don't like much. The only person who I truly enjoy is Asher, and I'm thankful she's here.

Well, at least someone is, I grumble internally. Ren's been nowhere to be seen all night, even though he promised he'd help. That we could do this together. He asked me to go with him, and since the moment the party started, he's been glued to Laina's side. Every time I've glanced over at them, she's been staring up into his eyes, blushing with a beautiful pink glow.

A little while later, I excuse myself. I'm hot and the dress is pinching my sides. It may be one of the prettiest things I've ever worn, but it's not the most comfortable. The party's going a lot better than I expected, but even so, I need a break to collect my thoughts. It's exhausting speaking to everyone. Socialising isn't usually one of my strong points, but for a wonder, I'm enjoying myself. I lean back against the wall, tucking myself into a little alcove, out of the way of any passers-by. Still, I can't avoid overhearing the voices of those in the hall.

"It's impossible that she could be the true heir of Merlin!" A low voice catches my attention. "Just a slip of a girl, not even grown!" It's a man, possibly Percival. It could be Lamorak senior, although I can't be sure.

"You doubt her because she's a woman?" The voice is high and lyrical, not Asher, which only leaves Lydia.

I scan through my mental notes. Lydia Geraint, a small woman with slicked back dark hair and pretty eyes. I liked her when I spoke to her. She was quiet and thoughtful, and she didn't look down her nose at me like some of the others.

"I doubt her because it isn't *true*. Merlin's power died with him. There is no heir, and it wouldn't be a ridiculous girl Joth pulled off the street!"

"If Willow finds a bloodline—"

"It'll ruin everything we've been trying to build!" His voice rises as my beating heart jumps into my throat. I clench my fists, my ragged nails biting into my palm.

"Not even you would go against the Templar!"

The man splutters, "Never think it! But that doesn't mean there aren't others who doubt as I do. Letting that girl attempt to take the magic, regardless of who she is, will be ruin for all of us. Think of our standing! All this talk of Morgwese and danger, it's all for nothing! She's no threat to us. Hundreds of years dead! This new heir could be the end of everything we have."

"Stop it!" Lydia snaps. "You go too far! We'll put it to a vote, as we do with everything, and the outcome of that vote isn't mine or yours to decide!"

"Maybe not, but you're a fool if you think this child will do anything to benefit us or the Pendragons. And you'd do well to remember that, if you like your title and estate."

Lydia huffs in frustration, and fading footsteps ring off the walls. My eyes burn with fury and I tip my head back against the cool stone. I knew the knights didn't really like me, but to hear it sugar-coated from Joth is entirely different to hearing it out loud. I feel like I'm being manipulated like a puppet on a string, dancing like an idiot to please them, when there's really no hope of winning.

"That's just politics, sweetheart." Dad's voice again. *"Don't let a stuffy old man ruin a lovely evening."*

"Merle?" The voice brings me out of my thoughts. Lore's standing in front of me, a quizzical expression on her face, "What are you doing out here? Everyone's looking for you!"

"I needed some fresh air."

"Come on," she squeaks, offering me her hand.

I don't want to take it, but my anger dampens as her bottom lip trembles. She must sense my rage. I lean down and hug her tightly.

"I didn't mean to upset you," her voice trembles in my ear.

"It isn't anything to do with you, Lore. I promise." I might be angry, but I won't punish this sweet girl for it. "Let's go."

She eyes me suspiciously, but then nods and takes my hand.

After an hour or so of wandering, when everyone's taken full advantage of the bar and become much merrier, Joth calls for more music. I keep scanning the room, looking for Ren. He's still enthralled by Laina. They're dancing together again, never taking their eyes off each other, never apart for more than a moment. I hate the horrible jealousy writhing in my stomach, which is only exacerbated by their closeness. His arm slung around her shoulders, hers around his waist.

Lux approaches sulkily, under strict instructions from Lore to ask me to dance. I can't help but laugh at his reproachful face, but I take him up on his offer. It'll help take my mind off Ren. We stand on the sidelines, slowly rotating. Halfway through our dance, someone clears their throat behind us, and when I turn, it's Owen Lamorak.

"May I?" he asks Lux, who gratefully agrees, running off to find his sister.

Owen stands in front of me and smiles. It changes the whole shape of his face; he looks much less severe. "Is that okay? Will you dance with me?"

"I'm not much of a dancer."

"I'm not either." He takes my hand gently and moves us a little closer to the centre.

I'm very conscious of the heat of Owen's hand on my waist and my hand in his. He isn't bad looking, and can only be a few years younger than me. I wonder why he and Ren aren't friends. "You aren't new to this, though, are you?"

"No," he shakes his head, "but I'm still only Dad's squire. I've just been given some of my own responsibilities."

"Responsibilities?"

"Yeah, like right now it's small stuff, helping with Dad's estate, keeping watch over the fae rings and the places where they might come through." He spins me under his arms and as I'm rotating, I catch sight of Asher on the sidelines giving me the least discreet thumbs-up ever. "Nothing compared to what you've been thrown into, though, right? It's hard to imagine not being born into this life."

"It has been a bit of a shock."

"Yes, and especially after what happened to your parents. I can't even imagine seeing something like that, one of those things—" he trails off as he sees the colour drain from my face.

I blink rapidly, trying to stop tears forming in my eyes. My words stolen from my throat. To him, to all of them, I'm just gossip. They've heard the fantastical stories, probably blown out of proportion by now, and don't seem to link them with real life. My mum is dead. Taken from me. Dad too. But they talk as if it was written in one of Willow's scrolls; a legend with no real implication. As if I'm not heartbroken every time they remind me.

Owen's saying something, his mouth opening and closing, but I can't tell what. I brush him off, wanting to be as far away from him as possible. I need to find Asher or Ren. Even Joth will do. Just a friendly face to reassure me that everything's okay. Making my way to the back of the hall, I scan the crowd, looking for my friends. Instead of reassurance, though, there's yet another blow. Pressed against the wall, out of the swell of the main party, but making no effort to be discreet, are two people. They have their arms locked around each other, their lips pressed together. Her hands on his face, brushing at his cheekbones and jawline. It's Ren. Ren and Laina.

The flash of anger that burns through me is so great I almost scream. I would have if all the air hadn't been sucker-punched from my lungs. The image of their twisting bodies stamped into the back of my eyeballs sends my remaining calm spinning into the ether. Sparks crackle up and down my spine in a raging tide. How can this be? After everything there is between us. My blood is fire in my veins, burning my reason to ash.

I've no right to be angry. Ren made me no promises, and he's given me no reason to believe we're anything but friends. Still, I thought he liked me. I must have misread the furtive glances and fleeting touches.

It's not even Ren I'm really angry at. I'm angry at the whole situation and how stupid I feel. I've attached myself to him like a life raft, expecting his life to stop as mine has, to exist only in relation to me. Now I understand his true role in this, which it seems was to help me until someone else came along to take over. Now Asher's here, his job is done. Tears of frustration burn behind my eyes again, and I bat them away.

No, no more of this. I will not be led along anymore, always relying on someone else to guide me. I'm my own person, and I can make my own decisions. If Ren wants Laina, then he can have her. If the knights want to gossip, or to label me incapable, then it'll be even more shocking to them when I fulfil the task ahead. They'll be sorry for doubting me then, when I'm one of the most powerful sorcerers on earth!

I'm lost in my little world when I collide with Asher on my way across the hall. She has to grip my shoulders to stop me from tumbling to the floor.

"Hey," she smiles, and then her face creases. "You all right?"

"I'm tired." I massage my brow again, unable to stop myself glancing in Ren's direction. Asher follows my gaze and her face pinches in a little, then it softens.

"Come and help me with the kids? It's way past their bedtime." She points to the corner of the hall where the three children are slumped. Lore and Eyrie have their heads close together, and Lux is blinking sleepily.

"Will anyone mind?"

"You showing your compassion by tucking the Pendragons safely into bed?" she snorts. "I doubt it."

As we approach the sleeping children, Lore's eyelashes flutter open. She smiles dreamily at me and then holds out her hand and I pull her to her feet. Lux gets up too and follows us out.

It's a great excuse to leave, and a great political move on Asher's part. I see members of the party giving me warm, appraising looks. At the foot of the stairs, we bump into Ren, who's thankfully alone. His hair is tousled and his eyes glazed. I think he's drunk.

"Do you want some help?" He strokes the top of Lux's head.

"No, thanks." I try to smile at him, but the muscles in my cheek grind together, refusing to be moved.

I can't be mad, I'm not mad. I'm humiliated though, and my heart hurts with the weight of it. The tears are back. I'm going to cry, and right now there's nothing I can do about it.

"Merlie, why are we stopping?" Lore twists her head. "I'm sleepy."

"I was just saying goodnight to Ren."

"Can we go?"

"Sorry, Princess," Ren grins. "Goodnight Mer. I'll see you in the morning?"

"Yeah," I nod, swallowing the lump in my throat. I barely keep from breaking down in front of him as I follow Asher up the stairs.

We tuck the kids into bed with very little fuss. Lux sleeps on his own, while Lore and Eyrie top and tail. I'm also ready to go back to my room and fall asleep as effortlessly as they have.

"I'll be here in the morning, if you need anything," Asher says when we're out in the hallway.

"Thank you for looking after me at the party."

She smiles sadly and squeezes my elbow. "I'm sorry you had to see what you saw, that things didn't go the way you wanted, with Ren."

If I wasn't still so bitter about it, and hadn't just given myself a pep talk about how I don't need anyone, I don't know if I'd be able to keep myself together. "Goodnight, Asher. Thanks again."

I should go back to my room. It's late and I'm tired, but as I near it, I know I can't sit alone in the dark. The air's too close, too hot, and I'm already burning. Instead, I race up to the Mews. It's so cold in the dark I have to catch my breath, the shock of it like plunging into an ice bath. I settle myself into an alcove, no longer caring about my pretty dress or new shoes. Now I cry, with no one to see or hear me. I cry for all that I've lost, and all I want that seems so far away. How can there be so many forces working against me? How is it fair to lose the boy that I like, and feel the chance of claiming Merlin's magic slipping away?

After my sobs have faded to sniffles and I'm about to go back to bed, I notice a glimmer of gold in the grounds. I lean as far over the edge as I dare, squinting into the gloom. There's definitely someone down there, running towards the gates. It's too dark to see who it is from here; too cloudy to see what they're doing. All I can make out is the irregular flash of light on jewellery, the soft crunch of stones underfoot.

It's probably nothing. And there's nothing to be done about it, anyway.

I drag myself back downstairs, still contemplating who might be out on the grounds at this hour. It could be anyone, Benjamin checking the gates, a guest leaving early. There's no point in wracking my already tired brain for answers I'll never find. The best thing I can do is ask Ren about—

I cut off the thought. Not Ren. Maybe Asher will know something. When I get back to my room, I find Mona waiting for me, a dressing gown pulled close around her thin frame. She eyes me for a moment, then says: "Yer no' to lettum get to ye. Their time's almost up, 'n they know it. That's all."

She helps me out of the dress and ushers me into the shower. When I return, she's gone. There's only a steaming cup of cocoa left behind.

17

I wake up late again after a fitful night's sleep, full of bad dreams and shadows. One dream was of a fine mist creeping through the Templar, settling on everything like gossamer spider webs. I could sense it looking for something, hunting for its prey. I'm about to pull my covers back up over my head and go back to sleep when there's a knock on the door.

"Come in," I say, hoping it isn't Ren. I don't think I could face him. My eyes are still puffy and I've got no good excuse for them. Luckily, it's not him. Asher's on the other side, a large mug in one hand and a hanger with a black cover over it in the other.

"You awake?"

"I am now."

She puts the mug into my hands. "How are you feeling about today?"

"Nervous. What's in the bag?"

Asher grins. "A couple of years ago, when I moved to the estate, I was having a clearout and we came across some old tunics, pristinely preserved—"

"Like the one you were wearing last night?"

"Exactly! There were at least three dozen of them, all different coats of arms. When I asked Joth what he wanted to do with them, he gave out the ones that belonged to the others, and kept some that he thought were Arthur's." She unzips the front of the bag to reveal a similar tunic, and with a little wiggle, it's free from its hanger. In Asher's hands, it's much easier to get a proper look at. The tunic has capped sleeves and is made of crushed velvet in the deepest indigo I've ever seen. The material is quilted, embroidered in criss-cross patterns with golden thread. A white linen shirt flows underneath, ribbons protruding from the v-neck.

"It's beautiful," I say, putting down the mug and brushing it with my fingers. It's ancient and probably worth millions to a museum. On the left breast, there's a symbol, a silver circle around a shining crescent moon that seems to radiate light. A flame burning in orange and yellow comes next, so rich in colour it might hurt to touch. And below that, thin spidery symbols that make a name for those who can read them. *Merlin.* Not a coat of arms exactly, but something important.

"It's yours." Asher pushes it gently forwards into my hands. "You don't need to be a genius to know that says Merlin, this thing has magic stamped all over it."

"I can't accept—"

"You can and you will." There's no room for negotiation in her voice. "I don't know anything about magic, really, or about what's in that cave. But this was his, and it's his magic.

It might be able to sense itself? I don't know. Maybe it's stupid—"

I cut her off by hugging her tightly. I'm not going to fight her. Not only because it's such a kind gesture, but because I want it. Selfishly and ferociously. Something of his that's now mine.

Like that magic will be.

"Get ready for lunch," she laughs in my ear. "It's important that you show your face before they go to vote this afternoon."

Asher says 'they' so freely, as if even after such a short time, there's a line drawn in the sand. There's 'us' and 'them', those who want me to be the heir, and those that don't.

It shouldn't be that way, my own small voice niggles at me. The 'us' should unite the Templar, not divide it. Especially with the forces at work to bring it down.

"I'll wait outside," she says and leaves me to get dressed.

I go to the bathroom and wash my face and tie my hair up on the top of my head. I want to wear the tunic, more than anything, but I'd never forgive myself if I spilled soup on it straight away. Instead, I dress in leggings and a hoodie. At the door I hear voices, Asher's and Ren's. My stomach does little nervous flips. Should I carry on as if I never saw Ren kissing Laina in the doorway? Can I? No. I think that much is obvious. My jealousy still wants to rush from me like a hungry river and devour her.

Get a grip. My voice is like steel. *Ren doesn't matter.*

"I'd started to think you'd keeled over," Asher says as I step into the hall. "This one looks like he's going to be sick any second."

I peek at Ren, and his dishevelled appearance goes a long

way to helping my mood. His face is deathly pale, almost green, cheeks flushed with pink as if he has a fever. Black hair spikes up around his ears, his dark eyes glazed over like he's struggling to keep them open.

"Bless." Asher grins and clasps her hands in front of her, mocking him.

"I don't remember anything," Ren shakes his head as we head towards the stairs. "What happened?"

After a moment of silence, I realise he directed the question at me. "How should I know? You'll be best asking Laina." I try to keep the tart edge out of my voice, but don't entirely succeed.

Ren's face creases in puzzlement but I turn away from him.

"You'll be fine after you've eaten something." Asher pats him on the shoulder when she realises that's all we've got to say to each other. "There'll still be breakfast, there always is when we've had a party."

She's right. The room where we usually eat is full of trays loaded with food. I pile eggs, toast, and tomatoes onto one plate, then croissants, butter, and jam onto another and go through into the hall. It's been transformed since last night's party, now sporting rows of tables where some knights still sit, munching on various food items.

"Over here!" a friendly voice calls from the far end of the room. Willow waving at us.

I'm more than happy to sit beside her and let her chew my ear off about history and bloodlines. Ren doesn't really say anything the whole time we're eating. He occasionally looks like he wants to speak, then confusion flashes across his features and he snaps his mouth shut.

After a while, Joth makes his rounds through the tables, stopping when he gets to us. "It's time for us to get ready for the vote, Merle. You should probably wait elsewhere. It could take a couple of hours, maybe even longer."

"What? Don't I get to be there?"

"No. It wouldn't be fair to anyone to allow you in, but I will plead your case, and I promise to do it to the best of my ability."

"And I'll give anyone who doesn't vote your way a hard kick in the—" Asher's voice is loud enough to have drawn attention, and she trails off under Joth's scathing gaze. She crosses her arms over her chest and mutters, "Well, I *will*."

At first I want to protest, but I should be grateful they're taking so long to decide my fate.

"You can come to the library?" Willow offers.

"All right. I've got some books to show you, anyway."

As everyone disperses to get ready, Joth pulls me to the side. "I'll do everything I can for you in there. So will Ren. It went well last night. I'm hopeful."

"Thanks." I want to be hopeful too, but I can't quite bring myself to do it. Joth gives me a rough hug before sending me on my way.

Ren's waiting for me in the hall between our rooms. He's doing his best to look nonchalant, but his spine is drawn as tight as a bowstring, fingers tapping nervously against his thighs. He twitches when he hears me, then slowly lifts his head until his eyes meet mine.

"You look better," I say.

He continues to stare, trying to figure something out. "I don't like Laina, not like that anyway."

"Okay." My palms are sweaty on the door handle,

heartbeat pounding in my ears.

"I mean it," he insists. His tone is low and dark. "I don't know why I don't remember anything, or why I'd be with her all night instead of you."

"It's fine. You don't owe me anything." My words are paper thin and on the edge of tearing.

No. That steel voice inside me snaps again. *Remember what you decided. We're not following anymore. He should have thought about who he wanted before sticking his tongue down her throat.*

"I know that!" He steps forward. "But I-I just—"

A bell tolls through the walls of the Templar, loud enough to make my teeth rattle in their sockets. Calling everyone to action I suppose. Ren scowls and clenches his fists.

"Ren, look, it really doesn't matter. We didn't— we're not—" Now it's my turn to go quiet, my cheeks burning with embarrassment.

"Mer—"

The bell rings again, cutting off his words.

"I think that means they want you."

"Mer, wait!"

I don't wait. Instead, I wrench my door open and stomp behind it, legs shaking underneath me. Can't he leave me to tend to my wounded pride in peace? It's embarrassing enough that I got the wrong end of the stick, never mind having to talk about it. I grab the books off my bedside table and wait a few more minutes before deciding it's safe to leave.

My head is full of Ren while I'm trying to find my way to the library. In my frustration, I take a wrong turn and end up in a part of the Templar I've never been to before. I'm about to head back to my room in despair when I hear rustling coming from one of the rooms. I edge forward and poke my head around the doorway on the right. The room looks to be full of old furniture covered in dust blankets, and the scrabbling sound is coming from Laina. The half-fae is hanging over the drawers, pawing through their contents and muttering to herself. She's more feral and beautiful than I remember, the angles of her face so sharp they could cut glass. The fae pauses for a moment and sniffs. I jump back, but I'm sure I'm too late. She definitely saw me. I start to shake all over when I hear her sniff again. What will I say when she finds me spying on her?

I'm about to step out and face her when Mona rounds the corner. Her nose wrinkles in confusion as she sees me hiding, but her eyes go wide as she looks over my shoulder.

"Quick," she hisses under her breath and waves me back towards the stairs. I rush past her and behind the wall, looking back over my shoulder. "Go on, I'll deal with her."

I nod gratefully and go back the way I came. I don't know what Laina's looking for, and I don't want to find out. The last person I want to see today is her. She might rub it in my face that Ren likes her better, and that's enough to make me furious all over again.

Nerves jangling, I trace a path back to somewhere I remember and finally make it to the library. When I find Willow, she's surrounded by stacks of paper.

"Hello?"

"Jesus Christ, Merle! Don't sneak up on me like that!" She pushes her glasses up on the end of her nose.

"I didn't mean to sneak."

"Then I guess I'll let you off." Willow purses her lips, her eyes wandering to the books in my arms. "Can I see?"

I gladly hand them over and go to make myself as comfortable as possible. It seems it's been a thousand years since I brought the books here, intending to give them to Willow, but she's fascinated by the drawings, running her hands over them with childish delight.

"Can I keep them for a while? I'd like to look at them some more," she asks after getting halfway through the first.

"Yeah, sure," I nod.

As the hours crawl by, I flick from book to book, unable to concentrate on anything other than the vote going on below. I must nap because when I look out of the window next, the sky is dark, stars winking far away. I watch Willow work for a while, and she lets me begin to translate some of the books written in Merlin's script. Eventually, though, I'm unable to bear the ominous wait any longer. What can they possibly still be discussing all this time later? Surely they know they need to let me in? I've got magic and time is running out.

After another half an hour, I excuse myself and go back to my room, throwing myself into bed. I lay awake for a long, long time, not even trying to sleep. It's as if I can hear every creak in the walls around me, every wail in the freezing wind. At eleven thirty, a low thrum of voices starts below and I sit up in bed. Two minutes later, the door across the hall slams into its frame with earth shattering force.

My heart sinks. Not good news then, if Ren's so angry.

In my bare feet, I slip out into the hallway, running down the stairs and sticking to the shadows. They look like reaching hands, trying to curl bony fingers around my throat.

Everywhere is empty, but Joth will be awake, probably expecting me. The door to his study is even open. The hinges creak as I enter, announcing my presence, and Joth looks up. In his right hand, he's nursing a glass of whisky. The left is running over a silver blade sitting on a velvet cushion. Huge rubies are embedded in the handle, the blade honed to an almost invisible sharpness. I can tell from the down-turned corners of his mouth it isn't what we wanted to hear.

"I'm sorry, Merle."

"What happened?" I'd already known, but to hear it out loud is devastating. Disappointment crashes through me, slow tears trailing down my cheeks. I don't even try to stop them. Why should I? I wanted it, to claim what they suspect to be mine, what I've been promised.

"There is no heir, and it wouldn't be a ridiculous girl Joth pulled in off the street!"

One of them said that, though I'm not sure who.

"I thought we had it. I truly did. You made quite the impression last night, and when we finally got around to taking the vote, we were an even split—"

I raise my eyebrows at that, entirely surprised. Then cold seeps into my limbs. If it was an even split, then they'll have called in Laina, she'll have been the one who decided. The ragged edges of my nails bite into the flesh of my palm. To take Ren wasn't enough then? She had to have this too?

"—we explained it all again, and she seemed to be favourable but, when the time came she said there wasn't enough evidence to suggest a faery attack—"

"She could be lying."

"She could be," Joth concedes, although he doesn't think she is. I can tell by the way the skin around his eyes creases, flinching like I'm ridiculous to suggest it. "Faeries can't lie as a rule, but seeing as she's half human, it's a possibility."

She was rummaging for something in that room, something she shouldn't have been. If only I could've seen what it was! It isn't fair, none of it is. I suck in a huge breath, but rather than it calming me, it ignites the fire in my chest further.

"We'll wait then," I growl stiffly and push my chair back. It scrapes against the floor like nails down a chalkboard.

"Yes," Joth answers. He intends to let me go with no further discussion, at least for tonight. I'm eternally grateful for his foresight. The only thing I want to do for the next half an hour is scream into my pillow. I don't look back as I march upstairs. As Ren did, I slam my door behind me, locking it in one swift motion. Then I dive back into my bed and cover my head with the pillows and blankets. I curse Laina under my breath, slamming my fists into the mattress. And the rest of them, those cowards who voted against me! Content to fade away in their comfort rather than face the problems right in front of their noses. It'd serve them right if I went into the catacombs on my own and—

I heave in a huge, deep breath. No. It isn't as desperate as that just yet. Willow might still find the missing links, or Laina might change her mind. Better to sleep on it, and if I still feel this way, tomorrow or the next night, I'll take my chances.

When I wake up again, it's the middle of the night and everything's pitch black. A light sheen of sweat covers every inch of my body. I've been dreaming like last night, but instead of mist rising through the Templar, I dreamed of a huge black Shadow prowling the floors. It didn't have the same hard shape as the other faeries I've seen, but existed in wisps and puffs of air. It passed by my room and stopped to inhale. Then it paused a little longer at Ren's door, laying its half-formed hand on the wood, carving four deep grooves with its claws. It faded and continued down the hall until it reached the stairs. The Shadow then raised its head and took one long sniff, its gruesome mouth parting in a smile, having found what it was looking for.

The twins.

The urge to check on them is so strong that I'm up and fumbling with my lock in thirty seconds flat. I step out into the hall, my feet frozen where they touch the bare stone. I don't see a Shadow, but there are four slashes in Ren's door. My heart pounds as I race down the hallway. I'm almost to the stairs when the screaming starts.

"Lux? Lore!"

I burst in to find all three of the children screaming. Lux and Eyrie cuddled together on the end of Lux's bed. They're both shrieking with their hands over their ears. Lore is levitating at least four feet off the ground. An enormous Shadow form floats in front of her, bathing her in deathly black light. A ribbon of crackling fire runs between them, painting the room with an icy-blue glow. Lore's eyes are rolled backwards so I can see only the whites. Her small mouth hangs open, hair fanning around her pale, stretched face. As the little girl gets whiter, the Shadow becomes stronger, moving from translucent to opaque with sickening speed. It's taking something from her, some vital life force. Sucking her soul dry.

My fingers tingle like they're on fire, cracks and pops

running down my spine. I focus on only one thing, getting Lore out of its deadly clutches. I throw my arm up and a charge pulses from my hand like white, electric fire. The Shadow shrieks as light spreads on its skin, crackling over its contorted limbs. It burns, shedding black flakes like snakeskin. Lore falls to the ground, hitting her head so hard it makes my ears ring. She twitches twice before going still. The Shadow retreats, screaming and holding its misshapen head in its hands before it melts back into the wall.

Lux gets to Lore before I do. He cradles her head in his lap, sobbing uncontrollably. Lore's eyes are firmly closed, but her chest is moving up and down. Eyrie is sitting on the end of Lux's bed with her hands clamped over her ears.

"Eyrie," I signal to her, "Eyrie, get Asher as quickly as you can and tell her to wake Joth. Can you do that, sweetheart?"

The little girl nods violently and gets up. As the sound of her feet slapping on the stone disappears down the hallway, I go to the twins and scoop them up in my arms.

18

L ess than five minutes later, Joth and Asher come bursting into the room. I've quietened Lux down, but Lore still hasn't moved. Her breathing is shallow and uneven, eyes rolling behind closed lids, pulse pounding at her wrists in a slow and steady beat. I was too late. As soon as I saw the marks on Ren's door, I should've run. If I had more control over my treacherous abilities, I could've stopped it! If more people had believed there was a threat, we could have put better measures in place to protect her.

They'll believe us now.

None of us here at the Templar are solely responsible for this, but we've each played a small part in it. Especially those too cowardly to accept what's right in front of them.

Joth drops to his knees and tries to pull Lore from me. At first, I'm reluctant to let go, but he reassures me with steady hands that it's okay. I relinquish my grip and he scoops her up, carrying her to the doorway where Benjamin is waiting to take her limp body and rush to wherever it is they're taking her. Lux trails behind them, still sobbing shakily. When Joth has his hands free, he offers one to the little boy and leads him from the room. I've not moved from the floor, staring down at the space where Lore's just been. Blood is rushing through my ears, the rhythm of my heart uneven in my chest. How did it get in? How did this happen?

"Hey, you good?" Asher asks as she crouches, and I nod shakily. Eyrie's pale beside her, clinging onto her sister.

"Are you all right?" I ask.

She nods, glistening tears balancing on her lower lashes as she whispers, "What *was* that thing?"

"No idea."

"Will Lore be okay?"

"Honey!" Asher swoops in and wraps her arms around Eyrie's middle. "Lore will be fine. Now it's time to go back to bed. Merle and I need to visit with Joth."

"But—!"

"But nothing." She kisses Eyrie's cheeks. "You're going to sleep in Willow's room, and Monty will be right outside. I'll take you."

I follow them down the hall and up the staircase. I've never been to Willow's room, but the giveaway is Monty standing dutifully outside the door in his full knight regalia, complete with sword. Sir Percival is the only person in the Templar, besides Asher and Eyrie, with dark skin. He has a bald head and brown eyes that are dark with sleep. He pats Eyrie on the head, smiling weakly, and then knocks on the door. Willow's in her pyjamas, her hair rising haphazardly around her cheeks. She's wearing big fluffy socks, one of which is falling off her foot, trailing behind her. When she sees me, she pushes past Monty and throws her arms around my neck.

"Merle! Are you okay? What happened? Where are the twins?"

"I'm fine. The twins are with Joth. When I got there, I was already too late. That Shadow, the fae, if that's what it was, it already had her."

Willow claps her hands over her mouth as Eyrie's eyes widen. "At least you arrived when you did. Who knows what would've happened."

We're all smart enough to know 'what would've happened'.

"Merle, Joth will be waiting for us," Asher says, breaking the silence.

I nod and step back from Willow. Asher gives Eyrie strict instructions to behave while she's away and to get some sleep. As we make our way to Joth's office, I keep thinking through what happened, seeing Lore hovering above the ground with the black shroud of death around her. The threat the knights thought so far away is now dangerously close. So close I can feel its breath on the back of my neck. It hurt Lore, and I wasn't quick enough. I've let her down, and while I'll take responsibility for my part in it, I'm not the only one to blame.

There's a horrible feeling hounding me, like I still don't understand the lay of the land here. I've been told just enough of the politics and customs to keep me quiet, but not enough to truly be of any help. Laina and six of the knights denied me entry to the cave. They denied me because they don't want their status to change; a call to action from their placid lives. But they must know something's wrong and that we're under attack. So why would they fight us? Why would they want us to fail?

Whatever the reason is, sickness is bubbling its way through the morals and obligation of the Templar, and it didn't start with me. And maybe I could stand it, not being given a fair chance, if I was the one to suffer for it.

The suffering of one of those who voted against me would be even better.

I'm so angry I can barely keep from growling as we stalk through the halls. Now they must let me in, now the knights must see it's too dangerous to stop me.

Asher's about to knock on the door, but I shake my head, moving past her and pushing my way inside. Joth's sitting at his desk with his fingers steepled in front of him. Ren's thrown into the chair opposite with red-rimmed eyes and pale cheeks. I lean against the wall, flicking looks between them both. I don't know who to trust, or if they're worth trusting at all. Neither can I be sure whether my judgement of Ren is clouded because I saw him with Laina. Even with waves of anger rolling through me, I won't complicate the situation further. If I can leave him out of it, then I will. I wait for someone else to break the silence.

Joth looks up from his fingers. "Lore is stable. We don't have a medical team here, but Sir Bedivere is a trained doctor. He's with her now."

"Is there any sign of her waking up?" Asher asks.

"Not yet." He turns his attention to me. "What happened?"

"I was dreaming. There was a Shadow in the Templar

walking through the halls, trying to find them." I remember it sniffing the air, tasting it, and shiver involuntarily. "I got up because I had a bad feeling, then I heard the kids screaming. When I got to the room, it already had her."

"Eyrie told me it's a good job you got there when you did," Asher chimes in. "She said it was *eating* her."

"Not eating." I shiver again. "But it was doing something. I could see it between them like a ribbon, but when I hit the Shadow, the ribbon broke, and it disappeared."

"Was it the same as the one I killed in your garden?" Ren asks.

"It was stronger. But I didn't kill it, it just faded away."

"How did it get in? Isn't the Templar protected?" Asher looks between our faces, and from the way hers drops, she must not like the expression on mine.

I'm starting to figure out what's going on here. The answer, the missing link, floating just outside my understanding. The way Laina was looking at Ren with those horrible familiar eyes, the faery charms, the magic. The knights voting against me, pushing me out. All the different pieces swirling there, almost whole.

I level my gaze at Joth. "There's something wrong and I think you know it."

"I don't—"

"You have to let me into the cave, into the catacombs at least. Right now."

"I can't." Joth shakes his head slowly. "I explained the rules—"

"Damn the rules!" I shout, shocking a jump out of everyone in the room. "It was different when they voted this afternoon. Entirely. Now Lore's hurt and we need to protect ourselves! Next time, that thing could come back and kill her!"

"The knights voted—"

"You knew they wouldn't allow me, didn't you? All this time you knew! The knights wouldn't want a stranger becoming as powerful as the magic might make me. Still, you let me make a fool out of myself!" I suck in a breath, suddenly on the verge of tears.

"Merle..." Joth rises from his seat, as if he's about to offer me comfort. That's the last thing in the world I want.

"Joth," I snap, "they might have been able to ignore it before, but they can't possibly now! You know they can't! That Shadow, faery, whatever it is, it almost *killed* Lore! Still you'd let the vote stand? Unless there's more, something you're keeping from me. I think there is."

"I'm not—"

"Don't lie to me!" I scream. "I heard them, Joth! I heard one of them on the night of the party saying they couldn't allow me in because it might upset their standing—"

"They would never!"

"Yes, they would," Ren says. He's been uncharacteristically quiet throughout the ordeal. "You know some of them are so stuck to tradition they'd cut their own hands off if it was required. Let her in, vote or not."

I steal a look at him, and he's staring right at me. He's pale with dark circles under his eyes, skin drawn tight over his clenched jaw.

"They still have the integrity to put their own standing aside," Joth says firmly. "I don't believe—"

"What, the knights wouldn't worry about me being a potential threat to their way of life? Whether my magic might mean their ruin? They wouldn't question Morgwese's existence, or that you're trying to upset their standing? Is that what you're telling me, even though I heard it? If the situation is as dire as you'd have me think, if we're about to go to war, why do you insist on lying to me?" I'm shouting, words spilling out of my mouth more quickly than I can take a breath.

"There have been some concerns raised," he concedes.

And with that, I'm done with this whole charade, all the politics and secrets. I thought I'd taken all the pain I could endure, but somehow there's more. His words are like an icicle through my heart. I thought he was my friend.

Just like you thought Ren liked you. But that wasn't true either.

"Why did you bring me here, then? Why did you let me look at this life when you had no intention of letting me have it? Why?!"

"I have a duty."

I stare at him, my mouth hanging open. I'm sick of this. Evading my questions with slippery answers. I have magic, we've all seen it, and I believe I'm Merlin's heir. I don't *need* them. In fact, they need me, and it's about time Joth remembered it.

"How dare you! I trusted you! When you knew they'd vote against me no matter what! I'm done, Joth, I really am. You've messed me around and lied, and paraded me in front of people who had no intention of trusting me! Honestly, I was willing to go this far. I was willing to listen while you levelled with me, to give you this one chance to be honest. But I see your loyalties don't lie with me."

"I don't..."

"*Stop it!*" The words rip at my throat and my hands tremble. Hot prickles ripple up my arm, and this time I'd

275

happily rip something apart. "Let me in that cave, right now, or we're done here."

Joth takes in a deep breath, and for a second, I truly believe he's going to change his mind, that I won't have to sneak in alone.

"No," he says.

I turn on my heel and leave. I run because I might not be able to control this horrible anger begging to be let loose. The burning at the tips of my fingers and the electricity rattling up and down my spine. A chair scrapes behind me, followed by footsteps. I'm at the bottom of the stairs as a hand grips my arm and spins me around. Ren stares at me, his eyes cold and almost unbelieving. I say nothing. I don't flush; I don't tremble; I hold his steady gaze and wait.

"You're really going."

"Let go of me." I'm not really leaving, not yet, but I'm too furious to face them. Tomorrow night, I can go into the catacombs and claim the magic myself. I can do it, I know I can. But first they need to see I'm serious, that I'm done with them and their strange ways.

"You can't! We can convince the others."

"No," I shake my head, "I'm done convincing. *I* need to be *convinced.* Did you know that all this is just a pretty lie? That the knights never intended to accept me?"

"Merle, I would never do that! I would *never* do that to you!"

I believe him, I do, but it's not enough. "Goodbye, Ren."

His cheeks flush red, eyes darkening so they're almost black, before he turns and storms off. I watch him go and then run upstairs to my room, throw everything into my bag, and head up to the roof.

19

I've been hiding in the Mews for almost an hour, watching the stars in the dark sky being replaced by the burning dawn, when I hear feet padding up the stone steps. It's apt that the sky should mirror blood on such a morning. The future queen has been struck, and even the sun knows it. I thought I'd been so clever coming up here, but if Ren's found me, the game's up. Maybe it's better that way. I keep picturing Lore's awfully slack face, her eyes rolled up to the whites, deathly pale. If I'm found out, maybe I'll get to see her.

Whoever it is bursts out laughing at the top of the stairs. Asher. "Oh man, you had me going, Merle! You should get an Oscar for that performance!"

"They bought it, then?"

"Oh yeah, hook, line, and sinker! Honestly, it's one of the best things I've ever seen. It's been years, probably millennia, since anyone's put their foot down with a Guardian like that." She wipes a stray tear from her eye. "And it's about time it happened. They're running around like headless chickens down there trying to figure out what to do now."

"You aren't."

"Well, I'm smart," she grins and sits beside me on the stone ledge, hanging her feet over the side next to mine. "There's no way you're leaving Lore, but they're so stuck in their traditions they sometimes forget humans have emotions. So oblivious to everything, they can't even *fathom* that things exist outside their own ridiculous, tiny world. Plus, someone may have given me some intel on where to find you."

"Willow?"

"Yeah, she's smart too. She hasn't told anyone, or at least no one else thought to ask," she shrugs. "What's the plan, then? You must have one if you staged an exit?"

"I have half a plan, maybe."

Asher levels her luminous green eyes at me. "I know you've only known me for a short while, Merle, but you need to trust someone. I can't help you if you won't tell me what you suspect."

She's right. I need help and I like Asher. More than that, I trust her. "All right. Some of this stuff I don't know for definite, some of it's only feelings."

"Then start with what you do know."

"I opened a fae ring. I've done it before when I was little, although I didn't know what I was doing either time. The Shadows are real, they're faeries. One of them tried to kill Lore, and one killed Mum. *I* killed *it.* Ren and Joth made it sound like I was welcome, that you all wanted me here, and that they'd teach me as we went along. But Joth keeps giving me little dribbles of information to pacify me. Every time I think I'm getting somewhere, he reveals something that wasn't there before. I have to open the cave and get whatever's inside, the magic, whatever that means, and I have to prove who I am to the knights. Willow's close to finding my bloodline, but she's not there yet."

Asher takes a moment to digest, staring into the horizon, the sun casting pretty bronze light on her cheeks. "How did you open the faery ring? I knew you'd done it, but Joth wouldn't say how."

"I cut my finger and asked for answers," I say, showing her the tiny white scar on the tip of my finger.

"No wonder they're losing their heads down there. A blood wish is a *big* deal. It takes a ton of energy to do blood magic, and it worked?"

"Yes."

"So you're powerful, without even claiming any magic from Merlin's cave! We can add that to the list of reasons of why someone might want to get rid of you. What about the things you suspect to be true?"

I bite the inside of my cheek, unsure of how to explain without sounding like a madwoman. "I think someone's been watching us, me, since I opened the rings the first time. That time I was an idiot, I wished to see a faery—"

Asher hisses in a breath.

"But I didn't know! Dad said it was just a game and—" I break off, shaking my head. It doesn't matter now what I did or didn't know, what Dad thought. "Willow said it's possible that someone knew about me and was sending the Shadows to mess with Mum and I. To scare us. It makes sense, doesn't it? Someone close, someone that followed me here? How else could the Shadow, the faery, have gotten in last night? I also have this!" I hold up my wrist, the silver charms glinting in the light. "Laina called it an '*Armilla*', some kind of faery charm bracelet. I got it from the Shadows before I knew what they were. They could be using it to follow me. There's someone working against us, and I suspect it might be Laina."

I see Asher's eyes flash with something I don't like, some kind of unease. "And you're sure your judgement isn't clouded?"

"What's that supposed to mean?"

"You don't need me to spell it out for you, Merle."

I sigh. I want to lie, to cover up what I'm feeling, but if I do, I'm no better than anyone else. "No, I'm not sure. I mean, I'm basing my hunch on things I've seen, like her rooting through some drawers and the fact she voted against me. But I'm not sure."

Asher regards me earnestly. "I'm not sure about her either. Sometimes she does strange things, but I put that down to her being part fae. She wanders off like she's looking for something, snooping. I caught her in Joth's office once too, going through the drawers of his desk."

That makes me feel much better about my own nagging concerns. Maybe I'm not just horribly jealous after all.

"Do the knights believe the Pendragons are in danger?" I ask. "Ren told me Morgwese is trying to get through from the fae realm. Is that a common opinion?"

Asher sighs and shakes her head. "Nope, not really. Like I told you, the knights are mostly old men, and they're set in their ways. They don't like change, and they don't like to act too quickly. They always want endless amounts of proof of everything and usually that's a stalling tactic. But they aren't here all the time. They don't see a threat to the twins because they don't *see* the twins." The sun's fully up now, and it bathes her face in cold autumn light. "If we had more proof of your line—"

"But I can open the cave!"

"You can't know that."

"I'm serious. I've seen it and I can."

"You might be serious, but you could also be delusional. How can you know? The knights would never have allowed you down there."

"Lore took me. I saw the writing and I have the key. There was a shape in the door that I think this fits into." I pull on the cord at my throat and let the ring fall flat in my palm. Asher looks at the ring in my palm for a moment, then back into my eyes. "I know the way, and I could read the script. I *am* Merlin's heir! I can feel it in my bones."

"Yes," she says after a second. "I can feel it in my bones too."

A wave of cool relief rolls through me. I didn't know how much I needed to hear someone outside my bubble say it; to be *believed.* "If Joth and Ren won't help, then we'll have to do it without them. Do you know what's in there?"

"Magic, supposedly."

"Yes, that's what everyone's been saying, but do you know what that means?"

Asher shrugs. "No. If anyone does, it's Joth and we'll get him to tell you before tonight. He will, even if he doesn't like it. He loves those twins more than his title, which is a rarity in this place."

"What do we do now?"

Asher contemplates for a moment. "Let's go to the library and find Willow, see if she can help. Once we prove your lineage, there's nothing the knights can do to stop you."

"Okay." I stand up, wincing at the sweet ache in my legs. I'm thankful for Asher's suggestion, as I'm freezing cold.

Together, we go back into the Templar to assemble our allies. Asher checks the coast is clear at every turn on our way to the library, but we see no one. In fact, the halls are eerily quiet as we walk through the vacant corridors.

"Where is everyone?"

"Probably in a meeting of some sort."

"Won't they be missing you?"

Asher bursts out laughing, the sound so loud she claps her hands over her mouth. "You're funny! Will they miss me? No, Merle, they're probably glad I'm not there to divide the vote."

"It isn't fair."

"Damn right, but that's how it is, and we won't change anything if we don't get moving."

When we reach the library, I climb up the ladder and peek my head around a stack of papers. Willow's at her desk, still in her pyjamas. She looks to be speed-reading through a book almost as big as she is. I cough lightly, hoping not to scare her. Her body jerks, but she doesn't look at me.

"It's about time you got here."

"Nice to see you too, Willow."

"Hmm." She regards me with cool eyes as she finally looks up. "You've caused them to go into quite a spin. Ren especially, I've never seen him so angry."

"I don't care," I reply, trying to keep my voice even. "They didn't want to be straight with me, so they deserve to spin a little. We were wondering if you'd had any more luck?"

"Oh, in all that spare time I've had?" she snaps and shakes her head. "I'm sorry, Merle. I'm under a lot of pressure. What happened to Lore is awful, and she's still shown no sign of waking up. Lux is beside himself. He hasn't said a word since last night!"

"I'm trying to help her."

"Which is why I've spent the last two hours trawling through this book! As for your question, I'm close. I was only missing three links, and now I'm down to one. A couple more hours and I'll have it."

"You're bloody wonderful!" I kiss her cheek and she blushes.

"We've got company." Asher pokes her head around the corner. "It's time to get going if you still want them to think you're missing, Merle."

"Go to Lux," Willow says. "He's been on his own with Lore for the last few hours, it's making him sad."

"Won't someone be watching him?"

"Yeah, but any knight can. Get Asher to take whoever it is off watch. She can warn you when someone else is coming," she says, rolling her eyes.

"Next time I need to do some plotting, I'm coming to you." I grin. "Thank you, Willow, I owe you one."

"You owe me hundreds," she smiles back. "Get going. I'll cover for you for as long as I can."

The trek to find Lux is as painless as it was to get to the library. Bedivere is on watch outside the twins' bedroom. He looks pale, his shoulders slumped forward. Asher waves me back down the adjacent corridor and goes to meet him. I can't hear what they're saying, but about five minutes later, she comes back.

"Coast is clear. He was nearly asleep on his feet, so it was easy enough to convince him to swap. Lore's condition is the same. Lux is still in there, just sitting."

"I'll check on him. Thanks, Ash."

"No problem."

As I enter, the room looks normal, and there's no sign of what occurred here less than seven hours ago. Lore's lying in her bed with Lux beside her. Her hair is splayed across her pillows, small hands clasped in her lap. She's so pale and still she could've been carved from marble; eternal and unwaking. Lux looks up, and on his face, there's only a flicker of the mildest surprise.

"Hi."

He says nothing. For a long moment, I think he won't speak at all. That instead, we'll just sit and stare at Lore's beautiful empty face. But when the silence is at it's most unbearable, he whispers, "You're supposed to be magic, right?"

"Yeah."

"Can you hear her too? It might be a twin thing."

"Lore?"

"Yes, Lore," he snaps. "She's trying to say something."

I move so I'm sitting beside him. When I put my hand over theirs I *do* hear something, but I can't make out words, it sounds like humming.

"Do you hear it?"

"A little."

"When are you going to wake her up?"

286

"Me?!"

"Who else would it be? Magic put her here, magic has to bring her back... and you already said you can do magic! Or did you lie?"

"I'll do everything I can."

"That's what Ren said, too."

I turn my head to hide my expression, the anger and confusion; the hurt.

"You're both so stupid!" He bites his lip and his cheeks blush. "You're trying to solve the same problem, but you're too stubborn to be friends and do it together! Lore always says we're stronger together."

"It's complicated, Lux."

"No, it isn't, Merle." He imitates my tone perfectly and my cheeks burn. "Even if you don't want to be friends, you're supposed to look after me and Lore! I want my sister back! I want her to wake up!"

He's right. Once again, I've been thinking of my own feelings over everyone else's, and I've been punishing Ren because of my anger and jealousy. But he's my friend, and I owe him an apology.

"I'm sorry, Lux."

"Don't be sorry," he wipes his sleeve across his nose, "just help us!"

I get up and squeeze his shoulders, kiss Lore on the forehead, and smooth back her hair. I trusted Ren enough to follow him here. Now I have to trust that I made the right decision. When I pull open the door, Asher turns.

"Everything all right?"

"No, I just got reality checked by a ten-year-old." I sigh and run my hands through my hair. "I need to find Ren."

"Yeah, I figured you would at some point. He was in Joth's office last. He doesn't always get to sit in on the meetings because he's still on 'probation'." She holds up her hands, seeing the question on my face and having no time to answer it. "He was waiting there."

I creep down to Joth's office and pause when I reach the door. There are muffled noises coming from inside, creaking chairs and hushed whispers. I poke my head around the corner and through the slit in the door, I see Ren's legs sticking out straight in front of him, his hands hanging down over the arms of the chair. Laina's perched in his lap, her body raised over them so I can't see either of their faces. My stomach turns at the sight of them.

I spin back around the corner and lay my head against the wall. My palms are sweating. I hate that I'm jealous; it clouds my judgement of everything. More noise spreads from the room, hands fluttering against the side of the chair. A sucking sound I don't want to know the source of. This wasn't a good idea. The best thing would be to walk away...

"*You saw more. Use your brain,*" Dad's voice snaps. "*Did that look like kissing to you? Does this sound like it?*"

As much as I don't want to, I cast my mind to the image. I've got no experience of even light make-out sessions, but I've seen enough Rom Coms to know the man's arms go around the woman's waist, that his body language shouldn't be so... un-wanting. And the sucking doesn't sound like kissing; it sounds like ripping. If I suspect Laina to be a spy of some sort, not to expose her would be wrong.

Just go in there. If they're making out, you'll look like a creep, but you've looked worse.

I brace myself and go in. Ren's right arm is still flapping

against the side of the chair, but his left is reaching for something on the desk. His fingers are trying to grip the jewelled knife, but they knock it spinning away onto the floor.

There's no time to think. Wishing for something more lethal, I grab the lamp off the desk and aim it at Laina's head. I don't know what I expect, but the lamp doesn't smash. Instead, when it hits her skull, it makes a sound like a cracking egg. She turns as if in slow motion, and in her anger, she's radiant. Her features are drawn together and much darker than the night before, black eyes bulging from their sockets. Her elongated fingers are gripped tight around Ren's throat. Then her eyes roll and she slumps onto the floor. As soon as her weight is off Ren's chest, he scrambles backwards so fast he tips the chair over. He falls hard, gasping for air and rubbing at his neck. When I'm sure Laina's out cold, I slump to my knees in front of him.

"Ren! Are you all right?"

He leans back against the wall, deep grooves and long red scratches on his throat. I put my hands on either side of his face and turn it to me so he's looking into my eyes. They're focused even though he's still wheezing. Little spots of blood have bloomed in the soft skin on his face, tiny burst vessels. If I'd been a minute later, I might've been faced with a corpse.

"Ren?" We're so close our foreheads are touching. The purple has begun to fade from his cheeks, leaving the skin deathly pale.

He nods and leans into me. "I'm good, I'm okay." Then: "Why the hell are you here?"

"I saved your life!"

"And that just about makes us even." He's still rubbing at

the welts on his neck. "I was waiting for the knights to come out of their ridiculous meeting, and Laina came in and... but she's supposed to be on our side... I don't understand."

"Well, I almost do. That's why I came to find you!"

"You know something?"

"I suspect a lot of things, and none of them are nice... I think there's a much larger problem than we first thought."

"Oh really?"

I swat him with the back of my hand. "How much do you know about faeries?"

"A lot more than I ever wanted to," he mumbles and looks at Laina's unconscious form.

"Can I ask a question?"

He nods.

"If Morgwese was a woman, a sister of Morgana and Elaine, she isn't a full faery, right? Or is she?"

"Is that important right now? I didn't intend to spend my morning giving a history lesson."

"Did you intend to spend it being murdered?" I ask in the sweetest voice I can manage. "Or was that scheduled for after lunch?"

"Touché," he concedes. "Legend says she's half and half. She wasn't always that way. Before the battle with her sisters, she was powerful, but she wanted more. She made a deal with the Unseelie Queen. Morgwese would restore faeries to their former status in trade for immortality and fae powers."

"Unseelie?"

"Mischief faeries, the ones that hate humans and mess with them at every opportunity."

I nod, as if I understand exactly what he's talking about. "How powerful would that make her?"

"Pretty powerful, probably the most powerful fae in existence."

"Powerful enough to exist outside the fae realm for a long time, hypothetically?"

"It doesn't sound very hypothetical," he glares at me.

"Answer the question."

"I guess... normal fae only have a few days, a week tops, before their magic fades and immortality catches up with them. But Morgwese? There's no way of knowing. Why?" Ren narrows his eyes. "What are you thinking?"

"I..." I begin, but someone's calling my name, running feet stomping towards us.

Willow bursts into the room waving a sheet of paper, Asher's on her heels. Willow's face is flushed, and she doesn't even glance at Laina on the floor.

"I found it!"

"What?" I say, my breath whooshing from my lungs in disbelief.

"I found it!" Willow says again, waving the crumpled piece of paper over her head, grinning from ear to ear. "I found the last of your line."

20

Willow throws her arms around my neck and squeezes me so hard she almost cuts off my air. "I was missing something from the king's court, back in the 1700s! I found a birth certificate, really interesting, dating to 1736 when —" she trails off, staring between our faces. "Not interesting?"

"Very interesting," I assure her. "But for later, right now we've got to show the knights."

"What happened to Laina?" Asher asks, nudging the fae's unconscious form with the toe of her boot.

"Long story," Ren says, rubbing at the marks on his neck.

"Which we'll explain later." I've been waiting for this moment. Now it's here, I'm ready to grasp it with both hands. "Is that where the knights are?" I point through the door off to the side of the study.

"They won't like it if you burst in on them," Asher says.

Ren's staring at me, his eyes burning coals. He nods, a single stroke of his head that tells me all I need to know. He's with me and that's all that matters.

"For God's sake, go on then!" Asher rolls her eyes, "I'll deal with the fae."

"After you, Merlin's heir," Ren says grinning.

Intending no courtesy, I push at the door, which sticks until a thump from Ren's shoulder shoves it open. The knights look up from the table, some of them shocked, others angry. Only Joth's face is still. I've not entirely forgiven him, and I still think he's hiding something, but right now he's the least of my concerns.

"What's the meaning of this?!" Lawrence Lamorak stands up in his seat.

I'm about to speak, to say the blissful 'I told you so', when Willow shoulders in front of me. Her voice rings clear and bell-like in the stone room. "The heir of Merlin requests an audience with the Knights of the Templar. She requests access to her birthright, a right which you can no longer deny her."

"This is ridiculous!"

"Willow has proof, and you can't stop me."

Willow slams the paper down on the wooden table. "Do you doubt my work, Sir Lamorak? Because if you do, you call almost every single person in this room into question, including you and your son."

"I would never..."

"Shut up." Ren's voice is like silk twisted over steel. "You've messed Merle around long enough. You have your proof, everything you asked for. Do your duty."

"Du Lac is right." Lydia Geraint stands up, eyeing me. Then a smile breaks on her face. "I accept your request."

"You can't..." Sir Alymere's voice joins the chorus, his cheeks reddening in protest.

"You will!" I say. "You will accept! You *will* let me into that cave, and you will let me do what you brought me here to do! You have no right to stop me."

"And we won't stop you." Joth's voice is calm in a storm of noise. "But you won't enter the cave until tomorrow."

"Joth!"

"Tomorrow," he says firmly, blazing eyes piercing into mine.

"With all due respect—" Ren starts, but Joth holds up his hand.

"It's okay, Ren." I squeeze his wrist. There's pride in Joth's eyes as I stare him down, along with something else, something he needs to tell me. "Tomorrow."

Willow skips back towards us and out through the doors as I give Joth one last look. Ren takes my hand and pulls me after Willow. In the study, both Asher and Laina are gone.

"That's the most exciting thing I've ever done!" Willow clutches her hands together. "I'm never allowed to speak to the knights like that!"

"You did great!"

"Now what?"

"We figure out what happens tomorrow. Check on the twins. I speak to Joth—"

"We," Ren butts in.

"I think it's best if you let me do it. He has something to say and I think he's afraid. Now he has to tell me, but he might be more forthcoming if it's just me."

"I—"

"I mean it," I say firmly. Although I've got to put what happened with Laina behind me; I'm still a little sore.

"Come and find me as soon as you're finished. We need to talk."

"Okay," Willow interrupts, drawing out the word. "I think I'm just going to leave you guys to it. I'll go back to my safe place to do some more digging."

I look back at Ren. "Go on, we can do this later."

"All right, I'll be up with the twins." As he leaves, he shines his winning smile at me and I can't help but smile back.

"You two make me want to throw up." Asher's voice startles me.

"Jesus! Don't scare me like that."

She snorts and throws herself into a chair behind the desk. "I put the fae in the brig. I guess that isn't what you call it on land, but," she shrugs. "And you might get rid of Du Lac that easily, but I'm not going anywhere until I hear what the big man has to say. You might need backup."

"Okay."

We wait for the knights to file out of the hall, some of them giving me scathing glances, others smiling, some not looking at me at all. Finally, Joth comes through and shuts the door behind him. He surveys Asher and nods.

"Do you want a drink, Merle? Lady Gaheris?"

"Like an alcoholic drink?"

"It's been a long night, and it's about to turn into an even longer day." He takes a decanter from the shelf behind him, along with three glasses. He pours and hands them out. Asher wrinkles her nose at the smell and downs it in one, while I hold the shining crystal tumbler in my sweaty palms.

"You were right, Merle. I have been hiding something, but it isn't what you think. It isn't sabotage." He sighs. "I didn't want to tell you because I didn't want to scare you, but you're apparently fearless."

"What is it?" He's wrong to call me fearless, but the things I'm afraid of outweigh anything I think the cave holds. Like Lore staying in the state she's in, like Ren being murdered by a rogue fae. Like Morgwese's imminent reign of terror, should I fail.

"It's about what might happen when you get into the cave." He turns his blue eyes to me. "I've told you about the magic."

"Yes. That somehow you expect me to get it, although I don't really know what that means—"

"Most of the knights think it's access to his things, his books, potions, and relics," Joth continues slowly. "But it could also be Merlin's power, his raw magic that's trapped down there. Willow thinks it's possible he transferred his magic to an object, or to the room before Nimue encased him in rock."

"What does that mean for me?"

"If it is the full force of his power, and it's been waiting down there all this time, as soon as a suitable host comes, it's likely to..." he breaks off and sips his drink. Nervous.

"It's likely to what?" I could claw his eyes out with frustration. When he looks back into my face, there are tears in his eyes.

"To speak plainly, because that's what you deserve, no one has ever been in there except Merlin himself. For all we know, his magic could rip you apart the second you walk in. If you aren't the true heir, although that seems very unlikely now, it will kill you. But even if you are, your body might not be strong enough to take it."

Now I understand why he didn't want to tell me, and the drink I wasn't sure about burns its way down my throat. Joth lets his tears track freely down his face.

No, no, no. It can't be! Yet another cruel trick in this horrible game! I clench my jaw against the unfairness of it, the bitterness sliding down my throat and choking me. How can it be so?

"So it might kill me?" I whisper when I can bring myself to speak.

"It might not," Asher offers.

"The choice is still yours, Merle. No one can make you go in there."

That might've been true this time yesterday, but with Lore in a coma and Ren's attempted murder, it's no choice at all.

I sigh and put down the glass. "I have to try, Joth."

He regards me for a long moment before he nods, then he reaches out across the desk and takes my shaky hands. His fingers are feverishly warm. "Thank you."

"Don't thank me yet." I try to smile, but my mouth doesn't pull up at the corners. "I need to get some rest."

"Of course," the old man smiles. "Tomorrow, then. I'll send for you when it's time."

Asher follows me out of the door and puts her hand on my shoulder, then pulls me into a rough hug. "I believe in you."

"Thanks, Ash."

"I'll tell Joth about Laina, then I'll take Ren off duty and send him up. I assume you're going to the roof?"

"Yeah." After today, I might never see the sun again, and I intend to make the most of what I have left.

When I'm finally comfy in my spot in the Mews, I let the gnawing emptiness I've been holding at bay consume me. The last few weeks have brought nothing but confusion and heartache, all with the promise of something better, and now that also seems out of my reach. I understand why Joth didn't tell me, even though I hate it at the same time.

I don't know if I've been used or not, or whether I've been led down a path by someone else's feet instead of my own.

"As much as you'd like to play the blame game, Merle, it isn't true." It's Dad's voice, the only one that could talk some sense into me. *"You can't escape who you are."*

Perhaps I can't, but I don't want to die for it. I don't want to go into that cave and turn to dust.

Tears form in my eyes and burn in my throat, and I let them fall. I might be the only chance we have at saving Lore and now that's in jeopardy, too. If I don't make it back, she might stay stuck in her coma.

Don't forget about the rest of them, Merle. You've got to save them from Morgwese, too.

Somehow, I find a laugh through my tears. As much as I want to let my fear and grief consume me, I can't give in to it. There's only darkness that way. If I continue to scare myself, I'll certainly fail. At least tomorrow I'll get my answers, or I'll burn, and then they won't matter anymore. I wipe my eyes and try to control my breathing.

In the quiet, there's a noise that's not quite footsteps. It must be Ren. I've become much better at detecting him.

Without saying anything, he takes a seat beside me, his feet planted firmly on the ground. I glance at him and his face is pale, the scratches on his neck standing out like screams.

"I know you aren't okay, so I won't ask." He reaches forwards to brush the remaining tears away with the pad of his thumb. I lean into it, the touch that I've been waiting for.

"I'm terrified."

"Me too." He drops his head, his forearms draped over his knees, hands hanging limply between them. He's so still he might turn to stone. "Asher told me what Joth said, about what might happen... that you might..."

"I have to go in there."

"No, you don't. If I'd known about this, I would never have come to find you, or invite you into this twisted place!"

"Yes, you would."

"No." I know he believes himself true, even if I don't. "No, you were right all along. You made all your choices based on half-truths, and I allowed it to happen. In fact, I encouraged it. I can't accept that you might go in there and... I won't accept it."

"Ren," I shift in my seat so that my crossed knees are against his thigh, his legs are shaking, "make peace with it. It isn't your fault, I don't blame you."

"Well, you should. If the worst were to happen, what would I do? How would I go on afterwards?" His voice trembles like glass on the edge of a high note, right before it's about to shatter.

"Like always. You'd continue to be a knight and protect the Pendragons with your life as I would do with mine, given the chance. Nothing changes."

"Everything changes! You changed it!" He whips his head

towards me, eyes blazing. "I didn't expect it, this. When Joth sent me to find you, I thought you'd just be another false lead. But not only are you *not* that, you're something else entirely!" He gets to his feet and starts to pace, talking fast. "Joth told me a story once, about when he met Morgana Le Fae. He said he took one look at her and had known in a second that the world wasn't the same anymore. She had such a power, such a magnetism, that everything revolved around her, and once he knew that, once he'd been pulled into her orbit, that's all there was." He takes a deep breath, slowing his movements entirely until he's standing in front of me again. He holds out his hands, which I take, then he pulls me to my feet. "That's what I felt when I saw you smash those cups. Everything changed."

"*I saw what you did,*" he'd said, with that beautiful smirk on his face and heat in his eyes. I'd known then, hadn't I, how drawn to him I was. How I've trusted him from the start. How I'd wished to see him over and over again.

"Stop it," I snap, on the verge of tears again. "Just stop it! Somehow, you've wormed your way inside my head and you won't leave! It's clouding everything! I can't trust my judgement because I'm thinking of you. I can't trust my feelings because I don't understand them! The only thing I can bring myself to trust is you! So you can't have doubts, you can't tell me you can't go on, because you must."

"Mer..."

"I need you with me. You understand the situation we're in! You said it yourself; I'm your last hope. I have to try, because I'd not risk you for anything, not even my own life."

He starts and looks into my face for any hint of deception, of untruth. I let him look because there is none.

"It's too dangerous to risk that for us, for me—"

"It's worth it."

"That's easy for you to say, though, isn't it? You might not be here tomorrow. What will happen if you go and—" he trails off.

"What will happen if I don't go down there at all?" I soften my voice as much as I'm able and he flicks his eyes up to mine. He knows the answer, as we all do. We know there's no choice in it no matter how much we want it to be different. "Tomorrow I might... tomorrow might be the last day. I don't want to fight anymore, I don't want there to be any bad blood between us."

"How could there ever be, Mer?"

I stand a moment longer, held in place by the look in his eyes. I can see every swirl of hazel in his brown irises, every shadow his lashes cast on his cheeks. "If the worst happens, you and Asher need to be ready. Get Willow and protect yourselves. Move Lux and Lore away from the rest of the knights. I don't trust them. They don't have the twins' best interests at heart."

"It won't happen."

"*If* it does. I'm only sure of the four of you, Joth included, even though I'm still furious with him. I know there's no reason to listen to me, but Asher... she'll explain everything if I..."

"You won't."

"Promise me you'll take care of them." I grip his fingers tightly.

"I promise."

302

We spend the rest of the day wandering the Templar like ghosts. We eat, we nap, we talk about nothing and everything. When it gets dark, we go up to the twins' bedrooms. Lux is lying next to Lore, his arms draped over her stomach. They're both sleeping, chests moving up and down in tandem.

"Do you need a minute?" Ren asks.

"No," I shake my head, "I just wanted to say goodnight."

I go to them and plant a kiss on Lux's forehead, something he'd never let me do if he were awake. Then I smooth Lore's hair back off her forehead.

"*I'm coming for you,*" I send to her, "*hold on.*"

Lux shifts and opens his eyes. "She says don't fight."

"What, sweetie?"

"Don't fight, that's all I can hear," and then his eyes slide shut and his breathing evens out.

I don't know what that's supposed to mean. Maybe she's talking about Ren and I, as we were fighting when she was last awake. Or maybe it's just sleep talk. I'm too tired to think about it now. Tomorrow will be the biggest day of my life and I need to get some sleep of my own.

"Time for bed," I smile at Ren.

"Yep." He follows me out and back down the stairs to our respective rooms. Outside the door, he puts his hands on my shoulders. "I'll see you in the morning."

I nod and put my arms around his waist. He wraps his own around my back and then kisses the top of my head.

"Promise me you won't die?"

"I promise I'll try not to."

He chuckles and releases me. I turn into my room and close the door behind me, heart beating hard. I didn't imagine Ren's feelings then? There *is* something between us, something hot and full of sparks. I turn towards the bathroom and the bottom drops out of my stomach, hands flying to my face to cover the sound of a scream.

"Din' mean to scare ye." Mona grins wolfishly at me from where she's sitting on my bed. Her eyes are sparkling with amusement.

"I don't believe that for a second."

"We've 'eard abou' wha' the old man said." She rises slowly and holds out her hand, offering me something. "Mi mam gi' me this when she died. It's bin pas' down for centuries between us, s'posed to 'ave been a gif' to my ancestors from Princess Anna."

She drops a delicate silver chain from her fingers; it's laced with creamy pearls. Cupped in her palm is the cross of a rosary; the silver is carved with intricate swirls, ancient and lovely.

"I can't—"

"I'd 'ave you take it into tha' cave." She drops it into my hands, closing my fingers around it. She covers my fists with her own fingers, squeezing. "An' when yer finished wi' it, I'd 'ave it back." Her eyes are sincere and sure. I understand the message loud and clear.

Promise me you won't die.

"I'll wear it."

Mona lets go of my hands and makes her way to the door. As she's about to close it she says, "Yer to prove 'em wrong. Yer to make 'em believe."

Then she's gone, the door resting in its frame with a soft click.

21

I wake up to the bell clanging through the walls. The same horrible noise that called the knights to vote, casting me out. Now my birthright is so close I can almost touch it. Even so, the sound, loud enough to make my ears ring, isn't a welcome one.

God forbid anyone misses my potential elimination.

"Good morning, sunbeam!" A loud shout makes me jolt upright, and Asher bursts into my room and jumps onto the bed. She's still in her pyjamas and her braided hair swings around her waist.

"Why are you so chirpy?" I sit up and brush my hair out of my eyes.

"Because today is the big day! The day you fulfil your destiny and get all your powers! Just like a fairy tale!"

"Or I'll get burnt to a crisp."

She blows air through her pursed lips. "Not gonna happen. I was thinking about it all night and it wouldn't make sense! I understand if I went in there, a lowly normal person, and it ate me up. But you? The proven heir of Merlin, no way!"

"I'm glad you're so convinced, it's a shame no one else is."

"Screw them! I believe, and I'm the only person you should listen to."

"How's that?"

"Because I brought you coffee." She points to a large mug on the dresser.

"I could get used to this. What time am I expected?"

"Whenever you want, it's your show, Merle."

I cross my legs and glance out of the window. It's raining although not heavily; the clouds are dark and full, painting the day with a pale light that doesn't fill me with much hope. Not that I'll ever see light again if the magic tears me apart.

"I want to go now." I'm on the edge of losing my nerve and the sooner I go, the better.

"Okay," Asher smiles. "You shouldn't be so worried, there's no way you can't do this."

I nod. Asher's confidence makes me feel a little better. I get up, finish my coffee, and pull on my jeans. The beautiful indigo tunic shimmers in my wardrobe, calling to me. When better to wear it? The ivory shirt is a little too big, but it's the softest material I've ever felt, like incredibly fine wool. The tunic fits perfectly. A high collar frames my jaw, making my face look angular and fierce. It's loose but not baggy, heavy enough for me to feel the weight of it pressed to my shoulders, but not in any way restrictive. I run my fingers over the shining moon and the burning orange flame. I'm sure it flickers red and yellow in the light. Under the flame is the word, the strange script that only I can read. *Merlin.* With strengthened resolve, I pull on my boots and plait my hair, the coil rough and thick down my back. The last thing I do is loop Mona's ancient rosary around my neck. It sits just above my heart, the pearls glowing.

Mum, Dad, I don't know if you're around, or if you can hear me at all? But I need you now more than ever. I need to know you're here.

There's no response, but I guess that's to be expected when talking to dead people.

I go out to the hall, and Ren's door is already open. He's sitting with his elbows on his knees and hands draped between them, as still as stone. When I knock, he twists his head and does a double take that's almost comical. A slow smile spreads over his face. "Nice top."

"You ready to go, Renwick?"

"At least if you die I won't have to hear you say that anymore."

"Always a silver lining."

He comes into the hall and laces his fingers in mine, squeezing tightly, eyes searching my face. "And you're sure you want to do this?"

Promise me you won't die.

"I'm sure."

"Let's go then."

We enter the hall to find the knights seated at the table. Joth is at the head, and the space at the other end seems to be reserved for me. Asher sits to the left, next to an empty place that must be for Ren. Mona, Etta and Benji are standing at the back of the room as they were on the day I met them. Hands clasped and eyes low. Except for Mona, that is. She drops me a sly wink, grinning wolfishly. The low hum of chatter dissipates as I enter and Ren steers me towards the chair. All the knights look at me, most of their faces blank and controlled. I change my expression to match, mirroring them.

Joth clears his throat, his eyes fixed on me. "Merle Wilde, you have requested, as is your birthright as Merlin Wyllt's proven heir, to enter the sacred Tomb of Magicks."

I stare at Joth long enough for Ren to kick me under the table. "I-I have."

"I've called this meeting to make sure you understand the duty you're undertaking by accepting this lineage. Upon bestowment of your powers, you'll be bound to the Pendragons, to serve them, and keep their secrets until the end of their lives or yours. You will act as an adviser and protector until you are no longer able. The Templar will employ you, and you must obey their law for as long as your service lasts. Do you accept the terms as I lay them out before you?"

I stare him in the face, my gaze unwavering. "I do."

"The Knights of the Templar accept your request to enter the cave. Should you gain the magic of your ancestor, the Templar accepts you as their adviser and confidant in all matters relating to the Pendragons and their kinsman." He stands. "Knights, upon Merle's ascendance, do you honour your sacred commitments and accept Merle's role within this Templar?"

"We do," they whisper in unison.

Joth looks back at me. "It's time, Merle."

I stand, heart beating hard in my chest, thrumming in my ears. There's no time for goodbyes, but I steal one final glance at my friends. Their faces are set and sure. I look away from Ren last, his smouldering eyes following me until he's out of sight. Joth ushers me through the doors into his study, and then to the room where the knights met yesterday. I think this must be what Lore called the Knights' Hall. On the wall is a huge wooden circle, a smaller version of the Round Table, split into twelve with a golden cup in the centre. In each of the segments is a coat of arms. Joth goes to it and, with some effort, rolls it to the left, revealing a small stone doorway. My nostrils twitch at the smell of ancient secrets. It's not as dark as the entrance that Lore led me through, but there won't be torches or guidance this time. At the thought of her, a needle of pain lances through my chest. I must succeed in my task. I can't leave her wherever she is, floating in the nothingness.

"This is where I leave you, Merle. Half the challenge is finding the cave on your own."

"Okay," I nod.

"You can do it, I know you can." He presses his palms into my shoulders.

"Okay." I can't help the smirk spreading across my face.

"No. I'm not supposed to help you. It's out of the question—"

"Okay." I step back from him and wave my hands in front of me in surrender. "If you say so."

"I do." His eyes soften as he stares at me. "Good luck, Merle."

I nod my appreciation, still smirking.

He turns to leave, then mutters something under his

breath. "Oh all right then! Go straight until you reach Merlin's face, chiselled into the wall. After that, take the right tunnel and then the middle one again."

I go to him and throw my arms around his waist, my anger forgotten. If this is to be the last time, I don't want it to be a bad memory. I want him to know I'm grateful for all he's done for me, and that I don't hold his actions, born of fear, against him. We're all scared.

He pats me on the back. "Remember, straight, right, straight."

"I've got it."

"You're supposed to bring something back!" Joth calls quickly. "Now, I've said enough. I better go before they realise I'm helping you. You can do this."

"I know," I nod. Before he has time to move or I have time to doubt my confidence, I duck into the gloom.

Joth's advice doesn't lead me astray. After ten minutes of walking, bumping into things and trying to feel my way along the passage in the half-light, I find the face of Merlin carved into the wall. I can't see him clearly, but from what I can make out with my fingers, he's not the nice, happy wizard in many of the pictures I've seen. Instead, he's wild. His hair is matted around his face, there are scars on his cheeks and his nose is bent at an odd angle, as if broken multiple times. As I could before, I can sense the way, a string pulling at the very fibre of my being. I take the right tunnel, then the middle one, and I reach the cave. It's exactly as I remember it, and my heart aches to think of Lore.

Now I'm close to the cave, the feeling of being pulled along is almost unbearable. Dragging me forward until I reach the writing on the wall, as bold as if it's only just been carved. I run my hands over it again to check that I haven't misread it, that I have an idea what to do. If not, I'll get stuck down here. I let the image formulate in my mind, and I'm relieved to find my memory hasn't deceived me: *Here is Merlin, cave of magiks, blood may pass.*

It's time. I look around on the floor for a sharp rock. I don't think the 'blood' mentioned on the wall is metaphorical. As for the key, I've had that for as long as I can remember.

I reach for the rough cord around my neck and lift it over my head, sliding the ring onto my middle finger. I twist it so that the stone is palm side, secure and waiting to be tried in the lock. I find a rock with sharp, jagged edges, and dig the sharpest corner into my finger, twisting it into the cut already there. It causes a burning pain but brings no blood; instead it leaves little flakes of red skin. I grit my teeth, bearing down again until the cut reopens with a fresh burst of agony. I bite my lip against a whimper and squeeze my fingers together to draw out more blood. The drops roll down my finger, lining my palm with crimson.

I take a deep breath. If this doesn't work, then I'm out of ideas.

I search for the indent in the wall and slide the ball of the ring into it. It fits! The oversized stone fulfilling its purpose. It glows in my hand, heat radiating from the point of contact.

I may not have come with papers, but I have my very own relics.

I press my other palm against the cool stone, smearing blood in a thin red line. I wait, holding my breath.

Nothing happens.

Panic blooms inside me, turning my legs to jelly. There's nothing more I can do. I have the blood and the key, but there's no movement in the wall. I must've been wrong about something. It all made sense! Maybe I can't read the words? Perhaps I could never read them at all.

Now I know how he must've felt, Dad, at the rings, when his wish didn't work. Excitement and nerves draining to cold, painful confusion. He would've expected it to do something, having been told of his magic blood. Then being able to see those awful Shadows instead. It's soul destroying, the horror dawning on me now. I can see why it sent him mad! Will that happen to me when I go back empty-handed? Not Merlin's heir after all, just nobody. Then I will lose Ren, and Lore, and Asher. *No. No. No!*

"Why won't you open?!" I shout, my throat burning with desperation and disappointment. I smack my free palm on the door and the sound echoes. "For God's sake, just open!"

The entire stone wall begins to shake, a crunching, grinding sound splitting the air...

Of course.

The door disintegrates in front of my eyes. It crumbles, dust filling the air, bigger chunks rumbling to the floor.

The cave is open! I've done it. I am the heir of Merlin Wyllt, and I can barely believe it.

I scramble backwards and tumble flat onto my back, which is better than getting hit on the head by a chunk of stray rock. My mouth and nose are full of dust, and I cover them with the collar of my tunic, trying to get a breath of clean air. My blood sings with anticipation, the cave calling to me. I clamber up, looping the ring back around my neck, and waving my arms to clear the air.

"Come, Child, you're home," a voice I've never heard before, but simultaneously the only voice I've ever heard, whispers around the cave. *"Come and let me give you all the wonders of the world."*

There's no music, of that I'm sure, but in my head I hear a chorus, a hum so sweet and familiar it brings tears to my eyes. I step forward and the sound intensifies, calling to me. My heart pounds in tandem with its beat. I'm whole, complete. Nothing else matters, nothing other than that sound and the thrum of magic. Sparks run up and down my arms, tingling in my spine and fingertips.

From where I'm standing, I see a stone altar, shelves of vials of different colours, and strange metal instruments twisted in looping swirls around clear glass spheres. Then there are the books. Dozens of them, identical to the ones in the library, creating a wall of red, blue, and brown.

One book lies open on the altar, its pages blowing wildly although there's no breeze. I step through the door and into the half-light of the cave pulled forward by that lovely, desperate hum. I'm reaching for the book with gold edges, the one on the altar. The trill of the air changes, its sweet melody entwined with a shrill, anxious note. It shifts, moving around me and taking on weight. In shape, it's like the Shadows, almost human in stature. But that's where the similarity ends. The looming outline is full of dots of light that spin like tiny suns, illuminating the dark space, so bright it almost blinds me.

Then it's reaching for me, so fast there's no time to move. It grabs my arms and flings me across the room. Where it touches me, my shirt peels away, skin burning. I roll over the altar and crash to the other side, winded, as I hit the ground.

As I push myself to my feet, it grips me again, shoving me back to the floor. I throw my weight against it, but I'm not strong enough. Everywhere it touches, fire rages through me, the humming in my ears turning to shrieks. I'm going to die here, turned into embers. Ashes and dust in the wind.

"*Don't fight,*" Lux's voice echoes in my head.

My throat is dry and aching in the heat. I can't breathe. I want to scream but have no voice.

Don't fight.

Maybe Lore didn't mean Ren and me; maybe she was talking about the magic? It's the only thing left to try as my whole body writhes in pain. The more I struggle, the hotter the fire burns. I close my eyes.

"*You are mine,*" I command. "*You are mine, and you will bend to me.*"

Then I lie back and open my arms.

There's pain, molten lava running through my veins, changing the very structure of my bones. I'm not going to make it. I was a fool to even think I could. My skin crackles as I embrace the shape, turning black under its touch. Who did I think I was, to wake this sleeping monster, to absorb a thousand years of unruly, electrifying power? My insides feel as though they're becoming liquid, my lungs are about to explode in my chest, and then, when the agony reaches its peak, there is nothing.

22

When I open my eyes again, I'm in a faery ring. My arms aren't split and black, even though red handprints mark my skin. They throb, a dull ache, like a rotten tooth or cracked nail. A cool breeze blows around me, picking up the tattered remains of my shirt, flying the ribbons like flags. At least the tunic has survived.

"*It's got magic in it,*" Asher had said.

The woods have been restored to their former glory. If they're even my woods. Everything's green and pink and purple. Foxgloves hang around my face, sweet with poison, and the birds call to each other overhead. This close to winter, there should be no colour. Everything is dead or in hibernation, waiting for the spring. I push myself into a sitting position, the aches of battling with the magic already setting in, and yelp with surprise.

Sitting across from me, with a small grin on his face, is my father.

This time, he looks exactly as I remember. Dark hair swept from his brow, square jaw emphasised by the flicks around his ears. There are lines on his cheeks as if he's smiled a lot, and he did. I know that now, even if it was lost at the end. Brown eyes regard me with an emotion that's entirely ours. It has no name, but it speaks of woods and rings, and thanking little river sprites every time we jump their stream. There's a stab of grief and nostalgia so strong I reel with it, but that's quickly replaced with warmth seeping from my heart to the rest of my body.

He's here! I can see him again, vital and alive. All those years wondering what happened to him, all the questions I have can now be answered!

My joy doesn't last very long. If I'm here with him, and everything is back to normal in the woods, I must be dead. The warmth spreading through my chest turns to ice. What we feared has come true. I won't make it out of here. As much as I'm happy to see Dad, I didn't want this. Six months ago I would've traded almost anything for this moment, to see him one last time. I wouldn't have even needed words then. Just seeing him smile or breath would have been enough. But now, now—

My thoughts slip to the twins; of poor Lore trapped in her coma and her brother's ebbing sadness; how I'll never be able to wake her. Joth and Asher, so confident in my ability, will be so disappointed. And Ren, Ren—

Promise me you won't die.

A sob wrenches up my throat; I know they'll go on without me, though that's not such a comfort as I thought it would be.

My father laughs; in the notes of it, underneath it, is that same lovely hum from the cave. "You aren't dead yet, Wild'un."

I shake my head in shock. To hear him speak again, in real life rather than just memory, knocks the wind from my lungs. I'd not forgotten what he sounded like exactly, but neither have I truly remembered the rise and fall of his voice. How his deep tones fill the space, and the light notes twist into words. It's surreal and something I'd never even considered I'd lost. Just to see him here, existing, has made this whole ordeal worth it. I rise onto my knees and reach out to him, but he shakes his head.

"We're in the in-between space. If you put your hand outside the circle, you *will* die and that's not what either of us wants."

"I miss you."

"I miss you too, Merle, more than anything." The lines on his face crease as his smile deepens. "I'm glad that you found your way without me to guide you. I suspected you would, but—" he shrugs.

"What happened to you?" The question burns inside me. There's so much I want to know. So much I still need from him. So much lost time I want back.

"It's too much to explain now, maybe one day, when we have an eternity. Right now you need to see something else, something much more important."

"What?"

"I brought you here because I wanted to see you, my little girl, all grown up." There are tears in his eyes and they grow in mine. "But when you close your eyes, you'll get another visit. I can't pass on the gift as it was never truly mine, but there's someone excited to meet you, now that you've freed their soul."

"I don't understand."

"No," Dad shakes his head, "no, sweetheart, but you will. The last time you were here, you wished for the truth. Now you've come into your birthright, it's time. All the masks will fall and you'll know everything. Then you'll wake up, you'll gain your powers, and at least make a start in undoing the damage done. Which sadly often seems to be the way with children and their parents." A wistful smile crosses his face. "You'll see everything. The road will be hard, Wild'un, but you can make it right."

"I don't want to leave you."

"Yes, you do," he responds, but not unkindly. "I love you."

"I love you too, Dad."

"Now close your eyes."

I take one last hard look at him, making sure I remember every detail of his face, his eyes, his nose, and I let my lids slide closed. Then I'm falling backwards like Alice through the rabbit hole, tumbling and tumbling faster and faster into the dark. As rapidly as my descent started, it stops. I open my eyes just in time to see blades of grass before I drop. The cold on my burnt neck is soothing, reducing the pain to a dull throb rather than a scream.

I sit up, disoriented. I'm in a forest, but not *my* forest. The trees are far too large and wizened, their trunks covered with luscious green moss, reaching far up into the clouds overhead. There's a stream, babbling over stones and rushing over roots. In front of me is an enormous boulder of the same rock as the cave wall, cream-streaked with pink and grey. As

I stare at it, it cracks, opening like a mouth, the ground shaking. If I wasn't already sitting I'd've been thrown to the floor.

When the rock is demolished, the man encased inside tumbles to his knees, spluttering. His long brown locks are streaked with grey, beard hanging almost to his waist. He lowers his head, shaking off the dust and debris, and then he takes a rasping, rattling breath. The entire forest responds in kind. Birds sing, the ground rumbles, and the wind whips around us and into his lungs. The Lord of the Forest is back, and everything from the dirt under his feet to the sky above him knows it. He raises his head to me as he exhales; the eyes that meet mine a shining gold.

"Who's there?" he questions, his voice hoarse and deep.

I know the great man on his knees. He's the man in Dad's drawing, even down to the woven shirt and the scar under his right eye. He's the man who started this, my great-great-great-great-grandfather, the most powerful wizard to ever have lived.

His brow creases again as he regards me, and then his eyes widen. "How rude you must think me, I haven't even introduced myself! It's been a long while since I've had company." He gets to his feet and towers above me. "I am Merlin, wizard, and advisor to the throne of Camelot. Long may it stand! And you must be..."

"Merle," I say and offer him my hand.

"Merle and Merlin!" His face splits in a broad, warm grin and he waves my hand away, and holding out his arms. "Blood of my blood! What a pleasure it is to finally meet you, and to be free of that cursed rock!"

I go to him and he embraces me, squeezing hard. My

head only just reaches the bottom of his ribs. "So you found your way into the cave?"

"Yes."

He puts his arm around my shoulders and leads me further into the woods. "I've been waiting for you for a long time."

"I know, it's been about a thousand years."

"A thousand? My God, I knew it had been an age but..." he shakes his head, "I don't imagine the knights made it easy for you?"

"They didn't."

"They've always been that way," Merlin sighs. "When Arthur passed, they ran Camelot into the ground with their rules and regulations, their 'moral superiority'." There's genuine sadness in his voice. "I hoped time would make them wise, but it seems even a thousand years wasn't enough."

"Some of them are wise. Ren Du Lac, Asher Gaheris, Joth... and the twins."

"The Pendragons," he nods slowly as my eyes widen in surprise. "I may have been encased in rock, my dear, but I've not been entirely idle. I still know the goings-on of the Templar. Like a hibernating bear I knew of your coming, and that you could set me free."

"Are you the thing I'm supposed to take back?" I say, remembering Joth's words.

"Somebody told you? Maybe they aren't all fools, after all. But no I must stay here, in the enchanted forest, not dead, but not alive. My magic will fade as it flows to you, and I'm happy for it to do so. I've been alive for far too long and seen far too much."

"I don't know how to be an advisor or a wizard!"

"When I was paraded before King Vortigern, I'd met only one other human being in my entire life." He grins. "If I could help Arthur build a kingdom, I have faith that you can accomplish the task before you. And I'll not set you on your way without a little help." He stops walking as we enter a small clearing. It's full of soft moss and ragged stones jutting from the ground. He descends on one of the flattest grey squares and I sit cross-legged in front of him.

"The knights will expect prophecy, which you shall have. In return for delivering this favour to the knights, I'll give you what you want. I'll show you Morgwese's work, her cunning plan, for I have seen it all." His voice falls. "I have seen it unfold like a tragedy and been able to do nothing."

Yes, I sag forward with relief. It's better than I'd dreamed, more information than I ever could've hoped for.

"While the magic adjusts to your bones, the very fibre of your being," he peers down at me, making sure I'm listening, "it will be wild. After an hour or so, it'll settle to its usual thrum, yours to train as you see fit. But for that one hour," his gold eyes bore into my soul, "enjoy it."

"But—"

"Hush," he raises his hand. "Our time is short. You've been gone a while. The knights will lose hope of your return. Give me your arm." He holds out his hands and I offer both of mine. He takes my left arm, the least badly burned, and flips it over.

"This may sting a little," he whispers, "and you must remember every word I say."

"I'll try."

"No, Wild'un you must." My nickname on his lips only reiterates the firmness of his words. Then he takes the index finger of his right hand and draws on the soft flesh of my forearm. It stings as he etches something into the skin. Then he speaks:

> *"When enemies come disguised as friends,*
> *the lines of blood will break.*
> *The mad will rule in the court of the dead,*
> *the tied will come undone.*
> *When dawn breaks on silver shores,*
> *the wise will lose their heads.*
> *The kingdom burns by the will of the damned,*
> *shadows thrown by wings of death.*
> *When the true are tested through the burn of flames,*
> *hope may be reborn.*
> *Only under redemption's scathing gaze,*
> *will the chosen rule once more."*

His voice is hypnotic, and the words fill me with dread. He drops my arm, and the symbol is the same as the one on my tunic. A circle with a flame in the centre, a crescent moon, and Merlin's sigil. I want to ask him what it means, but instead I say, "The Templar won't like that."

"They've never really liked much of what I've had to say," he grins, "but I don't dictate prophecy, I only deliver it."

"I'll tell them."

"It's time for you to go."

"How do I get back?"

"The same way you got here, you'll close your eyes and I'll send you." Merlin kneels in front of me.

"What about Morgwese?"

"You shall have what I promised."

Before he puts his hands over my eyes, I take one last look at his face. He seems to have aged ten years in only a few minutes, his hair now more grey than brown.

"Go with my blessing, Merle. And when you wake, may you receive all the answers you seek."

The heels of his hands press into my eye sockets, and then he pushes me back. The pressure is gone, but my eyes won't open. I'm falling again. Behind my closed eyelids, there are no floating chairs, bottled potions or hatters like Alice saw. Instead there's Ren and Lore and Lux. Shelby's greedy eyes and Laina's reaching claws. My father on the bridge in the park, rubbing his hands together to keep them warm. A figure approaches him, long slate-coloured scythes ripping at his throat, both of them tumbling over the edge. Shelby and a man with straight black hair and eyes like a beetle stand outside our house waiting for Mum. The man slides into my mother's body like a suit, strangling her cries for help with huge clawed hands. Laina in Lore's bedroom, hissing at her in a language that I don't understand. There's a baby boy with red eyes, like a demon. I see both Laina and another faery, who I know is Shelby because of her eyes, cooing over a cot.

That's where I saw them then, Laina's eyes. Why they were so horribly familiar.

She has long chestnut hair and sharp pointed features, grinning down at the baby who's gnashing at her with a mouth full of teeth. Both of them are laughing. I see myself through Shelby's eyes, prey easy for the taking, and stupid enough to bring a Pendragon straight to her. Then Laina running down the path from the Templar to the gates, whispering through the bars, but always being careful not to touch them. Shelby's ear is waiting: "*We have them, sister, all of them. Our wait is almost over."*

I see it all, and I'm being twisted out of shape, as if my organs are coming untethered in my midsection. I've been blind and far too trusting. I shriek into the dark. Shelby, it's her, it's always been her, manipulating me. Pretending that she cared. And I saw her. I *saw* Laina in the grounds that night; I knew something was wrong with Shelby. Waves of icy rage crash through me. For too long, she's played me like a fool.

My screams snap me from the vision. I'm laid on the floor where I remember falling, screaming so loud and long that my throat hurts and my stomach cramps. I'm still burning. My arms are on fire where the magic touched me, and my neck feels like it has been dipped in hot tar. The pain isn't enough to stop me from getting to my feet, but it's a close thing.

I check my arm to make sure I didn't imagine him; Merlin. His brand remains.

As promised, my limbs are buzzing with energy. My sight seems to have improved. There are silken cobwebs hanging from the roof and dust twirling in the light that weren't visible before. Footsteps pound above me and the rise and fall of voices.

One hour, he said. One hour that I can use to my advantage.

I push myself to my feet and start towards the cave entrance. The objects call to me, thrumming with power and wonder. I want to go to them, to feel them in my hands, but there'll be time enough for that later. My vision adjusts easily to the gloom as I race through the catacombs. I flee past Merlin's carved face and down the centre tunnels, bursting through the arch of the doorway into the hall, crying with joy. I'm really here! I made it back to Lux and Lore and Ren and Asher and—

Shelby.

That bitch has deceived me from the start. She and Laina, not truly Shelby and Laina at all, but Morgwese and Elaine. Blood sisters, half fae, half human hybrids from the dark ages, thrown back into the light. Now my vision goes almost completely black with rage. I knew Willow was right when she suspected someone had been following us, keeping tabs on me. But Shelby wormed her way into my heart so I'd tell her everything about us. I *loved* her, and all this time she's been using me. That's not all she's done though. She murdered my parents. She killed them both, even though she knew it would rip me apart. Even though she was supposed to love me too.

Shelby is Morgwese. Our mortal enemy. And I will have her head if it takes every living breath within me to retrieve it.

I shove through the doors, rage singing in my blood. The knights are exactly where I left them, muttering amongst themselves. When the doors swing wide, all of their faces turn, some of them shocked, others elated. Before I've taken the full measure of them, I'm in Ren's arms. His hands are on my face, pulling my eyes to his.

"You're hurt." His gaze is a mixture of concern and pride.

"Doesn't matter. There's trouble."

When someone clears their throat, Ren takes my hand. Monty Percival stands at the head of the table, peering at me with obvious disdain.

"I believe you have something for us?" His tone is hard.

"Can't it wait?" Ren starts. "She's hurt, she needs to rest."

I shrug Ren off and stamp forward, using the vacated chair as a stool and climbing onto the table. "I have prophecy for you, Percival, but first I've got business with a rogue faery. There's a spy in our midst, feeding information to Morgwese! She's been here the whole time, waiting."

"No, she—" Joth starts.

"How will we know you're truly the heir?" Percival persists.

I imagine a huge wind blowing him backwards, forcing him to be quiet. A low growl rips from my throat as he's shoved into his seat. The doors squeal on their hinges, thrown wide at my command.

"*It won't always work like that,*" Merlin speaks in my mind. "*One hour.*"

"I *am* the heir!" I stare at him, at all of them. Electric power fizzes up and down my limbs, crackling with static. It feels fantastic, like until now I've never truly understood how my body moves and fits together. My heartbeat thrums in my ears. Under that I hear the whistling of the wind outside, the pound of the rain on the roof. I pull back the remains of my shirt sleeve, showing them the brand tattooed there. "I *am.*"

"What about Morgwese?" Joth asks.

"He showed me; Merlin! I don't have time to explain now, you just have to trust me!"

Everyone's silent, staring at me, then at Joth, then back at me.

"I trust you in all things, Merle." His confident tone is enough to send a hush through the knights, his grin just as wide. "That's what I swore an oath to, and it's an oath I intend to uphold."

Now they look at me with a different expression, waiting for instruction.

"Whether or not you like it, Morgwese is here. She's waiting for me. I can send her back, buy us some time, but only with your help. If you're with us, ready yourselves with any weapons you have, anything that'll weaken the fae." I glare down at them all, finally settling on Percival. "And if you're against us, you should be gone by the time I've finished with her."

There's nothing for a moment and then a voice calls, "You heard her, get moving."

"*Not you, Gaheris,*" I think, starting towards her. "*You're with me.*"

Asher jolts like she's been shocked by a live wire, turning to look at me with wide eyes. It's barely noticeable in the sea of movement as the rest of the knights start to their feet, but one thing is obvious. She *heard* me. I *thought* something at her, and she actually *heard* me. I wonder if she might be able to send something back? But that's for later, when this madness is finished.

"Outside, twenty minutes! And somebody stay with Lux and Lore!!" I scream and then turn to search for Asher again in the crowd. She's already by Ren, and I jump off the table and race over.

"How did you do that?" she says, "with the mind talk."

"Mind talk?" Ren cocks an eyebrow.

"*She means this,*" I send to him.

Ren's eyes widen, his mouth sliding open. Then his lips transform into a grin. "Wonderful, another way for you to annoy me."

With the flurry of activity dying down, Joth finds his way to us. "I knew you had it in you."

"I don't have long with this magic. Merlin said it'll be stronger while it gets used to my body. It's the best chance we have of sending her back."

Joth brings his eyes up to mine, a hard expression dawning in them. "What do you need?"

A few moments later, we're storming towards what Asher earlier called the brig. I want to see the fae, to check that my suspicions are correct.

"More visitors?" she drawls as we enter the dungeons below, trailing off in an awful cackle. I ignore her, unlocking the door to her cell without the keys Joth offers. She's perched on a wooden bench, legs crossed at the ankle, leering at us. There's a thick gash on her head, auburn hair matted with blood.

"Are you Elaine?" I bark.

"You got the magic then?" she says almost lazily, as if she's asking where I get my hair cut.

"Are you?"

"I may have been known to go by tha—"

I lunge forward, grabbing at her throat, slamming her into the wall. She squeals in surprise. "Don't mess with me! I intend to let you live through this night, but it's your choice."

She considers me for a moment. I know, even though I'm not sure how I know it, that she's considering whether she's more afraid of me or her sister. Then she eventually says, "Yes. I'm Elaine, daughter of Garlois and Igraine."

"And Shelby, she's Morgwese? Isn't she?" I ask, her name ripping at my throat. I can barely believe the words as I'm saying them.

Too painful, my heart advises me. *Too painful to even think about.*

Ren sucks in a breath and Elaine thrashes underneath me. I push my forearm further into her neck, giving her a hard shake. "Answer me!"

"Yes! Yes!" Elaine sags against the wall, weeping what I assume to be tears of rage. I can feel it baking off her. Rage and fear. She'll have to face someone's wrath, and who knows whose will be worse?

I loosen my grip and turn to my friends. "I need to know how you sent her back last time."

"Morgana and Elaine did it," Joth answers. "They put her in a blood circle and cast her out. There were words. I knew once, but now I don't remember—"

"Tell me," I demand of Elaine.

"No."

"Tell me!"

She brings her face so close to mine our noses are touching. "You're just a party magician compared to my sister. I would rather bite off my own tongue than tell you. I won't help you."

"You're going to help me whether or not you like it," I spit. But she's not lying about biting off her tongue, and I believe if I press her, she'll truly do it.

"There are spell books in the library," Ren says.

I take in a deep breath. "Asher, stay with Joth and get ready to move the faery. I'll need her outside with the knights. And I'll need that knife, the big one with the rubies."

"Yes, boss," Asher says. Joth nods his grim approval.

I grab hold of Ren's sleeve, tugging him back the way we came. "Let's go find that spell."

23

We race back up the two flights of stairs towards the library, and by the time we're on the second floor, Ren's breathing hard. I'm not, and it's amazing. I don't feel tired even though I should be exhausted. The burns on my arms and neck barely ache. I'm electric and alive and—

Ren's slowed to a walk and has been staring at me for almost a minute. Maybe he doesn't realise how desperate we are, how little time there is to waste? His expression is a mixture of disbelief, determination, and something else, something hot. Even with our fate balancing on a knife's edge, I can't stop myself from taking his hand and pulling him towards me, from leaning into him, pressing my chest against him. His eyes go wide, and I can see every single strand of colour twisting in them, every reflection of the shimmering lights.

"I'm going to kiss you now, okay?" I say.

"Okay." His voice is husky as he closes the gap between us, dark eyes glittering.

My heart thuds against my ribs, hands shaking as they run up the length of his arms, then I rise up on my tiptoes and press my lips to his. Where they make contact, warmth spreads through me. It's like the magic in the cave, although this heat is much sweeter. The same melodious hum fills my ears. His hand finds its way into my hair, pulling on it gently. My arms lock behind his neck as I drag myself closer. I might never get close enough. Ren moans low in his throat, his fingers fluttering at my cheek like the wings of butterflies. With my heightened senses, the blood rushing through my veins sounds like a raging river, the beat of Ren's heart a pounding drum. It's exhilarating, and I want more of him, everything he has to offer. Then he's pulling away, breath hot on my cheeks, forehead pressed to mine, the tips of our noses touching. The knuckle of his finger brushes the underside of my chin, tilting my head so I'm looking into his eyes.

"You were gone a long time. You scared me. Please don't do it again." His voice is low and seductive.

"I won't."

He kisses me again. This time it's much more chaste, but still there's a flood of warmth in my chest. Ren offers me his hand, which I lost hold of in our tryst, and I entwine my icy fingers with his warm ones. When we get to the library, Willow's rummaging around, looking for something. She hears our footsteps and immediately looks up.

"I was wondering when you'd show up." She runs to me, Her arms squeezing tightly around my middle as we embrace.

"Thank God!"

"I came for information."

"As always." She raises an eyebrow and grins. "What are you looking for?"

"Joth told us about a spell that Morgana and Elaine used last time, but Elaine won't tell me what—!"

"Elaine's dead."

"No. She's *Laina*."

Willow's mouth drops open. "What? How?" Then: "I mean, now you say it, she really didn't try that hard to—"

"Willow, I need that spell."

"There are hundreds of books in here! We'll never get through them all!"

"No, but Merlin's magic might," I say and close my eyes. As I imagined the gust of wind blowing Percival back into his seat, I concentrate my mind on the spell, the particular hum of it resting in the pages of a book. I spin, scanning the shelves with my mind as I do. The vibration of the magic stays the same until there's a sharp spike on my left, a piercing high note that could shatter glass.

Veni. The word is in my thoughts before I properly understand what I want. *Come to me.*

I hold out my arm, and the book's spine thuds into my palm a second later. When I open my eyes, Willow's staring at me in shock, Ren's smirking like the cat that got the cream.

I lay the book on the table and hold my hand over it.

Ostende, my mind offers again. *Show me.*

The leaves of the book flicker, then the spine snaps open on a page full of strange words and symbols. I run my fingers over them and they stop dead at the top of the third paragraph.

Huic sanguis ego conteram recta tuum.
With this blood, I break your line.
Hoc sanguine, ut malediceret vobis.
With this blood, I curse you.
Huic sanguis ego mittam te.
With this blood, I cast you out.

Then, underneath,

Projiciam vos a facie mea.
I cast you out.

"That's it. That's the spell!"

"*The knights will need the last,*" Merlin says in my head.

"Ren, those last words, that last line. Do you see?" I ask, pushing the book towards him. He nods. "Good, remember it. We need to tell the knights, so they can help with the spell."

It's time to run, any advantage we had slowly falling away like sand in an hourglass. Elaine must've had some way to communicate with her sister, and I don't doubt she'll have told her about my intentions. When she sends word that the cave didn't kill me, Morgwese will come here herself.

I turn to Willow. "Stay here, stay safe. Maybe get to the twins if you can but—"

She's already shaking her head, sleek chestnut hair shimmering in the movement. "No, I'll come with you."

"It's dangerous!"

"Yes." Her eyes flicker with fear, but under that, determination. "But when I write our history, I want to be in it. I want to have done something brave."

Okay, I'm about to answer, but I'm cut off by another voice.

"*Merle,*" it echoes through the room, stabbing behind my eyes like thousands of tiny needles, "*Merle—*"

It's only a whisper, but it's so sharp it causes me to clap my hands over my ears. When I look around me, the others have their hands over their ears too.

Whatever I had to say will have to wait. Morgwese is here.

"*Come then,*" Shelby's voice reverberates around the room. Two of the windows shatter from its force. "*I'm waiting.*"

Power vibrates at my fingertips, running up and down my arms, begging to be set free. I understand blood. I know how to wish things in and out of existence. Things like arrogant, evil faeries.

"Come on." I pull on Ren's arm.

"Wait," he stops and grips my shoulders, "are you sure you can do this? That this'll work?"

"No. But I'm sure it's our only option."

He stares me down for a moment, eyes roving over my face as if he's committing all of my features to memory. "Then let's go."

Ren keeps up with my pace as we race through the hall. Excitement radiates off him, answering the call to action. There's no fear in him, no question. Willow's terrified but determined, the emotion bleeding into the air around her. We reach the head of the stairs at a dead run, and I almost go tumbling down them. At the bottom, the entrance hall is empty apart from Joth, holding the knife I asked for.

"Merle..."

I raise my hand to silence him. "I need you to tell me the true boundaries of the Templar, where the ground hasn't been blessed."

"The long grass, it's how we know the edge."

"One hundred percent sure?" I ask. Asher should be back in less than three minutes by my count, and we need to be outside before then. I command the front doors to open with my mind. They fly wide, rocking on their hinges, rain pounding into the hallway.

"*MERLE!*" Shelby's voice screams, deafening in its lunacy. I clamp my hands over my ears again and watch the others do the same. "*I'm done waiting, come to me!*"

"I'm sure," Joth calls over the noise.

"Tell the knights to hurry." I stand on my tiptoes and kiss his cheek. Then I turn to Willow. "Wait for Asher, come with her."

Ren grabs my hand as we run for the wild grass, our boots sliding in the mud. I almost fall, but he puts a steadying hand on my waist, pulling me to him. His lips find mine again, pressing so hard I can feel his teeth. But I feel it too, the call to battle, the pounding of our blood, the shriek of the wind. If this is to be the last, a war won and lost before it's even begun, then I'm glad it's with him.

"What are you going to do?"

"I told you." I pull the knife from the waist of my jeans. "Open a door."

"And then what?"

"The words! Make sure the knights know them. Like Joth said, it'll make a blood circle, hopefully strong enough to send them back!" I'm soaked to the skin, my hair plastered to my face. "Do you see Asher?"

"Yes, she's coming." He points, and I follow the length of his arm and see three figures hurrying towards us, one being dragged by the other two.

"Morgwese!" I scream. "Shelby?!"

In one flicker of light, there's nothing. In the next, she's standing before us, leering at me. Flicking her long pink tongue around her incisors. The faery queen doesn't look like much, in her flowing blue cardigan, powdered grey hair twisted into a bun. Still, the stab of betrayal through my heart is as painful as I expect. Shockwaves roll through me; anger, grief, rage. I bet she was laughing at me all this time.

"Hello sweetheart," she drawls. "Hello, my little Merlie Girlie."

Hatred swells in me, coursing through my veins like fire. I have loved her and trusted her and known her as a mother. I never questioned her interest in me. Why else would she care so much about a strange little girl? She slipped into my world so easily, hiding behind Nicky and Otto so I wouldn't notice the true nature of her existence. I was just so grateful to have somebody to lean on. The thoughts leave a bitter taste in my mouth. That Merle is gone. I am the heir of Merlin, and today, she'll see the full force of my power.

"Hello, Shelby."

"Oh, let's speak plainly, shall we?" She tuts, wagging a spindly finger in my direction. "You know I'm not that doddering old hag." She reaches up to her neck, plunging her long, needle-like fingers into the loose flesh there and pulling.

"Jesus Christ..." Ren whispers beside me.

Her face peels away with a horrible, wet, ripping sound,

like a thick rind being peeled away from rotten fruit. Underneath her mask is bloody and beautiful. Her features are elongated and dark, eyes like that of a bug, shimmering into the night, not flat and vacant but full of horrible intelligence. She sees all; she knows all. She is all-powerful. Her long auburn hair twists to her waist and snakes around her stomach.

"Morgwese."

"*Mother* is much more fitting, don't you think?" She grins like a loon. "Mother to the greatest children on earth, mother to you, and mother to those beautiful twins! Twins of my blood, twins of my line, twins of my flesh!" She barks the last words. There are too many teeth in her mouth, rows and rows of them like pins. She's insane, that much is clear.

"Mother?" I spit, disgusted. "You're no mother to me! I had a mother, who you took! And you will not have those twins!"

"I will!" I'm horrified to see she's laughing. "Oh, but I will, and there's nothing you can do to stop me!"

The hilt of the knife glitters as I slash it across my palm. Blood courses down my wrist. I switch hands and do the other, the same dark-red blood running and running and running.

"Asher!"

"Right here, boss!"

"When I say so, put Elaine in the circle."

"There isn't a circle!"

"There will be," I say, and Ren takes the bloody knife from me and slits his own palms. His unwavering loyalty fills me with resolve, and I don't know what I've done in my short life to deserve him, any of them. He hands it back to me, hilt first, and goes to flank Morgwese. I hand the blade to Asher, who follows suit. Then she passes the knife backwards.

"Not to her! Not to Elaine!" I scream.

But it's not Elaine's hand that reaches. They're smooth, brown hands. It's Willow. Not just her, but Joth and the knights. Only Bedivere, the faithful watchman, is missing. Everyone else has come.

"What are you doing?" the faery hisses, the mockery in her eyes now tainted by fear. "Stop that! Stop it!"

Morgwese takes a step forward, raising her hands in front of her. I see in her head that she intends to run. Under no circumstances can that happen.

Etiam, the magic offers. *Still.* I send a wave of sparks down my arm and directly at her, winding it around her torso, freezing the movement of her arms and legs. She's fighting me. The dirty yellow of her own magic pounding against my spell. She's strong, so strong my grip on her wanes.

She grins at me knowingly. "You're no match for me, *Wild'un.*"

For a horrible moment, I think she's right, that the sickness of her own magic will infect me. Poison me. Her spell is strong and deadly. But it's that word, *Wild'un*, that's undone her, igniting white-hot embers in my core. How dare she mock me! She won't be laughing when I send her back to the hell she came from.

One last push, I demand. *One more!*

I pour the molten anger within me into holding her. Her eyes widen as she scrambles backwards. Still, she fights, but now her efforts are useless. She underestimated me, and now she'll pay the price.

Her magic crackles and fizzles against my own. Elaine,

after realising her sister's peril, starts to mutter under her breath. She's no match for us though, her magic a weak, sickly trickle. I bat it away as I would a fly. When I look back at Morgwese, there's only panic in her eyes.

I take Ren's left hand in my right; he links to Joth, who links to Lydia and Percival and Tristen. The knights circle Morgwese/Shelby. Chanting the words the book gave us.

"*Projiciam vos a facie mea. Projiciam vos a facie mea.*"

Then the circle is full apart from Asher and I.

"*Projiciam vos a facie mea. Projiciam vos a facie mea.*"

Like whispers in the wind.

"*Projiciam vos a facie mea. Projiciam vos a facie mea.*"

Morgwese and Elaine both shriek in pain and terror. They're bound by the words of the knights, unable to move.

"*Wait, Asher,*" I shoot at her, "*wait for my say so.*"

The knights look to me, some terrified, especially Lamorak the younger, but they don't move.

"Put her in, Asher! Put her in now!"

Asher does, shoving the fae forwards. Elaine goes screaming, slashing at the air in front of her with one hand, covering her eyes with the other.

The pair aren't beautiful now, blind harpies trapped by the blood of the Templar. I reach for Asher's hand, our fingers almost close, but I slip on the slickness of her palm.

"Merle?" The voice is so familiar that it stops my attempt to try again. "Merle, why are you doing this?"

I turn my head with comical slowness, not wanting to see what I know is there. Unable to stop myself looking.

Mum is standing in the centre of the circle. She's in her pyjamas, her hair hanging loose around her gaunt cheeks, crying slow and full tears.

"What are you doing? Don't you love me, Merle?"

"It isn't real!" Ren shouts. "Mer, it isn't real! It isn't her!"

"Merlie," my mother sobs, "Merlie."

She looks exactly as she did that time in the hallway, waiting with wide eyes, for me to come and rescue her. I know it's not her, but at the same time, it is her, down to the finest detail. Even her tears and the soft curls of her hair.

A sharp pain snaps me back to the present, Asher squeezing my palm.

Mum's image wavers. Behind it is a decaying sack of skin, hair and teeth. I close my eyes. It's only an illusion, a good one, but still smoke and mirrors. Mum isn't here. There's nothing I can do to save her.

"*Projiciam vos a facie mea. Projiciam vos a facie mea.*"

"Huic sanguis ego conteram recta tuum,"I scream. *With this blood, I break your line.*

"Hoc sanguine, ut malediceret vobis." *With this blood, I curse you.*

Power ripples down my arms, through the knights, the floor shaking beneath us.

"Huic sanguis ego mittam te!" *With this blood, I cast you out.*

Morgwese and Elaine are on their knees, pawing at the ground as if that will save them from the blood magic.

"I, the Heir of Merlin, cast you back to the realm of the fae! My blood that runs in our veins, our hearts that beat as one, we cast you back!" I scream into the night.

The shrieks of the fae pierce the night, cutting through the rumbling of the earth as the knife had cut through our palms. The ground is open, cracking like a hungry mouth. Lines spread from where our hands meet and the blood falls, just like it did in the fae ring. They are sliding, sliding down into the cavern, screaming and clawing at the earth. The last scream is Mum's.

"Merle, no! Please, don't send me there! Merle, please! I'm your mother, don't send me back, please! I love you! Don't... don't... don't...!"

I wish you gone.

In one breath they're there, screaming, clawing at the ground, their terrible faces marked by pain and fear. In the next, with a final scream seemingly from the earth itself, they're swallowed. There's no crack, no sound. Only the pounding rain. Everyone looks to me, their faces taught, eyes wide and terrified. I've nothing to give them now. I have given all, and I'm exhausted.

After a full minute, when the air doesn't change, the earth doesn't open, and the rain doesn't stop, the knights drop their hands. When the circle breaks, I wait for the fae to return, for the mouth to re-open, for Elaine and Morgwese to spring back. They don't.

We stand staring at each other dumbly. Willow's crying. *I'm crying.* Did we win? We must've done, to all still be here rather than in piles of ash.

I sink to my knees, still not letting go of Asher and Ren, my arms hanging in a strange, limp 'Y'. Somehow we're all still together, the blood congealing in our palms. My entire body is aching, the burn marks throbbing, a horrible slow symphony that threatens to overwhelm me. The wild magic is gone, just as Merlin said.

"It's over," Ren falls beside me. "It's over."

I lean into him, wrapping my arm around his neck. It's not over, not really, but that isn't a conversation for now. I'm

346

shaking too much from the cold to answer him anyway, my teeth chattering.

Asher pulls us up. "We need to get you inside and let Bedivere have a look at you. Then I want to hear about everything that happened in that cave."

24

Ren pulls my arms around his shoulders and we hobble back towards the Templar. By the time we get there, he's almost carrying me. We wobble our way into the hall, chairs still strewn everywhere. Most of the knights have beaten us to it, already bandaging their hands. I want to thank them for their support, but have no words.

I throw myself into one of the vacant chairs, every inch of my body singing with pain now the adrenaline is wearing off. Ren crouches beside me, his features a mask of concern. He only moves from my side for a second when Mona pushes her way through, silently handing me a towel with her usual fox-ish grin.

I knew you could do it, That smile says.

"Hey, Lyle! We need some help over here, please," Asher calls from somewhere behind me, her voice pounding against my aching temples.

Sir Bedivere looks up from bandaging the hands of a tall knight with greying hair and flushed cheeks. Sir Pelleas I think. I didn't know Lyle was Bedivere's first name; I don't even remember half of their names.

Bedivere comes and looks at my arms and throat. He assures me that the wounds are not deep; the burns are superficial and will fade entirely. He cleans all of our hands and wraps them slowly. His own hands are strong and gentle.

"Who's watching the twins?" I ask.

He puts his palm to my forehead. "You're freezing, and exhausted, you need rest."

"I want to see them."

"Tomorrow," he insists. "They're sleeping, anyway."

"The old man's right," Asher says.

"Maybe." My very bones seem to ache as I move, everything so stiff and seized up. "We need to see Joth. I've got something for him."

"It can wait."

"I wish it could, but it's important."

Ren studies me for a minute, as do Asher and Willow. They must see the determination in me because no one argues further.

We make our way through to Joth's office. He's already waiting for us, five glass tumblers on his desk, full of amber liquid. This time I gladly take mine.

"Are you sure this won't wait until morning?" Joth asks as he sits. "You're dead on your feet."

"As I've told everyone else, it can't wait. Merlin gave me something, a couple of things you have to see." I need to show them the important stuff, the prophecy, the sigil, the vision he gave me.

I sit in the chair opposite from him and put my glass down. My elbows dig into my knees as I put my head in my hands. Even though the wild pull of the magic is gone, I can still feel it in my bones, tingling there.

"Merle?" Asher's voice is soft and close. She's on her knees in front of me. I sit up, my head swimming.

Joth's looking at me with concern, eyes flicking to the marks on my skin. Despite my exhaustion, a smile slips onto my face. Those marks are a reminder of something much greater. I have magic, we are alive, and for now, Morgwese is gone. "Would you hear his prophecy?"

"I would," he smiles. "And I would see his mark."

I lay my arm on the desk. The brand itches a little, but there's no longer any pain. He traces it with his fingers. I close my eyes, concentrating. It's important I get it right:

"When enemies come disguised as friends,
the lines of blood will break.
The mad will rule in the court of the dead,
the tied will come undone.
When dawn breaks on silver shores,
the wise will lose their heads.
The kingdom burns by the will of the damned,
shadows thrown by wings of death.
When the true are tested through the burn of flames,
hope may be reborn.
Only under redemption's scathing gaze,
will the chosen rule once more."

I open my eyes and stare at Joth's face, which is grey and pensive. "Did he give you any indication of what it might mean?"

"No."

"Well, it shouldn't be too hard to figure out," Willow huffs from behind us. "Prophecies are just riddles. We can put the pieces together."

"I'm glad you're so confident," Ren says. His hand finds the back of my neck, squeezing, as if he knows the exact nature of the ache that lurks there.

"We can start on that another day." Asher waves her hand as if she's brushing the task away. "What happened when you went down there? How did you know about the faery?"

I consider the questions for a moment. It'll take too long to explain everything, but maybe...

"Do you think you could show me?" Joth says, as if he's plucked the thought from my mind. "A witch I used to know was able to 'project' memories to other people, so to speak. Do you think you can?"

"Maybe." I wiggle the fingers of the hand already on the table, motioning for Joth to extend his own. "There's only one way to find out."

He puts down his glass and places his rough, warm hands in mine.

"I'm going to send you a picture. Tell me if you see it. Ready?"

"Ready."

I pull the image of my father standing on the bridge into my mind. There's steam coming from his mouth as he blows on his hands. He turns as he hears footsteps, making grooves in the snow with his heels. Then his eyes go wide as long steel-coloured claws swipe for his neck. Joth jolts, his hands releasing mine.

"Did you see it?"

"I did."

"Good." I draw my hands back and offer them to Asher and Ren, motioning for Willow to join the circle between Asher and Joth. "I've only got enough energy to do this once. If you break the circle, I won't be able to finish."

Both Asher and Ren lace their fingers in mine, then extend their hands to the others. Willow tucks her palm into Asher's immediately. Joth sighs and takes hold. I close my eyes and go back to the beginning. I show them everything. Dad falling into the water; Shelby and the male fae attacking my mother, taking on her form until there's nothing left of her. I show them the Shadow in my dream, stalking the halls of the Templar. The Shadow transforms into Laina when it reaches the twins' bedroom, speaking those harsh, guttural words I still don't understand. They see the baby with red eyes. Next is Shelby at the gates; her awaiting ear cupped by her palm as Laina betrays us. "*We have them, sister,*" she whispers, "*all of them. Our wait is almost over.*" I show them Shelby's eyes as she looks at Lore. I give them everything.

My mind aches as I pull my hands away. Asher lets go, but Ren does not. I don't open my eyes, instead I use my free hand to massage my aching temples and wipe the few stray tears from my cheeks.

In the quiet, there's only the rapid intake of their breath and the beating of their hearts. When I can't stand the sound anymore, I stare up at Joth. His face is set hard, his mouth a jagged line. He's angry. In fact, I think he might be furious.

Someone he thought we could trust has deceived him. We were all stupid enough to ignore the fae's threat when it was so obvious. It's not all his fault, but I don't say so. At some point, we have to take responsibility for our stupidity; myself included.

"Do you understand what I showed you?" I ask.

They all nod.

"I knew what to do because Merlin showed *me*. They were waiting, the faeries, and I let them through. Shelby, *Morgwese*, had been planning this for over a decade, and they played their parts perfectly. I never would have known about her—"

"Not true," Ren says. "You were on to Shelby. Something about her had started to niggle at you."

I shrug. It's too hard to remember what I thought before this morning, and everything changed.

Joth notices the slump in my shoulders and calls our meeting to an end. We all go upstairs together, my legs dragging. I'm still soaking wet and I want to get changed into my pyjamas and sleep for a hundred years.

They – my new gang of friends, friends I never thought I'd have and am eternally grateful for – drop me outside my room. Before we leave each other, we fall into an awkward hug. Our limbs tangled, crushed together in thanks and relief. After a few moments Ren breaks away, then Willow is gone, leaving Asher and me in the hallway.

"Are you okay?" she asks.

"I'm okay. Are you okay?"

She studies me intently, then her shoulders sag with a sigh. "I'm okay. That was a close one though right?"

"As close as it gets."

She chuckles and then stifles a huge yawn with the back of her hand. "Goodnight then, Merlin's heir. You can fill us in on the rest in the morning."

I wave at her and go into my room, stripping off my wet jeans and shirt and throwing them into a pile at the foot of the bed. Drying off and pulling on my pyjamas doesn't help warm me up as I thought it would. The shorts and t-shirts I brought are thin and full of holes. Eventually, I crawl under my covers, the bed feeling softer than it ever has, my aching limbs cushioned by every spring and bump. Still, I don't sleep. In the quiet, Mum's screams echo in my head.

"Don't Merle, I love you, don't, don't, don't!"

One more terrible gift from Morgwese.

Even though I know it's true, it's hard to believe Shelby could maintain the charade for so long. She was so convincing. I *loved* her. I should be embarrassed to admit it, but I'm not. I loved her and I miss her. Whether I like it or not, for years and years she was my confidant. She was there when I needed someone; she's wiped my tears and made me laugh more times than I can count. Her betrayal *hurts.* Having been led along and manipulated so easily *hurts.* There's grief now alongside my anger. No matter how tired I am, I know I won't sleep. I lie with my eyes open, staring at the ceiling. Wind whistles outside, the rain pounding the slate of the roof. It used to be too quiet for me to detect; not anymore. There's a creak in the hallway, someone coming towards my room, and I sit up. The hinges squeak as my bedroom door opens.

"It's rude to creep up on people," I say.

"I wasn't creeping, I was checking," Ren huffs.

"You couldn't sleep?"

"No, you?"

I shake my head.

"Anyway, I thought..." he trails off and blows his hair out of his face, then he shrugs and turns to leave.

"Wait," I whisper. "Don't go."

He turns back and smiles. I move over and make room for him to sit; he swings his leg onto the bed and lies on his back. We stay there for a while, not speaking, then he reaches for my hand. I grasp hold of his fingers and squeeze, never mind the bandages.

"Do you feel different?"

"Different?"

"Now you've got the magic?"

"I feel powerful." And I do. Everything around me sings and hums with new possibilities. Webs of magic are everywhere, waiting for me to wake them up and pull them into shape. Even if I can't make them do my bidding yet, I'll be able to soon.

And there's him. Ren. The one I have to thank for keeping me on track. Without him, I'd never have made it.

I bring my mouth to his, pressing against his full bottom lip. He responds immediately, our lips moving together with slow and delicate curiosity. His hand cups my cheek, thumb stroking gently up and down. I pull myself against him, running my fingers along the length of his arm until my elbow is looped around his neck.

When I eventually break away, his eyes are full of contentment and sleep. I want more kisses, but exhaustion pulls on me. There'll be time for that tomorrow.

He tucks his arm around my shoulders and I lay my head on his chest. His heart echoes, beating slowly and rhythmically like a drum. Eventually, his breathing evens out, and I know he's asleep. If this is my new life, I'm luckier than I ever dared hope. I pull myself closer to him and his arms tighten around my waist. I close my eyes and finally sleep.

I wake up the next day a little bit before Ren. He's lying on his front with one arm tucked under the pillow and I'm pleased he's not left like a shadow in the night. I sit up slowly as I don't want to wake him, but I needn't have bothered as the door bursts open, creaking in its hinges.

"Good morning, sun..." Asher starts but breaks off as she sees Ren stir, "...sun *beams*?"

I reach behind me and grab a pillow to launch at her head, but she bats it out of the way easily.

"If you didn't bring me coffee, I'm going to be pissed," I smile at her.

"We brought coffee. Even enough for Du Lac, though we expected to have to fetch him." She raises an eyebrow suggestively and heat floods my cheeks. Willow pokes her head around the corner and rolls her eyes when she sees us.

Ren pushes himself to his elbows. "Did you say coffee?"

"Yes, Romeo." Asher pushes his legs off the bed so she can sit and hands him a mug. I move mine so that Willow can join us.

"Why are you up so early?" I rub the sleep out of my eyes.

"One, it's noon, and two, we want to know what happened."

"You saw..."

"Not that part!" Willow snaps excitedly. "Before that!"

"Okay then, get comfy," I say before launching into the story of how I opened the door and released the magic. How

I spoke to Dad and Merlin and was given the vision in return for delivering the prophecy. We go through the vision again, although this time much more slowly, Willow jotting down things she thinks are important, nodding intermittently.

"And there was a baby," I finish, "a baby boy with bright red eyes."

"Mordred," Willow says. We all turn to face her and a pink blush flushes her cheeks. "Mordred, Arthur and Morgwese's son, supposedly. She seduced him using the same spell Merlin used on her mother for King Uther. After the baby was born, she raised him to become the next king, even if Arthur would never accept him."

"It's kind of poetic," Asher muses.

"They killed each other." Willow glances between us. "At Camlann. The battle for the rule of Camelot."

"Allegedly." I cock an eyebrow. "A lot of impossible things have happened recently, Willow, so forgive me if I don't take that as gospel truth."

She nods and brushes a strand of her long, dark hair out of her face. "I can look into it alongside the prophecy. I was feeling at a loose end now I've traced your line and Morgwese is gone."

"She isn't gone, she's just somewhere else." I scrub my hands through my hair. It's now almost one o'clock, and I'm starving. "Come on, I need some food."

"Oh yeah, that's why we came to get you." Asher stands. "Let's go."

The hall is almost empty, except for Lydia Geraint and Eddie Pelleas. I'm completely ravenous, and I eat more in five minutes than I have in the last two days. Shovelling down sandwiches and tea as if I've never eaten before. I'm about to refill my cup when Joth marches in. His eyes scan the room, and when he sees me, they light up. He waves his hands excitedly, a 'come to me' gesture that I don't disobey.

"Quickly." He grabs my arm and pulls me out of the room.

"What's going on?" I'm on high alert, waiting for a problem to show itself. Then Joth speaks and my fear melts like an icicle in the sun.

"She's awake. Lore's awake."

Willow, Asher, Ren, and I follow Joth as fast as we can. My heart is thudding in my chest. I can barely believe it! Ren grips my hand as we jog, the elation radiating off him.

When we reach the top of the stairs, the doors are already open. Lore's sitting in bed, as still as stone and beautiful as the dawn. Her grey eyes are a little red-rimmed, and her hair stuck up in tufts around her ears, but other than that she looks fine. Lux shifts from where he's been huddled at her side, turning to us with anxiety scrawled across his features. Ren and Willow rush forward, but that expression is enough to whip the smile straight off my face. Asher comes to a stop beside me. It seems she's picked up on the tension, too.

Lux obviously isn't happy. There's concern in his eyes, his mouth curled in a frown. He pulls on my arm so I crouch, dread churning in my stomach, cold seeping through my limbs.

"What is it, Lux?"

"She's different."

"Different how?"

His eyes fill with tears and his cheeks flush. "She doesn't remember me. She doesn't remember herself."

"What?" I don't understand the words, but

359

simultaneously I understand exactly what he means. That Lore's awake, but somehow she's not Lore.

"She doesn't remember." Tears spill down his pale cheeks. His eyes are sad and hopeless, a storm of misery.

"It's okay." I get up and smooth his hair with the palm of my hand. "It's okay."

"What's going on?" Asher starts, but I shake my head and move past her. I push my way in front of Joth, ignoring Willow and Ren's confused glances, sitting down in front of Lore.

"Tell me where you are," I whisper, the words shaking as they tumble from my mouth. "Tell me who I am."

"Merle," Joth puts his hand on my shoulder.

"Answer me," I insist, climbing up onto the bed so I can look into her eyes. "Tell me who you are."

Lore's eyes search mine, her expression blank. Then her face crumbles in on itself. First, her lips wobble, then she closes her eyes and balls her fists into the sockets. She rocks forwards and backwards, sobs ripping up her throat.

"I don't know!"

I wrap my arms around her to stop her from shaking and kiss the top of her head to calm her. It seems we're not out of the woods yet. Even though my little girl is back, she's not who she was before.

Lore is gone.

ACKNOWLEDGEMENTS

This special edition would not have been possible without YOU! Thank you to everyone who believed in my dream! I hope you have enjoyed the book and are looking forward to the next one!

With SPECIAL thanks to:

Carolyn Skeldon, Daniel Lopez, Craig Staiano, Alan Beaumont (T'old Bogis as Dad might have said!) & Tracey Beaumont, Jenny Beaumont & Josh Deakin, Jenni Strand, Gerald P. McDaniel and Seamus Sands.

With thanks to:

Rhianne Williams, George Smith, John & Maureen Gilbert, Vicky Calik, Fleur DeVillainy, Catherine Brentnall, Janet Barker, Carmen DaVinleam, Natalie Sheffield, Kayla Ann, Claire Aydogan, Kourtney & William Stauffer, Fleur DeVillainy, Ben Jacobson, Cate Dean, Lissette Buckley, Julia Rappaport, Melanie Briggs, Charlotte Mallory, Clarissa Gosling, Luke Mitchell, RC McKinney, Finley Wilson, David Riedinger, Brandon Baker, Stephanie Schwab, Emily Hodder, Tonel, Michelle Taylor, Inka, Preston Pfefferle, Dzsenifer, Nicole Kraehenmann, Renee Portnell, Leslie Twitchell, Rebecca Abrams, Samantha Engle, Anna Layton, Jessica, Casey, Jamie, Jordan and Oleksandra.

Printed in Great Britain
by Amazon